I'm Dreaming
of a
Wyatt Christmas

TIFFANY SCHMIDT

I'm Dreaming of a Wyatt Christmas

AMULET BOOKS • NEW YORK

PUBLISHER'S NOTE: This is a work of fiction. Names, characters, places, and incidents are either the product of the author's imagination or used fictitiously, and any resemblance to actual persons, living or dead, business establishments, events, or locales is entirely coincidental.

Cataloging-in-Publication Data has been applied for and may be obtained from the Library of Congress.

ISBN 978-1-4197-5401-2

Text copyright © 2021 Tiffany Schmidt
Illustrations copyright © 2021 Monika Roe
Book design by Hana Anouk Nakamura

Printed and bound in U.S.A.
10 9 8 7 6 5 4 3 2 1

Amulet Books are available at special discounts when purchased in quantity for premiums and promotions as well as fundraising or educational use. Special editions can also be created to specification. For details, contact specialsales@abramsbooks.com or the address below.

ABRAMS The Art of Books
195 Broadway, New York, NY 10007
abramsbooks.com

Knock, knock.

Who's there?

Kate.

Kate, who?

I dedi-Kate this book to my amazing agent and also to my babysitter/ballet expert (whose name I couldn't fit in this joke).

Kate Testerman & Haley Zelesko, this one's for you.

Babysitting Tip 1:

It's good to have a plan, but plans can change. Kids get bored, cranky, or just don't want to play the game or the craft you prepared. It's important to be flexible.

"**M**y blisters have blisters." I scrunch my toes, then wince as that pulls the skin tighter. Even on their best days, my feet don't look cute in flip-flops, but right now, after I cut corners breaking in a new pair of pointe shoes, they're worse than normal. At least it's November, no longer flip-flop weather. But still—*ouch*. I put another Band-Aid over an especially angry spot on my big toe.

"They're gross, Noelle," Mae Primavera says. Normally I want my best friend agreeing with me, but this time I wouldn't have minded the lie. "Put those things away."

I ball the bandage wrappers in my hand. "Can't." The Primaveras' house is strictly shoes off. "I don't have any socks." I never do. Like always, I'd swapped my pointe shoes for slouch boots at the studio. Trading those cardboard, glue, and satin torture devices for the ratty size-too-big shearling boots that had been my mom's was essentially a cozy foot hug, but it's also a reminder that she's gone. When they become tattered beyond fixing, there won't be another pair.

It feels impossible that this September I started high school without her—that I'm going to celebrate another round of holidays without her—and yet I'm at a Christmas kickoff planning meeting. It was her favorite holiday, and every year since she died I've vowed to celebrate it bigger, *better.*

"Wait! I can fix this! I have something for you." Our friend Autumn Hayworth-Macintosh hefts her backpack onto the couch beside her and begins to sift through it. I swear she could survive a week lost in the wilderness off the contents of her bag. Not that she'd ever get lost, because she probably has three map-apps on her phone and two spare battery packs. "I saw these last week when I was shopping with my moms for favors for this weekend's parties and I couldn't resist!"

Autumn holds up a pair of fuzzy chenille socks—they're printed with Nutcrackers. I squeal and make grabby hands. She laughs and pulls out a tiny pair of scissors—of course—to snip off the tags before tossing them over.

"I love them." I hug the socks before carefully easing them over my toes. "I've got something for you three, too, but I want to wait for Coco."

Since she has her backpack open, Autumn pulls out her planner and colored pens and lines them up on the Primaveras' coffee table—shifting some half-done chemistry

2

homework and tucking a receipt in a splayed romance novel so she has space. "Surprising no one, Coral isn't here yet. I knew I should've stopped at her house on my walk over."

Coco Sanderson's real name is Coral, but the only people who ever call her that are announcers at swim meets and her best friend when she's annoyed that Coco's late—which is most of the time. I think she does it on purpose to give Autumn something to grumble about. Grumbly Autumn is a kitten practicing her pounce—adorable and harmless, but totally convinced she's ferocious.

"I already texted, she's two minutes away." Mae does a happy wiggle in her chair—it's the massive leather wingback her parents have used for years of family photos. They dot the walls of the family room: starting with baby shots of Mae's oldest brother, Trevor; then toddler Trevor carefully holding Rachel; then Trevor *and* Rachel cradling the twins: Hudson and Booker. My favorite photo has all four of Mae's older siblings brawling over which of them gets to hold her swaddled bundle. Even in that picture—where they're practically playing tug-of-war with her receiving blanket—she's sleeping peacefully among their chaos.

I was here last weekend when they shot this year's Christmas card photo—all of them in ridiculous holiday sweaters, crammed in that chair. Trevor complaining about his drive back to college, Rachel roaring that someone was pulling her hair. The twins being the pullers and, based on Mae's I-refuse-to-laugh face, likely ticklers as well.

I love this family but know Mae's happy wiggle has to do with having the chair to herself, the fact that her house is miraculously quiet right now, and the latest text on her phone—"Coco's three houses away. I can't believe we finally managed to get everyone together."

"Seriously," says Autumn. "I knew we wouldn't have as many classes together in high school, but I barely see you all."

I look down at my new fuzzy socks. While they'd never say it, this is mostly my fault. Coco's swim schedule is no joke; she practices at least three hours a day. But some days I'm at the studio for five. And between dance classes and nonstop babysitting jobs, *I'm* the biggest complication in coordinating our schedules.

But—I reach down and pull a baggie from the backpack beside my chair—"At least I come with cookies! Rosa and I baked last night and Ms. Hernandez insisted I bring some home. Help yourself."

They're red-and-green pinwheels. I have several cookie and one playdough recipe memorized. None of them are fancy—not like the things Autumn bakes. Mine tend to involve crushed candy canes and Santa cookie cutters. And if Ms. Hernandez was surprised that Rosa and I made Christmas cookies before Thanksgiving, it's only because she's new in town. Most people in Juncture, Pennsylvania, know that Noelle Partridge's Christmas season begins mid-November and stretches until the last seconds of the year.

If Mae's family were home, she'd be diving for cookies before they're all claimed. Since they're not, she waits for Autumn to stack a few on a coaster before passing her the bag.

Mae's siblings—plus their equally boisterous dad—are off doing a "Polar Plunge." Looking around the family room might make you think they stopped mid-task and decided to go jump in a freezing lake, but this charity fundraiser has been on their calendar for months. Leaving chaos in their wake is a lifestyle for five-sevenths of the Primavera crew, and chaos makes Mae itchy. So she opted to stay home and let her mom photograph it without her. Also, we all know they're going to reenact it once they return.

"I'm here!" Coco calls from the foyer as she lets herself in, stopping to shed her coat and shoes and pat the Primaveras' golden retriever, Remy, who is ancient and slightly deaf, which is the only reason she didn't pounce on the word "cookies." Remy follows Coco as she joins us in the family room, so Autumn has to grab her cookies off their coaster while Coco flops on the couch beside her and steals one. "Someone baked? Yes, please."

"Me and Rosa Hernandez." Though I'd also made peppermint bark with the Dylan kids the night before and snowflake-shaped sugar cookies at the Smiths' on Thursday. Stress-baking is a real thing, okay? I learned it from Autumn. Maybe now that we're all finally together, I should use the chance to ask for some advice.

The first half of the reason for that stress is the list burning a hole in my backpack beside the brochure that's responsible for the second half. It's a list I look forward to all year, but I look forward to making it with my dad. This fall, he's been glued to his phone, his tablet, or his laptop. It's "One more minute, kiddo," or "Maybe later, kiddo," "Tomorrow, kiddo. Promise."

Clearly he's invented a new definition of "tomorrow"—one that means "a time that never arrives." "Promise" now means "probably not." And if we haven't had time to make our list of Christmas plans—which until this year I thought was a pretty sacred tradition—when could I possibly talk to him about the brochure for Beacon Ballet Academy?

Autumn *might* get what it's like to have a parent suddenly go MIA; she's the only kid of "workaholics"—her word. Momma Hay and Momma Mac are party planners who own their own business, but they seem to be a sort of *steady* workaholics. Always busy, but never *too* busy to, say, remember to pick up their only daughter from the same dance studio she's been attending since she was four . . . Good thing it's walkable from our apartment.

Mae would not get it. Her parents have five kids, an elderly dog, and full-time jobs—yet they still find time for family dinners, Polar Plunges, and trips to the ER whenever the twins decide to test the rules of gravity or logic. Seriously, if a body part can get stitches or an object can be used as a lightsaber or parachute, they've done it.

Coco definitely wouldn't get it—her family should give anti-stress classes. All of them are ridiculously relaxed. Well, relaxed in all instances except Coco's swim meets and during game night. Then they're competitive gremlins.

"Are you excited?" Coco asks me. She's settled on the couch with Remy's head in her lap and a cookie held out of the dog's reach. It takes me a blink to remember why she's asking, why we're here. So, yeah, this isn't the time. We can talk absentee Dad and Beacon another day, because Autumn's tapping her planner and she's already added Santa stickers to the pages.

Today's special and I'm going to enjoy it, dang it. I give a happy little squeal and kick my legs, "It's the official start of Christmas season!"

Coco and Mae laugh.

"It's not official until there's something on the calendar," says Autumn. She's sitting on the edge of the couch, her legs crossed at the ankles. With her red hair pulled up in a bun and dark-framed glasses, she looks like a fourteen-year-old librarian or executive. Comparisons that would delight her, so I make a mental note to say so after she's done updating the planner that runs her life—no, let's be accurate, it runs *all* our lives. She's got Mae's vlog post schedule in there and Coco's swim meets, and for me, she's got my *Nutcracker* performances, which is what she's tapping. "Before I pass the floor to Noelle for all other things Christmassy, we need to pick a date to watch her dance. And we need to get to the show earlier this year. I don't want to be stuck sitting by the door to the bathroom again. It was so distracting with all those little kids, pregnant moms, and grandmas going past us."

My dance school's show is held in a historic home that seats only ninety people. Which is plenty for a studio our size—we don't even have enough dancers to perform the whole ballet. The tickets printed on Miss Janet's office printer will read "Selections from *The Nutcracker,*" and the forty-ish students at Spirit School of Ballet will beg everyone they know to pay ten dollars to come sit in a folding chair and watch them dance their five minutes in the hour-long show. The seats aren't assigned and there are only three performances—the merits of which Autumn, Mae, and Coco are debating with an intensity that's usually reserved for class schedules or pizza toppings.

I love my friends.

"Not the matinee. That's the one all the younger siblings come to, and it's always loud and distracting," says Coco.

Personally, it's my favorite show. I love watching the toddlers in the audience stand and butt-wiggle as they attempt to copy moves they'll be doing a year later. But Coco is the non-babysitter among us. The only one who didn't take the town's training class last summer, doesn't have sitting jobs in Autumn's planner, and couldn't sing the theme song to every show on Disney+.

"So, first night, when they're still working out the kinks?

Or second night, when the youngest are exhausted and over it?" Autumn asks.

"Oh, remember when that angel sat down and refused to finish her dance?" says Coco.

Maisie Pullman. Poor thing had to be carried offstage and had fallen asleep in the backroom before curtain call. Though based on the "We don't enforce a bedtime, she'll let you know when she's tired" policy her parents shared when I'd babysat, it's possible her crash had been less recital-driven.

"I vote last night," says Mae. And it's settled. She's never going to be the loudest voice in the room, but my best friend is our decider. Autumn's already picking up her red pen—it's my designated color in her planner and it's going to get a workout today. She jots Noelle/Nutcracker 5pm in the square for the third Sunday in December.

"I'll get the tickets," she says. "You can pay me back later."

"I'll get them," I protest. "You shouldn't have to pay to watch me do *The Nutcracker* for the millionth time."

Mae waves off my suggestion. "Remind me, who are you this year? Sorry, I forgot."

I snort. "Totally understandable." I've been practically every role in my eleven years at Spirit School of Ballet. From Snowflake to Clara to the Spanish Dancer. There was even the year I was Dew Drop Fairy *and* Columbine doll, because poor Nikki got food poisoning. Since there's no guys older than eight at our tiny studio, I've played Rat King and toy soldiers. If I were taller, I'd likely have been the Nutcracker.

Instead Marcie's dad has gotten roped into it three years running. This year he says he's going to attempt a demi-plié and a soutenu—so honestly, it might be worth coming just to see that.

My dad did the role once—back when I was a nine-year-old playing Clara eleven months after Mom died. Back when he constantly told me we were a team and that he was my biggest fan. Now I can't imagine him having the time to prance around in the Nutcracker costume, and it's been months since we've felt like a team. He hasn't told me he's my biggest fan lately, but I know that hasn't changed, even if everything else has. I swallow against a tightening in my throat and answer, "I'm the Sugar Plum Fairy."

Mae's forehead is hidden beneath her straight brown bangs. They're new, along with the bob she had cut before we started high school two months ago. She'd wanted to look older, but she's five-feet nothing and baby-faced, so all they're doing is hiding a forehead creased with confusion. "Weren't you Sugar Plum last year?"

I nod. But there's only so many roles and that's the hardest. While it's nice to be the best dancer at Spirit, it's also starting to feel a bit like wearing a shirt that's two sizes too small. Even my teacher, Miss Janet, has been making comments like, "It's time for a new challenge for you." "You've really grown up this past year." "I think you're ready." Hence the Beacon brochures I've started carrying around.

The last two times we discussed the elite dance academy

three hours away in DC—when I was ten and she suggested their summer intensive, or the time she brought up their full-year residential school when I was entering seventh grade—I'd dismissed her suggestions: "I'm not ready to dance full-time or move away from home." But back then Dad and I were still a team.

My sigh is hidden beneath Autumn clicking her pen. She points to me. "Okay, Noelle, it's all you—what's on the Partridge Christmas Extravaganza plan this year?"

This is the only time Autumn cedes control of the calendar, and I usually bring my A game. Normally Dad and I spend weeks drafting *Noelle Partridge's Plan for Spreading Christmas Cheer, Because Christmas Is the Most Wonderful Time of the Year*—that's its official name. For short we call it "the Extravaganza." Only this year I had to create it by myself and it doesn't feel so extravagant.

Dad's the one who finds amazing things like the stop-motion Christmas carol video contest we won last year. Coco came up with the coolest plot about a cursed reindeer who's turned into a snowman after he accidentally ran over "Grandma"—and Autumn's attention to detail had been perfect for frosting the sugar cookies we used for our scenes, tracking all the tiny adjustments between each of Mae's photographs.

Dad's the one who taught us to ice-skate and drives us to the rink for their all-carols skate night. He's a judge for our gingerbread house contest and a taste-tester for anything we bake. He's chaperoned each of our caroling expeditions, and he's a member of some online forum about Christmas lights, so he maps a route to see the best ones within an hour of our small Pennsylvania town. He even made scorecards so we could rate the houses on "theme," "use of animatronics," and "synchronization of music" and on a scale from "garish to glorious."

He's usually copilot of the Extravaganza . . . but this year I'm flying solo. Dad works from home, and right now he's *always* working. There's a sign on his office door that we'd made back when I was little and couldn't tell the difference between true emergencies and feeling lonely or bored. One side says, INTERRUPTIONS WELCOME, but now it's perpetually flipped to read, DON'T COME IN UNLESS YOU'RE BLEEDING OR THE APARTMENT'S ON FIRE.

But lately lonely almost feels like a real emergency. If we hadn't already established protocol that states "paper cuts don't count," maybe I'd have given myself one with the empty notepad, just as an excuse to interrupt. And now Mae, Coco, and Autumn are all looking at me, expecting something amazing. I swallow.

"To make things official, your first Christmas present of the year." At least I hadn't messed this up. I rummage in the front pocket of my bag for the gifts I've been saving since I scooped them up on clearance last January. I toss a tiny tissue paper twist to each of them. Coco has to stretch to keep hers away from Remy, who assumes all things are food. To be fair, I added a red spiral to the center of the wrapping, so they look like peppermints. But when the girls unfurl the tissue paper, they're enamel pins.

"I love it," says Mae. Hers is Santa's sleigh above the globe, with dashed lines showing all his routes. It says: *Travel goals.*

Autumn is laughing as she pins hers—a checklist that reads: *Naughty, Nice,* and *To-do* with the third one checked off—to her backpack. "It's perfect."

Coco's is . . . *cocoa.* A snowflake mug with whipped cream and a candy cane sticking out. She fastens it to the drawstring of her hoodie. "You're the best!" I grin until she adds, "Now tell us what's on the plan!" and my satisfaction with having nailed their presents evaporates.

"Well, we've got all the usuals." I curl my knees onto the chair so they can't see all the scribbles and question marks on my notebook. "We'll do gingerbread houses on Christmas Eve Eve, and Ice House just posted the carol skate nights; either the third or the tenth."

"Third," Autumn says, adding it to her planner. "Swim meet on the tenth."

Coco's just pulled her long, blond hair out of its messy knot and thankfully it's not damp enough to smear or drip on the pages as she leans over to see the calendar. She nods and begins to finger comb her snarls. "Snowflake Invitational at Carmen."

There's a tiny red heart on the next block over, but no one mentions it now. They'll call and text that day to make sure I know they're thinking of me—but it's been almost six years since Mom died and we're still figuring out how to make grief less awkward and awful. If that's even possible. I rub my Achilles and try to ignore those thoughts like I do sore muscles—they're always there, but there's nothing I can do to stop them, so I might as well keep moving.

I clear my throat. "There's the movie marathon the half day we get out of school." But that's a given and already on Autumn's calendar. "And fudge fest—I like what we did last year when everyone brought a new recipe to try. There's seeing Santa, caroling, the town tree lighting, the Primaveras' seven fishes, karaoke and Boxing Day Brunch, seeing the lights. For new things I was thinking we could make hot cocoa mix and deliver it to neighbors or teachers or something. I found this cute idea about putting it in mason jars?"

My voice trails off. I know it sounds like a lot, but there's nothing *new*, no showstopper. It's *The Nutcracker* without Sugar Plum, *Swan Lake* without Odile. Based on their silence, my friends are expecting me to continue. I don't blame them; mason jars don't exactly scream "wow factor."

"Oh." Mae is the first to figure out I'm done. She swings her legs off the side of her chair and sits up. "I can't wait, Noelle. But about seeing Santa. What if this year, we . . . *don't*?"

Coco nods. "I kinda agree. We're freshmen now."

"I'm not saying we have to believe," I protest. "But it's tradition."

"Yes, but it's also *our classmates* who are hired to play the elves." Autumn exchanges looks with Mae and Coco and I sink down in my seat.

It's not like I'm excited about perching on the lap of some guy who's probably been peed on by nervous toddlers, but I want the picture. We have years of group photos at McTavishes, the local farm that does the whole Santa getup—horses outfitted with jingle bell harnesses pulling wagons past cornstalks painted like candy canes; the barn that's converted to Santa's workshop, where elves pass out cocoa while you wait to pose and say, "Naughty list" as they snap your photo.

"I just think we're too old." Mae's forehead is so scrunched I can see it through her bangs. "It'd be embarrassing."

"Fine." I cross it off with an angry slash.

"If it's that important—" Mae begins, but I shake my head, wishing I'd stopped home to shower after dance so my hair could be down. Instead it's trapped in its usual sweaty bun and everything I'm feeling is on display.

"Anything else you don't want to do?"

Coco slowly raises her hand. "Don't be mad, but I can't do fudge fest."

I tighten my grip on my pen. That was supposed to be a rhetorical question. Everything left on our tiny list (except for the stupid mason jars) is tradition. Fudge fest has always been Coco's *thing*. We destroy her kitchen in the process, and any fudge that isn't consumed we send to work with her parents or in college finals care packages for Mae's brother Trevor and Coco's big sister, Monica. "No fudge fest?"

"My coach . . ." Coco's eyes are glued to a particularly gnarly snarl and her broad shoulders are curled in. "She's got me on a nutrition plan for the next two months. It's not, like, a diet. And it doesn't say 'no cookies' or anything super-strict like that—so maybe we could make regular cookies? It's just something we're trying. To see if it makes any difference in my times for the winter season." She tugs her fingers free of her hair and looks at me. "I love fudge fest—but when have I *not* eaten five pounds of it in a single day? It always ends with me lying on the couch saying how sick I feel and then I'm sluggish and sugar-hungover the next few days. You all can still do it, but I should probably skip it this year."

I'm not sure how I feel about Coco's new coach—she's full of rules and big promises that if Coco follows them, she'll make the National Junior Team. But if skipping fudge fest helps Coco hit her goals, then we can all have a little less sugar and condensed milk this year. The second strike-through on my list doesn't even sting. "Okay, skipping fudge fest, and seriously, no worries. But . . . that's all I've got so far. I still need to find our razzle-dazzle."

They're trying to be subtle about the look they're exchanging—at least I think they are? They're not very good at it.

But every lifted eyebrow and lip nibble is them saying

they care how I feel. That even if Santa and fudge aren't on their lists this year, I still am. It's more than I can say about Dad lately. It's more than enough.

I'm trying hard not to get teary-eyed about it, because there's zero chance they'll interpret that as anything but hurt. I exhale slowly. *Think good things:* Nutcracker. *The piney smell of rosin. The clack of pointe shoes. Applause. Little kids laughing backstage at my jokes. Fresh gingerbread.*

Mae must lose the stare down, because she's their spokesperson. "Noelle, I always love your huge Christmas plans, but maybe this year simple is better? We've got more homework and Coco's swimming more, and Trevor's coming home from school, and Autumn's family is going into peak holiday party season."

"I'll ask my moms in case they know of any cool events," adds Autumn. "But I'm okay with what we have."

Coco stretches a long leg over to pat my foot with hers, and I try not to wince as she bumps my blisters. "Like they said, this is a good start. We just have to be, you know, open to possibilities."

I'm nodding and nodding—like a dashboard bobblehead on a gravel road. It's not that I agree that strongly. It's just—I love their support and I love them, but . . . Christmas is supposed to be *special*, not for settling.

"Who knows," Coco adds, giving my foot another playful kick. "Maybe this year will be less sitting-on-Santa's-lap and more meeting-someone-under-the-mistletoe."

I snort. We're all single. Perpetually so. Besides me, Coco's the only one who even has a crush. And hers is off-limits and uninterested. So, not all that different from my own love life. "I think the chlorine's getting to your brain."

"I don't know," she singsongs, and grins. "There's a certain boy who sits behind Mae in English class who'd like to be the candy to her cane."

Mae rolls her eyes. "You're ridiculous, he's annoying, and I'm uninterested. Subject change, please."

"Who?" My eyebrows float up with all sorts of questions. I'm not in their class, but I want a seating chart, stat!

Mae ignores me. "How long can you all stay? I was going to watch a documentary on the Azores, but that's really all I've got planned."

She's moving crushes and Christmas off the table, and eventually I'll circle back to both—but not today. Not until I figure out something to make this year special. If I don't . . . my throat tightens at the thought . . . if I don't, it'll still be Christmas.

"Noelle? Can you stay?" Mae prompts.

Apparently Autumn and Coco are all sorts of available. I'm not. I glance at my phone. "For fifteenish minutes? Mrs. Kahale is picking me up to babysit."

I brace myself for their groans and they don't disappoint. I won't let myself look at Mae, who's got to be smirking. I don't even peek when she says, "Oh, the *Kahales*? Hmm."

"All you do is babysit," grumbles Autumn. "You *can* say

no, you know. I do it all the time. I don't know how you're juggling it, plus dance, plus school."

She's not wrong, I don't ever turn down a job unless I'm already booked, and since I spend so much time at a dance studio full of small children, my schedule fills fast.

But there are bigger answers here—not just my inability to say no. My hand strays to my bag, thinking of the brochure inside that I need to place strategically in Dad's office. "Beacon," I say. "It's so expensive."

The Primaveras' family room goes so unnaturally silent that Remy sits up and barks. This time my friends aren't exchanging looks—they're studying their hands, their feet, the floor.

"That's still a thing?" asks Coco. "You haven't mentioned it in a few weeks."

I laugh uncomfortably. "Probably because we've barely seen each other."

"But you're applying?" asks Mae. "You said you weren't sure."

"I'm still not." I cross my feet and wince as sore spots rub. "I think so? Maybe."

Autumn's cleaning her already-clean glasses with a microfiber cloth from her bag. "What's your dad say? My moms would lose it if I asked to move out now—they're already sappy-sentimental about college, and that's four years off."

Dad would have to *know* about it first—but then . . .

would he lose it? That was the big question. I almost wanted him to. To announce we couldn't break up the team and he needed me at home . . . but lately that seemed unlikely.

"It's, like, the Harvard of dance schools," I say instead of answering Autumn. "No one ever says no to Harvard. Wouldn't you want to go if you could get in? And there's no guarantee I can."

Autumn nods reluctantly. Mae bites her lip.

"Only if it was the best place for me," says Coco. "Which . . . Harvard? No way."

"Yeah," I say quietly. "But what other place is there for *me*?"

"Spirit's really that bad?" Mae asks. She's curled up like a pill bug, her cheek on the armrest, and that wasn't how I'd meant it—I hadn't even meant to say it. But it was an easy exit to this conversation.

"It's no Beacon. Nothing else is Beacon." I shrug. "But Beacon doesn't have you three and I haven't even signed up to audition—so don't worry about it yet."

Besides, I'm already worrying enough for all four of us and we only have thirteen minutes. I swing my new fuzzy socks onto the coffee table, using them to nudge the remote toward Mae. "Is the Azores warmer than Pennsylvania? Because, you know how I feel about the cold." They laugh at my grimace and I exhale. Crisis averted, or at least delayed. "If so, I say we start the documentary now and pretend we're all there."

Twelve minutes later, I'm ready to pack a bag and fly to the island chain that's halfway across the Atlantic where there's no ballet decision pressure or absentminded Dad who's going full-Maurice from *Beauty and the Beast*. There *are*, apparently, volcanic hot springs. I can get behind those—but a beep from Mae's driveway pulls me out of a hot springs fantasy about how good that would feel on my tight Achilles.

"I bet that's the Kahales." Mae's grin is undiluted mischief. She may not be as wild as her siblings, but she has the Primavera smile—and it's a good reminder that not everyone in this room is clueless about my crush. "I'll text you later. I want updates on how things are with Holly and Jack . . . and *Wyatt*."

Autumn and Coco are too busy debating if they'd rather go to the island of Terceira or São Miguel to notice Mae's glee, but I stick out my tongue. When she texts me later, I'm definitely getting teased about being in love with a boy I've never met.

Babysitting Tip 2:

It's natural to have favorite babysitting clients—and perfectly okay . . . as long as you don't make it obvious to the families who aren't your fave.

Mae keeps threatening to steal the Kahales as clients in the hopes they'll bring her along on one of their trips back to O'ahu to visit Mr. Kahale's family, but there's zero chance I'm ever giving them up. Not because of any imaginary trip to the Hawaiian islands (they've never asked—though they do bring me back great presents, like the bracelet I'm currently spinning around my wrist). The Kahales are my favorite babysitting clients for many, many reasons—some of which I'll never admit out loud. But this is my last Sunday with them for a while. From mid-November through March they head to Vermont to go skiing every weekend.

Well, every weekend except the one of *The Nutcracker*. The youngest two Kahales are both in Tuesday afternoon classes at Spirit. Jack's making his four-year-old snowflake debut in this year's show, and eight-year-old Holly is the most enthusiastic soldier in the battle with the Rat King.

They're the best family. Mr. Kahale tells dad jokes and trots his kids around in piggybacks. He overpays, pretends never to have small bills, saying, "We'll settle up next time," but then repeating the same routine then too.

Mrs. Kahale is a national treasure. One of those people who truly listens, pays attention, and is uncannily observant. She offered me a ride home from dance the day I had staggering cramps, makes sure her fridge is always stocked with my favorite black cherry seltzer, and complimented a new pair of jeans I wasn't sure about—all without me asking or even hinting. She's the only person I've really talked to about my hopes and fears about auditioning for Beacon. The type of person I could totally confide crushes in . . . except not in this case.

Because mine's on the oldest Kahale kid—Holly and Jack's fifteen-year-old half-brother. With all her observational superpowers, I hope Mrs. Kahale never figures out that it's *her stepson* who makes my heart pirouette.

Wyatt Kahale is the perfect guy. Or, at least, he's the perfect dancer. I should know—I've watched every clip of him performing on Beacon's iLive channel and tracked him on his classmates' social media. Wyatt doesn't have accounts of his own—at least, not that I can find—and in a field where you *want* fame and attention, that's almost as rare as his talent. Maybe he just doesn't need it? Or doesn't want to be distracted by vlogging and follower-chasing like his classmates?

Speaking of chasing—today had included a long round of "puppy tag" where I pursued Holly and Jack while crawling on my knees (*ow!*) and barking, because whoever was "it" had to pretend to be a dog, followed by hide-and-seek, a dance party in dress-up clothes, then twenty minutes of vrooming trucks. My sore legs are grateful to finally be sitting in butterfly stretch on the yellow-and-cream rug in the Kahales' family room with four-year-old Jack beside me. And if my eyes keep straying from the wooden puzzle pieces scattered on the ottoman to the frames on the mantel, well, I've earned a peek or two at Wyatt. Jack doesn't need my help. He can put together the forty-eight pieces of the excavator picture by himself. I know because we've already done it—twice. Plus, he just batted my hand away, saying, "I'm doing it. Don't look. I'm surprising you."

Which, that's practically permission to turn and study Wyatt's form in the third frame from the left. It's sandwiched between a photograph of Holly in ski gear and one of all three kids on a white sand beach.

I could lie and say it's Wyatt's grand jeté I find so captivating—I mean, yeah, his extension and lines are perfection—but, hello, cheekbones! Hello, muscles. Hello, hello brown eyes a few shades darker than his skin. Hello, full lips I'd love to watch say hello back to me.

"Stop it, Jack!" Eight-year-old Holly's shout comes from the play tent in the corner. She'd retreated there when Jack's truck game involved running *over* anything in his path. (We declared the tent a "truck-free zone.") She's much happier on a pile of floor pillows, reading her library book. It's the newest in the series of graphic novels about a vampire who becomes an accidental spy that every elementary schooler I babysit for is obsessed with. "It's not funny anymore."

Her criticism is completely accurate and understandable—even if it's not exactly gentle. Jack has been repeating the same knock-knock joke for the past five minutes, and cracking himself up every time. I'd offered to tell him another one, but, no, he just really liked my first.

He sticks out his tongue without looking up from his puzzle and says the punch line again, *"Annie body seen the turkey?"*

"So!" I stand and plant myself between Holly's glare and Jack's giggles. "Who wants a snack?"

"Annie body want a snack?"

Holly practically growls as she shoves a bookmark between her pages.

I glance across the open floor plan to the microwave's clock. It's four thirty-seven and their parents will be home by five. They're picking up dinner, so this is dicey timing snack-wise, but Holly gets *hangry*. If you wait too long to feed that sassy, affectionate, competitive string bean, you do so at your own peril.

"How about an apple?" Her parents can't get mad if I spoil dinner with fruit.

"Will you cut it like a tube?" she asks, and Jack pipes up, "Me too!"

I groan inwardly. It's super annoying to carefully core an apple while leaving the rest intact. I should've known better than to show off that skill when I was here last week. I've already sworn them to secrecy, because I'm not doing this at every house I sit at. Only here.

"Sure."

"I'll come help," says Holly, vaulting out of the play tent still holding her book. "Do you think I can finish forty-three pages tonight? It's due back to the library tomorrow and Mrs. Emerick says I can't renew because there's a waiting list. I was going to finish last night, but Wyatt called, and then—"

"Oh?" I'm passing by a set of family photos—and seriously, who could blame me for the glance I shoot their way? It's drive-by admiration of the most photogenic fivesome on the planet. One picture's from their backyard on Easter; there are egg hunt baskets behind them. The other's a hike in Hawai'i—Mrs. Kahale's pale skin is hidden beneath a huge sunhat, Holly and Mr. Kahale have walking sticks, and Wyatt's got a Beacon water bottle in his hand and his brother on his back.

"Why'd Wyatt call?" I ask. The best part of eight- and four-year-olds is that I don't have to be subtle. I can ask about their half-brother and they're never suspicious. Fine, that's not the best part. The best part is their laughs at my cheesy jokes, their hugs, or how Jack sucks on the tip of his pointer finger when he's thinking. How Holly sits like a cat—in positions that look so uncomfortable—but that she springs from with an astounding grace she never demonstrates at dance class. How she'll chatter a whole conversation, from library books to a commercial she saw, to whether driveway chalk is worth it, since it's just rained away. Then pause and expect responses on every single topic.

"It was a vid-call from between classes," she says, pausing to wash her hands—and the apple—with soap.

I take the fruit and give it another rinse as she explains— at length—about the bookmark her friend Imani made her and how she couldn't find it and then lost the book while looking. "And then I found the *book*, but not the bookmark. But it was my turn to talk to Wyatt and he only had three minutes until his partnering class. He didn't sound excited about it."

I picture Wyatt sitting on the floor in a studio hallway. You can practically read how intensely serious he is about dance from the lift of his chin and the look in his eyes. Or, at least I can. Probably because my own passion for it recognizes his. I can only imagine what it would be like to talk to someone else who eats, sleeps, and breathes ballet. And believe me, I *have* imagined it.

He's probably used to it—living at Beacon, surrounded by peers all equally driven—but I still like to think there'd be some special spark of connection between us. That if I audition and get into his school—tuition magically not an issue—that he'll fix that intense brown gaze on *me* and realize that we're fated, refusing to pas de deux with any other partner. Our fish dives and press lifts will be the stuff of glowing reviews and legends . . .

Or, you know. Maybe he'll say "hi" to me in the hallway and I'll die from the shock of it.

I set down the paring knife, because on second thought, this isn't the sort of conversation I should be having while holding a sharp object.

"I bet he just wanted to talk to you," I say, giving Holly a side squeeze. "Who wouldn't? Or maybe he didn't seem excited because he was tired."

Because how could he *not* be excited? I'd sell my pinky toe to take a partnering class at Beacon. Well, not literally, because I need it for balance. Beacon is one of the top five ballet schools in the country. I know Wyatt realizes how lucky he is to go there, because he's featured in last year's recruitment video pretty much saying so. *"Beacon removes all the distractions and lets me be a dancer. I get to learn from the best and live with peers who push me to achieve more and get stronger—because that's their goal too."*

Or something like that—it's probably not verbatim. It's not like I've watched the video on repeat.

At least not in the past twenty-four hours.

Fine, not since this morning when I was dithering over the application again.

It's not my fault the video is right next to the Submit button. My mouse just slipped. Twice.

And what he's saying—I want that. There's no way I'm getting from Spirit School of Ballet in tiny Juncture, Pennsylvania, to any sort of professional company. Meanwhile Beacon has its own company and is a direct feeder to all of the major ones.

Partnering class? I sigh as I core Holly's apple. There are exactly five male students at Spirit. One of them is Jack. They're all under eight. No partnering classes for me.

But when I daydream about pas de deux—which is a perfectly natural thing for a dancer to do—my imaginary partner always has Wyatt's face.

"I want mine cut in three circles," says Jack. He tucks in his thumb, then holds up pudgy fingers. Looking from them to me, he amends his answer. "Four. *Four* circles. You know Wyatt's in *The Nutcracker* too."

I hand Holly her apple, then begin his. "Oh yeah? And, good job picking up your puzzle, buddy."

Holly lowers her apple-telescope from her eye and frowns. "But he isn't going to make it home for our *Nutcracker*. That's why he called."

I drop the knife into the sink with a clatter. "Wait! Was he going to?" Wyatt. Wyatt Kahale had been planning to attend a show where *I* would be dancing? I press a hand to my pounding heart, forgetting all about the sponge I picked up to wipe off the cutting board. Well, that's an attractive wet spot on my shirt.

"He wanted to. But the day he thought he could come, he can't. Something about his mom."

"But we're going to him show," Jack tells me.

"*His* show," I correct automatically. Not that he's listening—he and Holly have both turned their snacks into trumpets and are parading around the island.

Beacon is famous for its version of *The Nutcracker.* I've heard and read about it but have never seen it. For a moment I consider if this could be my razzle-dazzle Christmas activity—figuring out a bus or train to take us the three hours from Juncture to DC . . . but that would only razzle-dazzle me. I can't ask the girls to sit through the ballet twice.

"You're so lucky you get to see it." My voice is wistful as I drop the cores in the countertop compost bin. "Take so many pictures."

"Did you want to go? We would've gotten you a ticket." We all whirl toward the voice as Mr. Kahale sets two brown bags of Thai takeout on the counter.

"Hi, loves." Mrs. Kahale gives Holly a hug. "We didn't mean to startle you. You probably couldn't hear the door over your . . . apple music." She winks at me. "Noelle, I'm sorry I didn't think to ask you about Beacon's show. Of course you'd want to see it and we would've loved to have you come with us."

"I don't want to see him—I mean *it*—I mean, why '*of course*'?" It's a good thing Jack has distracted his parents with leaping hugs, because unlike eight- and four-year-olds, they're *not* oblivious and I'm acting super paranoid. If they ever learn about my crush, I can never come here again.

Mrs. Kahale sets Jack on the counter beside the take-out bags and lets him rip them open and pull out cartons. "Because it's *Beacon*."

Right. Because of the *school*, not the boy. The school I've told her I'm trying to psych myself up to audition for. I exhale and hope my cheeks aren't as bright as they feel. "It's the dream," I say softly. "A very expensive dream."

Mrs. Kahale tucks one of her red curls behind her ear while giving me a concerned look. She lifts her eyebrows at her husband and he scoops Jack off the counter and sets him on the floor. "Hey, loves, can you set the table quick? We need to talk to Noelle."

Holly and Jack exchange a look that's all teeth—well, except for where Holly is missing two of hers—but it's a delightfully conspiratorial grin. Whatever I'm about to hear, they already know, which is all sorts of shocking. We've spent three hours together and they didn't drop a hint—they might be better secret keepers than my friends.

I hold on to their grins as I follow their parents to the foyer for privacy. They wouldn't look so gleeful if this was bad news.

"We have a favor to ask you," starts Mrs. Kahale. "We

know it's a big one, so there's no pressure to say yes. We won't be mad if it's a no."

"Of course not." Mr. Kahale looks at his wife and they both draw in a breath. There's a decorative mirror on the wall behind them, and my reflection is staring back at me with wide, impatient blue eyes. She too has straight, brown hair that dried in a bun but was taken down to wear a dress-up hat, so it falls in weird creases and curls around bony shoulders in an oversized sweater.

"You know we have the cabin in Vermont," says Mrs. Kahale. "And that Holly joined the ski team this year."

"Yes." I smile. "She showed me her new helmet and told me all about her coaches."

Ballet is not Holly's first love—that would be hurling herself down mountains. I don't see the appeal of a sport that practically welcomes frostbite, or in Holly's stories about "frozen boogers" and "massive wipeouts."

"It's a huge commitment," Mr. Kahale says. "More than we fully comprehended when we gave in to her begging. Jack . . . he's not such a fan of the cold."

Yup, that's my boy. Because, same. He's all about puzzles and dress-up and proximity to snacks. I adore him . . . but I'm still not sure where this is going.

"Holly needs to be there over break. It's nonnegotiable. But Jack—there's no way he's going to tolerate being on the slopes that much. If Ginger and I are playing taxi and entertaining Jack, we won't have any time on the mountain."

"What Nick's trying to say"—Mrs. Kahale playfully pokes her husband—"is we want you to come with us. The cabin has plenty of room, a big cozy fireplace, and you wouldn't be working the whole time. Jack has half-day lessons."

"Do you ski?" Mr. Kahale asks. "Because the powder at Kringle is phenomenal." I shake my head and he changes tack. "We'd happily pay for your lessons. Rentals too. And babysitting, of course. We learned from last year that too much family time is . . . too much. You'll save our sanity if we can sneak away to the lodge to get a drink. Or not spend our whole day getting them in and out of boots."

Mrs. Kahale places a hand on his arm. "You're going to scare Noelle off. It's not as bad as he's making it sound. But the kids' schedules don't match and Nick's a bit of a ski nut, so he gets antsy if he's that close to a mountain and not on it."

"I'd never skied before college. I'm making up for lost time," he says with a grin. "Anyway, it would be so helpful if you could come with us. The kids would love it."

I'm trying to picture—*any of it.* The closest I've ever gotten to a ski resort is watching Christmas movies. I can't imagine myself in the picturesque lodges or among the Hollywood-perfect couples walking around in posh snow gear with ski poles slung casually over their shoulders. And I really can't imagine Holly's and Jack's playful energy in those serene settings.

Mr. and Mrs. Kahale exchange worried looks. "We'll pay you time and a half," he says. "For fifteen hours each day—though we really don't expect you'll be working even half that."

Time and a half times fifteen hours? I thumb my cell phone in my pocket. The calculator app could tell me exactly how mind-blowing a figure that would be. It's more than I'll make in a month of weekends. It'd cover pointe shoes for a year. Maybe even . . .

"Do you leave Black Friday and come back Monday?" I guess we could leave Thanksgiving night if needed. Dad and I don't do anything fancy. But I need to know how many days—it's the third variable to complete the equation and calculate if this is Beacon-possibility money.

My eyes go wary in my reflection as I catch the guilty look that passes between them. "Why don't you go check on the kids," Mrs. Kahale tells her husband. "They're being suspiciously quiet."

He brandishes crossed fingers as he backs out of the hall.

She laughs lightly and nods toward the dining room, sliding into a chair on the left side, leaving me to sit at the head of the long table. While I've spent plenty of time sitting across from Mrs. Kahale—lingering long after I'm technically off the clock—these conversations are at the kitchen table or island. And they're grumblings about my dad or school or ballet. Beacon.

These chairs are heavier, the setting more formal. The conversation too. "You've been telling me lately how preoccupied your dad's been with work—and how much it bothers you. And maybe that's changed or isn't relevant here—but it made me think you might be open to this trip. Though I completely understand if it doesn't work out."

I feel like I'm looking at one of Jack's I Spy books, trying—and failing—to find the catch. I give up, wrinkling the autumnal tablecloth as I lean forward. "What am I missing?"

"This trip is over winter break, not Thanksgiving. We'd leave right after early dismissal on the twenty-second and come home on the thirtieth." Mrs. Kahale squeezes my hand. "You'd be gone for Christmas."

Babysitting Tip 3:
You don't have to say yes to every job.

The answer is "no." It's so obviously no that I have to try not to laugh. Babysit at their ski cabin and miss *Christmas*? The day I look forward to for the other three hundred sixty-four? Not a chance.

But do I *tell* Mrs. Kahale no?

Absolutely not.

She's leaning forward and Holly's peeking around the corner, holding out crossed fingers. I don't want to disappoint, so I hesitate.

Mrs. Kahale nods sympathetically. "I know it's a lot. I wish the schedule fell differently. We tried to run all the scenarios—but the cabin's six hours away in light traffic, and Holly has a race on the twenty-third and mandatory practice on the twenty-sixth. We can't wait to go up or come back to get you after the holiday. Do you maybe want to think about it and talk to your dad, then get back to me?"

I nod and practically knock over the heavy dining room chair in my haste to stand. "Yes! That would be perfect. I'll think about it."

I think about it as Mr. Kahale overpays me, as his wife drives me home, talking about Jack's *Nutcracker* costume and Holly's latest Christmas request—for a book that's not out yet. "I think she's testing the boundaries of Santa," Mrs. Kahale says wistfully.

I think about it as I climb the stairs to our apartment and unlock the door. "Hey."

Dad's sitting on the couch. He looks up from his laptop when I walk in. "Long day at dance?"

I shrug as I slide off my boots. "I saw the girls and babysat the Kahales."

"Ah." He opens his mouth like he might say more, then shakes his head. "Dinner's on the stove if you didn't eat there. Chili."

Dad and I don't really talk about my schedule anymore. Not since our big fight in September—when he'd left me waiting in the rain after dance—and once I walked home, furious and dripping, had the audacity to ask, "Where were you?"

He claims I never told him I'd added extra studio time, but I swear I did. And things escalated to, "I'm in high school now—I don't need to check in every five minutes or ask your permission to make decisions about *my* life and schedule."

And him responding, "So, I'm just your banker and chauffer? I don't exist just to pay for dance and drive you around."

I'd wrung my soaked shirt out on the floor. "Clearly. But don't bother. I can walk home from Spirit if it's too much of a burden for you."

Dad's face had darkened. "I didn't say it was a *burden*, but how much does this new class even cost? Noelle, the bills from the ones you're already—"

"It's *free*," I'd snapped. "And it's not a class. I just told you, it's *studio time*. Studio B is empty then anyway, so Miss Janet is letting me use it."

"Fine, but I don't know how you can expect me to keep track of all this—your dance, your babysitting, your social events—"

My teeth had been chattering, my Achilles aching, and my feelings hurt. He'd *forgotten me* and hadn't even apologized! "And yet, Autumn doesn't seem to have a problem doing it. Maybe you need to take organization lessons from a fourteen-year-old." I'd slammed my bedroom door to end the conversation.

I'm still thinking about this two months later; maybe he is too as he watches me fill a bowl with chili. Or maybe he's already back to thinking about work. Things have been different between us since then. The closest we've come to revisiting the topic were the few times he's asked if I want a ride from dance—I always refuse and he doesn't push. It's pretty clear where I get my stubborn streak.

And also clear why I haven't brought up Beacon. I don't know if he'd support it, or reject it, or if me leaving now would shut the door on us ever being a team again. I glance at him, looking for any hint he'd attended the school's "Webinar for Potential Parents" that I'd signed him up for. He would've gotten a reminder email this morning and all he'd had to do was click a link . . .

"Did you do anything interesting today?" I prompt.

Dad's pretty firmly situated on the couch. Glasses smudged, drinks and dishes scattered among his piles on the coffee table. Crumbs on his shirt, coffee rings on his papers. "Huh?" He tilts his head toward me, but his eyes don't move from the computer in his lap.

"Never mind." I grab a spoon, the bowl, and my backpack and head for my room, calling over my shoulder, "Homework."

He lifts a hand from his keyboard in acknowledgment.

That's what passes for conversation between us lately. It isn't exactly a recipe for a "Holly, Jolly Christmas." Despite this, I pause algebra homework to text Mrs. Kahale a polite no, but thank you. Even if Dad's Captain Distracto, he's still my dad, still the only other Partridge left. And it's *Christmas* for frost's sake!

Her reply is immediate: I understand! No worries! You're still our favorite.

Followed by: Jack wants me to ask if you'll have a new joke on Tuesday.

His dance class ends right as mine begins, but he doesn't need to wait until we're passing in the hall. I text back: What kind of music did Pilgrims listen to? Plymouth Rock!

The response is a string of random emojis, so she must've given him her phone. I set mine down smiling and make a note to look up a good one for Tuesday, because at least *someone* can't wait to talk to me.

Mine and Dad's interactions over the next week are limited to things like him asking if I want to add anything to the grocery list and if I'm okay with ordering premade Thanksgiving plates from the store's catering department. Black cherry seltzer, orange juice, tampons, blister Band-Aids, and "Fine, but if they do the mini-pies for dessert, anything but pecan."

Or, me asking when we'll go get our Christmas tree, and him answering with a vague "Soon." Even though *he* is the one who usually quotes Mom's advice: "The best ones are gone before Thanksgiving," adding his own, "If we wait too long the field gets tromped up and then I'm lying in mud while sawing it down."

But I guess he's going through a pro-mud phase? Because Thanksgiving comes and goes—premade plates he heats up while on his phone and practically swallows without chewing so he can get back to work—and we still have no tree. We also still haven't talked about Beacon, despite the three new flyers I've strategically placed by the coffee-maker, on the back of the toilet, and on top of the car keys he left on the counter.

I spend Black Friday moping. It's a day we're usually glued to computer screens, competitively scouting the best bargains on things we have no intention of buying—"You found an inflatable flamingo-shaped pool float for a hundred and six? I've got it for eighty-nine. Beat that!" We'd polish our Christmas playlists and finish the day with leftovers and decorating—starting with the tree. Before Mom died, she and Dad would slow dance to Bing Crosby by the glow of the tree's lights and I'd sit on the couch and giggle, pretending to hide under a blanket when they kissed.

This year I'm lugging our tubs of Christmas gear from our storage unit in the apartment building's basement by myself. Dad must have headphones on, because he doesn't hear me yell when I pinch my fingers between the doorframe and handle or drop the bin so it lands with an echoing thud. It's the one with our lights and stockings and tree-skirt—not the ornaments or Mom's snow globes—so I doubt I've damaged anything except my fingers and maybe the floor, but his office door doesn't even crack open to check.

I do the best I can: tacking up the garland with attached clothespins where we display Christmas cards, hanging our Advent calendar on the back of the door, slipping reindeer seat covers on the kitchen chairs, and swapping out our plain blue towels for ones printed with snowmen. I stick up snow-flake window clings, run lights along the railing of our small balcony, arrange the Santa and Mrs. Claus salt and pepper shakers on the table.

But it feels weird to be doing it on my own, and when I lift the triple layer of padding and reveal Mom's collection of snow globes—the ones I've seen so many times as well as the ones still wrapped and numbered—I cover them back up and carry that bin to the corner where the tree *should* be standing. There are some things I can't handle solo.

Dad wanders out midafternoon; for once he's not attached to any sort of device. He looks around and whistles. "You've been busy out here, kiddo! It's looking good."

"Thanks." My voice is tight—he's saying the right words, but I don't want his admiration, I wanted his *help*.

"I'm going to make a turkey-stuffing sandwich. Want one?" He points over his shoulder at the kitchen.

"I already ate."

"Oh." He looks at his watch and scratches the week's worth of scruff on his chin. Even Thanksgiving didn't merit shaving. "I guess I lost track of time. I'm sorry, kiddo. I know I've been busy lately—it's just . . . This is the real thing. I can feel it. All this time I'm spending now—all the things I'm asking you to be patient about—they're going to be worth it."

I've heard this before. Dad used to be an IT guy until Mom died. Then he decided, "Life's too short to spend in a job that's soul-sucking"—and he quit to be his own boss. It's been six years, and with every doohickey or app he invents, he's convinced *this* time will be his big win. I should get "I can feel it, kiddo, our luck's about to change" printed on a double-sided magnet, with the reverse labeled: "dud pile." Then he can just flip it to show which stage we're at.

He's never been *this* absentee before, and I'm over being patient, hearing broken promises, and buying his hype. "So I guess that means we're not getting our tree today?"

He looks down at his feet. "Soon, okay? I promise."

My stomach sours at words I can't bring myself to believe. Maybe his does too, because he heads back to his office without lunch.

As soon as his door closes, guilt settles in, so I make the sandwich and deliver it to a distracted, "Thanks, kiddo," but I'm angry too, so I also retaliate by putting that song about the Christmas donkey on repeat, aiming my speaker at the wall my bedroom shares with his office—then hopping in the shower.

Afterward, when I head to Coco's house for the Sandersons' annual game night—which always starts in charades and ends in good-natured shouting—I leave the bin containing our Christmas ornaments in the middle of the hall outside Dad's office, where he can't avoid seeing it and being reminded of the tree we don't yet have.

Five days later, it's still there. And I've got five layers of bruises on my legs from tripping over it. For the sake of my shins, I move it to the corner beside Mom's snow globes. Not for the first time, I wonder if there was any point in turning down the Kahales if Dad's not going to notice or care if I'm here for the holidays.

But he will. He'll burn out on this project too. The prototype will explode or melt or shatter during some critical part of his beta testing, or the app's code won't run. I don't even know what he's invented this time, I just know I'm sick of the whole process. The grand promises, the grand failures. The grand loneliness of our apartment.

"You okay?" Mae asks after school on Wednesday. I'd been staring into space, trying to decide if a cloud looks more like a Christmas bell or an angel's skirt. They're all reminding me of cookie cutters. The ones we won't be using since our fudge fest replacement day of cookie-baking had to be canceled—Coco's coach called at dismissal to say she'd pulled some strings and set up a practice with a former Olympian to work on Coco's turns. Apparently the guy is booked for months and was only available last-minute.

Which, great for Coco, less great for us. Especially since we can't move to Autumn's kitchen, because her parents are handling some sort of catering emergency. I only caught the words "crab puffs everywhere—shellfish allergy!" before Autumn disconnected and said, "I should head home to help."

So I may have visions of sugarplums dancing in my head, but there won't be any baking in ovens, and the start of my Extravaganza is pushed back another two days to skating.

"I'm fine," I tell Mae.

But it's December first—twenty-four days from the best holiday of the year and thirty days from the worst. My loathing for New Year's stems from when Mom died and less than a month later it was suddenly, "Oh, she died *last year*." Like somehow a new calendar was supposed to make my twenty-day-old grief less all-consuming. Like, "fresh starts" and "looking ahead" were things that erased her gaping absence in my life. If I had my way, New Year's Eve and its dropping balls and resolutions would take a permanent time-out and tinsel and twinkle lights would be year-round decorations.

But this year no one is looking Christmas-cheery, so clearly I need to try harder. After Dad goes to bed, I sneak into his office to hang a strand of lights and drape some garland. I'm not a total heartless Scrooge; I'm careful not to disturb the piles and notes that cover his desk as I set down a handmade card.

If you have to work this hard, you should at least have a festive work space. Love, an elf.

I wake up to a Post-it note on my door. Thanks, kiddo. You're the best. Promise we'll do Christmas stuff soon. He'd signed it —D and drawn a doodle of an elf in a tutu.

I smile into my OJ and Cheerios, but when I knock on his office to say goodbye before school, the twinkle lights are turned off. "You don't like them?"

"No, I think they're great—but staring straight at them was giving me a headache."

"Oh! I can move them." I cross the office to where I'd wound the strand around the curtain rod. The dangling cord bumps his lamp, which pivots and clinks against his mug.

Nothing spills. Nothing even splashes. But I watch his ears redden. "Noelle! I'm trying to work in here. You have school. Just leave it."

My brain deletes those last two letters. *Just leave.*

I do.

Babysitting Tip 4:

If you're enthusiastic about something,
the kids will be too.
If you really sell it, even clean-up can be
made into a fun game.

I'm not sure what Christmas curse I've bestowed upon myself. Did I trip an elf? Insult a reindeer? Give Santa food poisoning with last year's milk and cookies? I must've done something karmically criminal, because my Extravaganza events continue to flop.

"You're sure she's coming?" Autumn asks Mae for the third time. We're all standing on the sidewalk outside the band room—it's where Mae's sister, Rachel, had agreed to meet us after her trumpet rehearsal. She's supposed to be driving us to Ice House, but their carols-skate started fifteen minutes ago and the Primaveras' kid-car, a hand-me-down minivan, is MIA.

"I can call her again, but if she's in rehearsal, her phone won't be on." While Mae dials, Coco's stretching her arms in wide circles, trying to loosen a shoulder muscle that's been bothering her.

"My coach doesn't want me to go," she confesses while Mae bobs her head impatiently to indicate the phone's ringing. "She's worried I'll pull or hurt something if I fall. What if she's right? Autumn had that bruise on her butt for weeks last year."

There's no good way to answer that. I can't promise she won't fall, but I also shouldn't point out that Autumn's not exactly coordinated and that tripping over the benches *before* even getting in the rink is the type of accident that happens uniquely to her.

Mae lowers her phone. "She's not answering."

We wait another five minutes before giving up and walking to the Primaveras'—where the kid-car is in the driveway and Rachel is on the couch watching a movie with her girlfriend, Frances. She doesn't pause it when we enter, doesn't look over when she asks, "Why do you keep calling me? It's annoying."

Coco nudges Autumn, who nudges me. We take a synchronized step backward—it's time to go. Mae might be the quietest Primavera, but it's about to get all sorts of loud in here. Somebody should probably warn Frances, but . . . *Not it!*

"We're going to head out," Autumn announces. "Text us later."

Mae is hands-on-hips, shaking with fury—though some of that could also be from our walk in thirty-eight-degree temps. She nods, but doesn't take her dagger eyes off Rachel, who finally pauses the movie and asks, "What? What's your problem?"

We shut the front door before Mae can give that explanation, but the sound of shouting is audible by the time we reach the end of the driveway.

"Yikes," says Coco as she slings an arm around my shoulders and squeezes. "But caroling will go better. My mom's super excited we asked her to drive this year. She won't forget."

We asked her because Dad's "too busy," and I nearly wept from relief when she said yes. I *did* weep when she followed up by emailing me a video of Coco and me singing carols back in kindergarten. On it, Coco's giggling more than singing and I'm dancing across the school stage. Mom's voice is full of amusement as she tells someone—probably Dad—"She's fine. She's feeling the music. Let her be." My breath caught as Mrs. Sanderson turned the camera as she added her agreement, "Exactly!"

And there was Mom—on my screen. Looking younger than in my memories, but with that same smile. "I love our girls' spirit," said Mrs. Sanderson. The camera flipped back to where I'd roped Coco into turning "Frosty" into some sort of Hokey Pokey, but Mom's clear as a bell when she says, "Me too. I just love them."

I hug Coco now as tightly as I did back then. I'm not normally huggy, so Autumn or Mae would get suspicious or nosy as to the *why*, but Coco just accepts it. She squeezes back. "I guess I'll go do some shoulder PT."

And I guess I'll accept the last-minute babysitting request I'd been texted while waiting at school. Why not? At least the Kingmans' house has a fully stocked kitchen. Guess what, Jalen, we're making cookies.

I bring a tub of frosted trees and snowmen in the car the next day. And while Mrs. Sanderson doesn't forget, she also doesn't control the weather. She frowns past the wiper blades as she parks in the sprawling neighborhood I'd chosen for this year's caroling. "Are you girls sure you want to go out in this?"

Raincoats squeak when everyone turns to look at me. "We've got boots and umbrellas," I say encouragingly. "We should be fine, right?"

"Right," says Mae, but she doesn't sound convinced.

Neither does Mrs. Sanderson. "Okay, but I'll be here. Call if you want me to come get you."

"It's impossible to be unhappy or cold while singing," I tell them as we climb out and pull up hoods and umbrellas. My words are half carried away in a gust of wind, and the hair blowing in my face blocks me from seeing their dubious expressions, but Buddy in *Elf,* my favorite Christmas movie, says singing is the best way to spread Christmas cheer, and he's never steered me wrong before.

The temperature is just warm enough to keep the rain from turning to snow. I'm hoping it will drop those few degrees and we'll have perfect fluffy flakes as a backdrop to our singing. It snowed two years ago while we were caroling, and that night was pretty much magic. One of the houses we'd knocked at had been having a Christmas party—they'd loaded us up with snacks and to-go cups of cocoa. At another house, kids had stopped building their snow fort and joined in our songs. I have that picture hanging in my room.

But instead of turning to snow, the rain becomes sleet, my hands become numb, and my nose and ears begin to burn.

"Noelle," Coco begins cautiously as we knock on our fifth door. It's also our fifth house where no one answers, and as we turn to leave the porch, Autumn has to make an emergency grab for the railing to keep from slipping down the stairs. "I don't know if it's safe for us to be out here. The sidewalks are super slick."

I'm not mad at Coco. I tell myself this three times before speaking. Because she's not wrong and she isn't only saying it because she's worried about getting hurt for her precious swimming. The sidewalk really is becoming an ice trap and *I* should be equally concerned since twisted ankles and pointe shoes don't mix.

"Too bad we don't have our skates today," says Mae.

"Can we just sing in the car?" suggests Autumn through chattering teeth. "And maybe stop at Cool Beans for hot cocoa and home for dry clothes before the tree lighting?"

They're miserable. The realization that they're just *tolerating* these traditions started by my mom, not *enjoying* them, is a gut punch. My voice is barely steady as I say, "Yeah, of course." When Mae looks at me with concern, I fake a smile and add, "You know I hate the cold. Let's go."

We don't carol in the car. There's no way we can over Mrs. Sanderson's questions, our chattering teeth, and the roar of the cranked heat. I don't feel like singing anyway.

Today's the day the Kahales headed to see Wyatt dance. They'd chosen the matinee for obvious kid-bedtime reasons, but I don't remember when it starts. Has he already performed? Is he onstage right now? I spin the bracelet they'd given me around my wrist. I haven't been to their house since the ski trip invitation. The kids sent me a string of turkey and pie emojis on Thanksgiving, and I responded with a joke (*Knock, knock. Who's there? Hank. Hank, who? Hanksgiving Day!*). We see each other in passing at Spirit—but they've been gone skiing on the weekends. I miss them. I'd give a lot for one of Jack's hugs right now.

But it's the tree lighting in Juncture tonight! Sure, we're cranky and cold and potentially frostbitten, but the skies will clear, the town band will tune their instruments, the elementary school chorus will give an adorable performance, and it will all build to that moment of magic when Santa comes down Main Street on a fire engine and the enormous tree in town square is illuminated. We'll take selfies—so many selfies to make up for the ones we don't have—laugh and clink cocoas, and sing along with "O, Christmas Tree."

As I'm thinking this, my phone buzzes. I dig it out of my pocket and unlock the screen. Juncture Update: Due to inclement weather, tonight's tree lighting festivities will be postponed. For more information . . .

Autumn must get the same alert, because she pats my shoulder from the back row. I bet she's navigating to the town website with her other hand and wishing she had her planner so she could compare her calendar to theirs—but I already know the rain date. It conflicts with my *Nutcracker* shows. No tree lighting for me.

I shut my eyes and take some deep breaths. This holiday season seems to be daring me to become a grinch, but I'm not giving in. So Christmas spirit is a bit harder this year, so what? I've got a baking cabinet and a Pinterest account. I can make this work.

Since it's my turn to host tomorrow—for the stupid hot-cocoa mason jars—I've got some serious planning to do to make them less stupid. I open my eyes and my Pinterest app, pulling up my Christmas inspiration boards. There's going to be so much snowflaking holiday spirit in my apartment, they're going to breath it in like smog.

I scan the links I saved and can practically picture it now. I'll greet them with the adorable elf-ear headbands, a cup of eggnog, and a slice of fruitcake. A new playlist of Christmas bops. Autumn can be in charge of measuring, I'll pour. Coco can be on ribbons, Mae can make cards.

I'll put some holly in their jolly if it kills me!

It does go like that . . . sorta. I have the hot glue gun burns to prove I worked hard on the headbands. They're somewhat lopsided but mostly cute. The fruitcake is slightly oozing . . . but it smells okay. And the eggnog . . . okay, that's a fail. I don't love it at the best of times, but the kind Dad bought is gingerbread-flavored and made with coconut milk. It tastes like sunblock and cinnamon had a very weird baby. Despite this, I'm hopeful.

What I hadn't planned for was Autumn to scowl as she stuck on her headband and ask, "This won't take long, right?" in a voice that screams *Let's get this over with.*

"You got somewhere else to be?" Coco teases. She's pretending to enjoy the fruitcake but really crumbling bits into her napkin.

I swoop in with the garbage can. "You don't have to eat that." I just tried a bite and am not sure I'll ever recover. Turns out its reputation is totally merited. "There are cookies—" I point to a reindeer-shaped jar by the microwave and Coco gratefully switches to those after discreetly dumping her eggnog in the sink.

"This is giving me a headache." Autumn whines as she pulls off her elf ears and rubs her temples.

"Oh." This isn't the cranky-kitten Autumn we're used to. She's pale and pinch-faced and seems truly annoyed, so I don't complain about the fact we haven't even taken an "elfie" yet. Instead I turn off my pop-carols playlist, because I doubt it's helping.

She sighs and rubs her temples. "What do we have to do?"

I know the hot chocolate mason jars aren't going to win any awards for coolest idea ever, but Autumn's annoyance is quickly evolving into the type of snarly that has the rest of us exchanging looks. And her catching them—which doesn't help matters.

The project is literally just pouring layers of cocoa powder, powdered milk, sugar, and marshmallows into jars, but she critiques Mae's measuring ("Haven't you heard of leveling?") and Coco's pouring ("The goal is to get it *in* the jar"). She reties the bows, reletters the cards we're attaching, and makes no attempt to disguise her relief when the two dozen finished jars are lined up on my table. "My head is pounding. I've got to get home and lie down."

It isn't until the next morning, when we wake up to text messages from her—I have the flu or something. I spent the whole night throwing up ☹—that any of it makes sense. Because our sweet Autumn is the world's worst sick patient.

Coco actually responds Ohhhh! So that explains yesterday! before adding a heart and Feel better.

But since patient zero had her hands all over the cocoa, the jars of germs will be heading to the trash instead of to our teachers. Sure, Mr. Krieb's pop quizzes are evil, but I don't wish all-night vomiting even on him.

But you know what? I don't even care anymore. When "The Most Wonderful Time of the Year" comes on my holiday playlist, I practically scream, "Turn off the music!"

Then I have to repeat the words at a normal volume, because my phone doesn't recognize my angry voice.

Most wonderful? Yeah, that singer can go choke on a candy cane. I sweep the mason jars from our counter into our garbage can—enjoying the sound they make as they clang and smash. I mean, *why would* this idea go well? Nothing else has.

It occurs to me that maybe I'm irritable because I caught whatever Autumn has, but I don't think so. I slam the lid on the garbage can, then sink to the kitchen floor. It feels gritty, and when I raise a hand to wipe my eyes, I can't, because it's coated in coffee grounds and other crumbs. Vacuuming is on Dad's list of household chores, so clearly he's not doing those either. I blink back tears and lower my head to my knees.

Mom used to say, "Some days you've got to hit the Reset button. Get back in bed, pull up the covers, and have a do-over."

I want that. Not with a day, with the whole holiday season.

Instead I get Dad wandering in with his headset on and coffee cup in hand. "So the phone call on the twenty-fourth? Yes, definitely. Can you hang on a sec? Thanks."

There's a pause where he fumbles with a button. "Hey, kiddo, could you do your stretches somewhere else? You're blocking the coffeemaker."

Stretches? I fight the urge to slam my door after I storm past him to my room. Why bother? Christmas isn't Christmas if no one wants to celebrate with me, and what's the point of slamming doors if no one's going to care?

Yet, a week later he's knocking on my door, wearing the blazer he saves for my recitals and his interviews. He's carrying a cellophane-wrapped bouquet and we're just supposed to pretend everything's normal between us because it's the anniversary of Mom's death?

Saying any of this feels disrespectful to *her*, so I don't. Instead I sit quietly in the car beside him as we drive to the cemetery, rubbing my Achilles and sleepwalking through our traditions—like if I tread lightly, I won't sink beneath the surface into the dangerous emotions below. Grief always feels private, but more so this year. And, no, I'm not pulling back my mask and exposing all the messy vulnerability beneath it. He doesn't deserve that. So when we sit in a booth at Mom's favorite restaurant and it's my turn to recount some treasured memory, I repeat the same one I shared last year. I don't owe him more than that. It's already unfair he's got more years to choose from.

As soon as we're home, I'm peeling off my dress and throwing on a leotard, lying about "an important rehearsal— the show's only a week away, you know"—then practically jogging to Spirit. I haven't booked studio time, but Miss Janet won't turn me away.

There's classes in both practice spaces, but I don't care.

Anything that gets my body moving will help me turn off my brain. I throw myself into helping with the five-year-olds. Making them laugh with jokes and by exaggerating the mistakes in their form so they can give me corrections. "*No! Turn your feet out. Don't bend your leg. Your arms are all droopy. Like this—*"

By the end of the hour, they look so much better and I feel better too. While Miss Janet dismisses them to their parents, I run through my solo on demi-pointe. I'm just about finished when Miss Janet reenters the studio. She's got to be nearly fifty, but the only lines on her dark skin are smile ones. "That section before the manège is looking better—you don't look as nervous about what's to come."

I lift a foot and wiggle my toes. "It's easier not to be nervous when I'm wearing slippers." I hadn't bothered to change into pointe shoes since the studio's about to close.

She raises an eyebrow as she powers down the stereo, beginning her process of resetting the classroom for the morning. "Accept the compliment, Noelle."

"Yes, Miss Janet." I look at the floor, absently spinning my bracelet around my wrist and rubbing my left calf with my right foot, even though my Achilles isn't bothering me right now.

"There are so many opportunities for you with ballet. I hope you're thinking about your future. Once the *Nutcracker* chaos is over, I want to sit down and discuss some possibilities with you, okay?"

I nod. *Beacon.* She obviously means Beacon. I wonder if she has any clue that third time's a charm, that when she suggests the school for me again, this time I'll likely agree.

In the week before the show, dance is the only thing holding me together. While Christmas can go bah its own humbug, everything *Nutcracker* related is going super well. I mean, our dress rehearsal flops—two angels fell off the stage, one of the mice forgot her steps, and there was a terrifying moment when Kenzi tripped over nothing while en pointe—but according to dance superstition, a bad dress rehearsal means the show's going to shine. And the first two do.

So of course I wake up with my period on the day of the last performance. Cramps, bloating, and bleeding pair so well with a *white* tutu. It's not like I can wear period underwear beneath or black shorts over it, like I typically do during this time of the month. There are more than fifty turns in my variation—am I going to spend every one of them wondering if I look like shark bait?

It makes me think of Mrs. Kahale and how the last time I was feeling this crampy at ballet, she'd noticed and insisted on driving me home. Taking a detour though Cool Beans to order me the most ridiculous—and delicious—whipped cream sugar bomb of a coffee drink. "This is what I always treat myself to when I have mine. Doctors say to drink chamomile and avoid salty foods—good for them—I swear by a caramel mocha frappe and corn chips."

I want those delivered to my bed. Along with a glass of OJ and a side of pain meds. A hot-water bottle. A cool hand on my forehead. Basically, I want my mom. And a promise that if I double up with a thong panty liner and tampon, that nothing will leak or show or do anything to take the audience's attention away from the choreography I've worked so hard to master.

But those are all impossible things. I can't even guarantee Dad will make it to tonight's performance. He's already missed the first two.

I'm sitting at my desk, putting on stage makeup when Dad knocks on my door. "Need some clean tights?"

While he may be wearing his "lucky" coffee-stained sweatshirt for the third day in a row, the rest of our clothes are clean. Laundry is his de-stressing hobby, and from the number of times I've come home to fresh sheets in the past couple of weeks, I know his new project has to be close to total collapse. I wish it'd hurry up and land on the dud pile so he can pick up a freelance IT job, work a regular schedule, and let me have my dad back.

But more than I wish that, I wish he'd let our laundry stay dirty another day and instead spent that hour at one of my shows. My hand trembles on the liquid liner I use to camouflage the glue line for my fake eyelashes, so I lower it before I have to start the whole process over. I'm pretty much done anyway. I pick up my makeup setting spray, shut my eyes, and spritz it in my face. It's a weird feeling that never gets less weird but helps everything stay put when I sweat. The pause while I wait for it to dry helps me force down all the angry words gathering in my throat.

Dad's waiting for an answer, but my teeth are gritted, so I reach down and pull up the leg of my pants to show him the tights I'm already wearing.

"Okay, cool." He sets the bin of folded laundry on the floor inside my room. "I guess I'll get back to work."

It's not "cool." Nothing about today is. I tug the leg of my trashbag pants back into place—they're not *made* of trash bags, that's just what they're called, and they're designed to keep dancers' muscles warm. Right now I feel boiling.

"Sure," I snap as I click the lid back on the spray—my makeup will stay put, but these feelings won't. "I know how busy you are. And since you're *so* busy, I'll make things easier for you. Don't come to my show today. I don't want you there."

"Noelle?" Dad looks shocked as I slam my makeup drawer. Not that it stays closed. I've warped the track by using it to break in new pointe shoes—closing them in it over and over until the toe box softens.

I keep moving, grabbing my ballet bag and water bottle, shoving my feet in my boots, and yanking my coat from the hook by the door. Then I pause for a second. Waiting for him to contradict me, to tell me *of course he'll be there*, or at the very, very least, offer up the French swear word that all dancers say for good luck. It's the ballet equivalent of "break a leg," and there's no way he'll let me walk through the door without saying it.

Right?

But when I glance over my shoulder with my hand on the knob, he's still standing by my room, rubbing a tired hand over the stubble on his chin and blinking bloodshot eyes. "In this house we don't fear failure, we fear . . ."

He's waiting for me to fill in the blank. I narrow my eyes and spit out the words I've heard so often, "Not trying."

"This time it's going to be different," he says. "I just know it."

Babysitting Tip 5:
When in doubt, tell a joke.

Istill get nervous before every performance. Even when I know the steps forward and backward. Even on the third and final show. Even when the stage is only a slightly raised platform. The fight with Dad makes things worse. It was a lie; of course I want him here. But now if he doesn't come, I can tell myself he'd been planning to and only stayed home because I told him to. The thought of him not seeing me perform makes me feel how Autumn must've when she had that forty-eight-hour bug last week.

So I do what I do whenever my stomach starts to twist—find a small person to distract me. It's not like I have to look far. They're all over the storage room that's normally used to house the folding chairs now filling with a chattering audience.

"Hey, Fern," I call to a tiny angel who's struggling to tie the laces on her ballet slippers. As I crouch and take over the task, I ask, "Why did the walnut cross the road?"

She giggles. "I don't know. Why?"

Before I've given the punch line, there are two more

angels, a snowflake, and a mouse waiting to hear it. "To escape the Nutcracker."

Their laughter settles some of the butterflies in my stomach. So as I fix buns, try baby wipes on stains—this is why we don't drink *fruit punch* juice boxes while in costume!—I tell more. My stash of cheesy humor keeps growing, because many of my babysitting clients gifted me joke books along with cash for Christmas.

"What kind of nut won't work in a Nutcracker?"

My favorite part is when kids try and logic the punch line, so I don't interrupt as Lucia and Fern debate and announce, "Coconut! It's too big."

"Oh, good one. I was going to say 'donut,' but I like yours better. A coconut wouldn't fit at all." While they're coming up with more answers, I sneak into the hall to see how close we are to raising the curtain. Well, not "raising the curtain," because there isn't one, but starting.

The Jane Dewitt Memorial House—which is where our performances take place—is a local historic building. Autumn insists "memorial house" makes it sound like a funeral parlor. She's not wrong.

There are signs advertising tours, but I've only ever seen the auditorium, foyer, bathroom, coatroom, and storage-room-slash-backstage. None of that is historic. I mean, I guess renovations done in the '80s—1980s—are pretty old, but according to the plaque outside, the rest of the house is a century older.

The auditorium is painted cream and mint green. It's got puffy floral curtains that look like a fabric version of flower-scented air freshener, which is how the room smells. The ninety-six chairs I set up in eight rows of twelve with an aisle down the middle are almost full. No, ninety-five chairs, because I moved one to the foyer so Kenzi's grandmother would have a place to sit while collecting tickets.

"Are we ready?" Miss Janet asks, coming up behind me to take her own peek.

"Seems like it," I reply. "Hannah Goldman's mom sent her with a coloring book and markers. I swapped them for crayons, but the sooner we start, the less chance the angels go onstage looking tie-dyed."

"I heard about Masie's juice box." She shakes her head and laughs ruefully. "At least it's the final show. Did I see your dad out there?"

I'm not sure how to answer that, so I go with honesty, almost choking on it. "I hope so." But the girls are here, seated in the second row, laughing about something on Coco's phone with a bouquet tucked under Autumn's chair. Watching them is enough to push back the tears that would destroy my careful makeup.

Directly in front of them are Mr. and Mrs. Kahale, tripod set up. Seeing them calms me too. They'd given me a huge bouquet of flowers after the first show. The accompanying card had read, *We are so proud of you!*

I'd needed to hear that.

"Well, I think it's time for me to stop watching the audience and get onstage." Miss Janet brushes her hands down the front of her silk jumpsuit. "Do you mind getting the first group lined up?"

"Sure." I spin toward the storage room, where the noise and activity level are growing increasingly chaotic. My stomach is twisting again and the Sugar Plum Fairy doesn't appear until the second act, so after I shepherd Clara, Fritz, her parents, and the rest of the partygoers into a line, I hunt down my favorite joke buddy.

"Hey, Jack, what do you call a dancing sheep?"

He stops driving his cement mixer over the radiator and looks up with expectant eyes. "What?"

"A baaaa-llerina," I bleat.

He doubles over. "Good one." Then turns to repeat the joke to everyone in earshot. There's no space in this tiny room for parent volunteers. Miss Janet's assistant, Miss Haley, is in charge. Me and the other older dancers pitch in keeping the kids calm while not missing our own cues.

My favorite place to help is the corner in the hallway. From there I can make sure the littles don't fight while they're waiting to scamper onto the stage. More importantly, I'm right here when they come off again—on a performance high, beaming and squealing when they run to hug me.

From my spot I can scan most of the audience, but I don't see Dad. I push that from my mind and focus on kids and cues.

At Beacon, there are real dressing rooms. Mirrors and makeup tables. Costume racks. Prop masters. There are stage lights, curtains, live music. Programs that weren't photocopied at the local office supply store and hastily folded by the first five dancers to show up. At Beacon there'd be the full ballet, not just "selections."

But if I were at Beacon, I wouldn't have Jack Kahale holding my hand in the hall. Squeezing my fingers and whispering, "Get him, Holly" as he watches his sister's adorably fierce (but strictly choreographed) battle with the Mouse King.

I wouldn't get her leaping hug as she dashes offstage. Her faced pressed tight against the sweatshirt I'm wearing over my costume. She crushes down the front of my pancake tutu, making the back flip up. It's not until the rest of her classmates decided to pile on in a group hug that I get nervous. That's a lot of makeup surrounding my pale tulle.

But there is one other thing Beacon has that I can't find here—the oldest Kahale boy. After I collect their prop swords so there's no backstage battles and Holly and the other soldiers rush off to watch Hannah play Animal Crossing, I ask Jack, "How was Wyatt's *Nutcracker*? Do you like watching or dancing it better?"

"I like their flipping guys. Why don't we have those?"

Yeah, the Russian dance was never a "selection" Miss Janet included. Probably because we lacked the stage-size or talent to execute it well.

"Wyatt was good," Jack adds as an afterthought. He squeezes my hand and says, "You're good too. I like you as Sugar Plum Fairy better."

I know his ranking's based on loyalty and not accuracy, but I crouch and hug him anyway as the dancers clear the stage at the end of the first act. This kid is the best. "Thank you."

He shrugs. "Your costume is sparklier."

Since there's no curtain to shut and no set pieces to change besides removing the small artificial Christmas tree from the corner of the stage, the intermission between acts serves mostly as a bathroom break for the audience. One for me too. Thank goodness Miss Janet told me about a separate one-seater, because do you know how hard it would be to maneuver in a stall in a tutu? Double thank goodness nothing's leaked and I'm not about to turn this Christmas ballet into a gory Halloween spectacle.

And then—I'm onstage! It's anticlimactic. My only job in the opening of the act is to welcome Clara to the Land of Sweets and begin the dancing festivities in her honor.

But I'm not leaving the stage for long—it barely feels worth it to put my warm-ups back on, but of course I do. A few songs later and it's my big moment. There are so many kids in the hallway at this point and there are tugs on my costume and overloud whispers of encouragement as I take a deep breath and strip off my trashbag pants, sweatshirt, and warm-up booties. I stretch my ankles, shake out my shoulders, and nod acknowledgment to the French swears and other sweet words.

But as soon as I step into the rosin box, the rest of the world fades. I forget to search for Dad in the audience, because I'm lost in my head, lost in the music—finding the precise moment to pull on my performance face and step onto the stage.

In a full production, the Sugar Plum Fairy owns the stage for more than eleven minutes—there's her romantic pas de deux, then a respite during the leaping dance of the cavalier, *then* her big solo, and finally the up-tempo coda where she and the cavalier partner again.

Without a partner, those eleven minutes become two. They're a beautiful, lilting two minutes and the dance is demanding, but it's only two minutes. I want so much more.

Because this is what I live for; it's when I come alive. Practice is for determining the precise angles of wrists and timing of steps, finding my spot for turns, and blocking out leaps. Performance is for taking those thousands of tiny decisions and calculations that I've rehearsed to the point of muscle memory and making them sing. If I need any motivation to lift my leg higher, exert on my turnout, or land lighter in my jumps, all I have to do is remember that Wyatt Kahale was *almost* in this audience and imagine that he's actually here. I picture his full lips pressed tight in concentration as he studies the girl who's stolen the show at his younger siblings' ballet. Maybe he'd shift in his gray metal chair and do some imagining of his own—of himself partnered with me.

The idea makes me sort of breathless, which isn't ideal as I head into the hardest combination of my dance: the thirty-two counts of continuous turns that end the song. It's a dizzying sequence of pirouettes, fouetté, chaîné, and piqué turns that form the manège—which just means it makes a big circle around the stage.

I force all thoughts of Wyatt Kahale from my mind as I sight my spot—the first of the five focal points I'll use to keep my bearings as I spin and circle. I close my rib cage, lift my chin, and rise to relevé, going en pointe to begin my turns.

I'm stepping out, and out, and out, my head twirling, my core aching, stepping out—and then I'm done. I end in fourth position, trying to catch my breath without looking like I'm gasping. The applause creeps up on me slowly. It's not that the audience is slow to clap, I'm just slow to hear it. But when I do, it feeds a hunger deep in my aching muscles. The sound is a rush of adrenaline, of satisfaction, a craving for more, even while I'm still in the midst of it.

Curtain call is a blur of restless little feet in ballet slippers, and giggles, and wobbly, knobby-kneed curtseys. Jack takes a few extra bows. We give flowers to Miss Janet and Miss Haley. Parents stand—first to clap louder, then to look around for dropped gloves and to gather their belongings. It's a Sunday night, a school night, and most of the under-ten students are overtired and exhausted from having three shows this weekend. It doesn't take long for back-stage to empty, until all that's left are forgotten slippers, empty snack wrappers, and a collection of stray sequins, feathers, and bobby pins.

Normally I'm the one who stays and gathers all the recital detritus that will fill the lost and found. Usually I help pack up props, give the old wooden Nutcracker a kiss as we enrobe him in bubble wrap and say, "See you next fall." Then I'd head to the auditorium and pick up discarded programs and help fold and stack the chairs on their wheeled carts.

But tonight I don't even wash off my makeup. I throw my trashbag pants and a sweatshirt over my base layers, swap my pointe shoes and warm-up booties for shearling boots, and hand over the Sugar Plum Fairy's tutu. Will I see it or the Nutcracker again next year? I don't know.

And I still don't know if Dad is here, but my friends are waiting on the other side of the foyer. I'm one quick stop in the coatroom away from heading out for stuffed French toast. I yank my jacket off a hanger and turn to leave, almost walking into Mrs. Kahale.

"Oh. Hi!" I say.

"Noelle, as always, you were breathtaking up there," she says warmly. "I was just telling Nick that there's not a girl at Wyatt's school who comes close to having your stage presence and grace."

"Thanks." I feel my cheeks flush from the praise I want so much to believe. If I decide to audition next month, I may call and ask her to repeat it. I shuffle my feet. "Were you able to find a sitter to go skiing with you?"

"Oh." Mrs. Kahale's smile gentles. "We didn't ask anyone else. We wanted *you*. I completely understood that it was a long shot and why you couldn't come, but there was never going to be anyone else."

It's my turn to say a startled "Oh."

"Noelle, you're more than just a babysitter to us—I hope you know that."

I touch my wrist, but it's bare. I'd taken my bracelet off for the performances. The bracelet that Holly and Jack picked out on their trip last summer—the one that says "hula" (*dance*), "pā'ani" (*play*), and " 'ohana" (*family*).

There's a dry cough behind me, and Mrs. Kahale and I turn to see Dad coming from the bathrooms. "Hey kiddo; Ginger."

My hand drops from my wrist, the soft sentiments of the moment hardening. "You're here?"

"Of course I am. I was just stacking the chairs," he says. "Where were you?"

His shrug is infuriating. I can't tell if he's being oblivious, or if he's already forgotten that the last time we talked—yelled—I told him not to come. Or that "of course" doesn't work when he's missed my last two shows.

Who knows what this coatroom was in the house's historic life, but now it feels like a trap. Even though there are two exits, there's no escaping this conversation. One of the doors heads from the hallway to the bathrooms, the other into the foyer, where Autumn and Coco are bent over a phone and Mae is watching me. She can't have a clue what's going down, but she nods encouragingly.

I'm so angry and so tired of being angry. Dad doesn't get to tell me he'll "never miss a show" and then miss two-thirds. He doesn't get to guilt me about not staying to stack the chairs when I'm the only one who always does. He doesn't get to wear the Santa pin I made him back in sixth grade on the collar of his coat when he's participated in no other Christmas events this year. *It's a week until Christmas and we don't even have a tree.* Mom's snow globes are still in their box. I don't even know what invention he's working on, but I'm so tired of feeling like it's more important to him than I am.

I touch my empty wrist again. *Dance. Play. Family.* "You know what," I say to Mrs. Kahale. "I've changed my mind. If the offer still stands, I'd love to come."

"Really?" Her face lights up. "We would love to have you."

I narrow my eyes at Dad and drop the gauntlet: "I'm going away for Christmas." I add, "With the Kahales." If he minds this, he'll definitely object to Beacon—and if not . . . No. That's impossible.

I wait for his reaction, but he just says, "Huh?"

Mrs. Kahale's eyes are wide as she's taking in my crossed arms and his blank expression. She pauses slightly before giving my dad the explanation she must infer is needed. "We invited Noelle to come skiing with us over the break—well, maybe that's not quite the right way to phrase it, but we asked her to join us as our babysitter. If she'd like to learn to ski, we're happy to cover rentals and lessons and whatever she needs."

Dad's forehead is creased. He's scratching his chin, even though he must've taken a few minutes to shower and shave off the stubble. "Do you want to learn to ski, kiddo? I always meant to take you but just never got around to it."

"That's not the point!" I hope Mrs. Kahale knows I'd never use that voice with Holly or Jack. But this was me making a major bluff, and he's supposed to call me on it. He's supposed to say "no." To throw back his head and laugh. *No way, kiddo. You're dreaming if you think I'm letting you wake up to stockings and waffles in any bedroom but your own.*

"Did you hear me say I'll be gone for Christmas?"

He doesn't react. Unless not-reacting is a reaction. And because he's not reacting, Mrs. Kahale adds more details. "With Holly's ski-team schedule, we'll leave straight after early dismissal on the twenty-second to drive up to Vermont. Then come back on the thirtieth. I know it's a lot to ask, and if the holiday is truly the only sticking point, maybe we could look into a flight for Noelle into Burlington on the twenty-sixth. If they're not all sold out. It's about two hours from there to the cabin, but we could—"

I'm scrutinizing his face, waiting for the moment this all sinks in. He's going to be so mad, and the thought makes me almost giddy. For the first time in ages, I won't be the only one feeling that way.

Dad nods as he comes out of whatever thought loop he's been stuck in. "If that's what you want, I think it's fine."

"What is?" I ask, because he can't mean—

He shoves his hands in his pockets. "Actually I think it's a good idea. I'm going to be busy and this keeps Noelle from being bored or becoming a nuisance. Dance is pretty much wrapped up until the new year. So, yeah, *go*. This is a great opportunity, kiddo."

"But—" *Nuisance?* At some point I'd begun petting a faux-fur coat like it's a cat.

"Christmas is just a date," he says. "We'll celebrate when you get back." He's nodding, adjusting some sort of mental abacus. "Since this is what you want, I support it."

What I want. It feels like I'm standing on a fancy stage, like the one at Beacon, the kind that has a trapdoor. And it's just opened beneath me. I was right—this coatroom is a trap. One I'd set for myself. I just hadn't expected Dad to spring it.

"Oh, Noelle!" Mrs. Kahale squeezes me in a hug, then clasps her hands to her chest. "Jack and Holly are going to be so excited. Thank you! Thank you both. You've just made their Christmas." Her eyes go soft as she adds, "I promise we'll do our best to make yours wonderful too."

I smile weakly and hold up a one-minute finger to Coco, who's tapping an imaginary watch on her wrist, patting her stomach. "Sounds . . . good."

"I'll let you get to your friends, but we'll talk tomorrow to nail down all the details, okay?"

I tell her "sure." Tell Dad I won't be home late. Tell myself this is all going to work out somehow. I could cancel on the girls. I could cite cramps or exhaustion—neither of which is a lie. I could go home, hash this out with Dad, come up with a better solution, then call Mrs. Kahale.

Instead, I flee to my friends.

They're all, "*Hey there, prima ballerina,*" and Coco's thrusting flowers at me. I take a moment to pretend to smell them and compose my face. When I look up, I say, "Stuffed French toast?" And we're spilling out into the night, their laughter and chatter loud enough to disguise that I'm not joining in.

At least it does for the five minutes until we're seated in a booth, but as soon as we place our drink orders, Coco turns to me. "Okay, what's wrong? You just killed it on the stage, so why do you look like someone told you Santa's not real?"

I mouth "Sorry" to the family one booth over, the dad having turned around to glare, but Coco doesn't notice because she's still waiting for my answer. "I'm—I'm going away for Christmas."

"Your dad's taking you somewhere?" asks Coco. "Cool."

"Really?" Autumn looks surprised.

"Where?" Mae's gone dreamy-eyed. "I've always wanted to do a Christmas trip—the German Christkindlmarkt, or somewhere warm with palm trees . . ."

"Not with Dad," I clarify as our waitress delivers four mugs of cocoa. "I'm going to babysit for the Kahales at their ski cabin." Saying it aloud feels weird, and wrong, and final.

"You're missing Christmas to babysit?" Autumn scrunches her nose. "How long will you be gone?"

I stare in my mug. "All break."

Autumn sets hers down with a clank. "But what about our plans? They're *your* plans. They're in my planner."

A tiny part of me is like *Now you care?* Because this is more enthusiasm than she's shown for any of the activities that bombed so far. But I've picked enough fights today, so I sip my cocoa and shrug.

"The *Kahales?*" Mae's eyes are narrowed. "Are you kidding me?"

"No." I sputter into my mug, spattering whipped cream and chocolate as I realize the conclusion she's drawing. "It's not what you think."

She hums and rolls her eyes.

"What am I missing?" Coco asks Autumn, who gives an annoyed shrug.

"He won't even be there," I insist. This is true; I confirmed with Mrs. Kahale that it will only be the *four* of them plus me.

"He, who?" asks Autumn.

"Wyatt Kahale." Mae pronounces his name like a fungus.

"Who's Wyatt?" Coco eats the whipped cream off her drink with a spoon, leaning in like she's watching a soap opera. "I thought the small one's name was Jack or John or something."

"It is," says Autumn, looking between me and Mae.

"It has nothing to do with Wyatt!" Now I'm as pissed as she is. Thanks, best friend, for jumping to conclusions and assuming I'd ditch them—and my dad—to go hang out with a guy. Even if he is perfect.

Coco reaches a long swimmer's arm across the table and bops me on the nose. "Who. Is. Wyatt?"

"He's the kids' older half-brother," Mae explains. "He goes to Beacon and Noelle is in love with him."

"Not cool," I tell her, before turning to Coco and Autumn. "And I'm not. I mean, he's a good dancer, but I've never even met him."

"Oh! *Ohhhh!* Is that why you're so obsessed with that school?" Coco sinks back in the booth in dramatic relief.

"It's a good school," I say defensively.

"A good school with a hot guy." Coco gets out her phone. "What's his handle? I want to follow him."

"I haven't found it." When Autumn narrows her eyes suspiciously, I add, "Really. If you do, let me know."

Coco says, "Bummer," but she doesn't get how weird it is that I haven't. Most dancers have one—*I* have one. Because if you're chasing companies, chasing fame, you need to be findable. I've only found Wyatt—untagged—in the videos of his classmates.

"So, to recap—" Autumn asks the waitress to give us

another minute before turning back to me. "You're abandoning us and your dad on your favorite holiday to babysit in a ski cabin, when you don't ski, don't like the cold, and you don't have any ulterior motives—but apparently you *do* have a crush on some guy we've never heard of?"

Well, when she puts it like that, it doesn't sound great. I thought the question was rhetorical, but they're all staring at me expectantly. I chew on whatever's left of my stage lipstick and shrug. "Basically, yeah."

"What's really going on?" asks Mae. "Why would you agree to this?"

"It will pay for so much of Beacon. And I really didn't think my dad would let me go." My voice wavers. "But he didn't even hesitate—so maybe it's a good trial run. If I can't handle a week away, I can't handle a whole school year. But if I can . . ."

"I thought you hadn't decided about Beacon?" Mae's voice is wavery too.

"I'm thinking"—I take a deep breath—"I'm thinking I should at least *audition*. See if they'll take me." I don't know if I'll get in, if I'll qualify for scholarships, or how I'll begin to pay the rest of the tuition. But I know that what Miss Janet said at the beginning of the night applies to me too—*I need to stop watching and get onstage.* I need to take a shot, like Dad always says, *In our family we don't fear failure, we fear not trying.*

"But—"

"I get it." Coco cuts Mae off. "This is your version of the National Juniors. And if you want this, I want it for you." I open my mouth to say *thanks* but she's not done, "But, *ugh* to you missing Christmas! I don't know how to Christmas without my Noelle!"

I blubber "Thanks" as the waitress approaches, then wisely decides to back off again.

"Have you signed up to audition?" Autumn asks.

"Not yet. I keep pulling up the application, then chickening out."

Autumn nudges my phone toward me. "Do it now. No more chickening. We're all here for you."

The site is still up in my browser. The answers on auto-fill. The audition's in DC in late January. All I need to do is press Submit.

I glance at Mae. Her eyes are wet, but she nods and reaches for my hand. "Hit the stupid button already."

Coco reaches across the table for Mae's other hand, then links with Autumn beside her, who touches my arm as I click Submit.

We're silent for a long moment, then Autumn pulls back and asks, "You're allowed visitors, right? Not in Vermont—there we'll just have to do lots of vidcalls. But at Beacon? Because I already looked up how we'd get there. It's a bus from Juncture to Philly, then a straight shot on the train to DC."

I laugh. "I want all the visits—but I have to get in first! And they're really, scarily selective."

Mae's still squeezing my hand, but she drops it to elbow me instead. "Of course you'll get in. Shut it with the negative talk about my best friend."

We're all giggling when the waitress returns. "You girls know what you want yet?"

I do.

Things aren't fixed with Dad or certain with Beacon, but this moment with this trio is sweeter than the stuffed French toast I'm about to devour.

Babysitting Tip 6:
Do not teach them any song, tell them any joke, or read them any book that you're not willing to sing, hear, or reread a hundred million times.

Winter break officially began twenty-eight minutes ago. Except for bathroom breaks and to get more food, Mae, Coco, Autumn, and I will likely not be leaving our seats for the next six hours. The big difference is that their seats are cozy spots in the Primaveras' family room, where they'll be parked for the duration of the Christmas Movie Marathon with plates for cookies, bags of popcorn, and a few interruptions from Mae's twin brothers and Remy.

My seat? It's the in back of the Kahales' Mercedes SUV, en route to Vermont. I'm squeezed between Jack's car seat and Holly's booster. The row behind us is folded down to fit all the luggage, the floor in front of me is crowded with bags of snacks and activities for the kids. Though the only activity they have any interest in is the same one occupying my friends. I know this not because of any deductive genius but because Holly is pointing at the built-in screens, chanting "movie, movie," while Jack continues his progress through "99 Grape Juice Boxes on the Wall."

"The screen time rules haven't changed. We're not putting on a movie until we're past halfway," says their mom.

Holly huffs, crosses her arms, and falls silent for about thirty seconds before turning to me. "Will you come watch me ski? I'm learning to do moguls. I'm really fast. My coach tells me I'm pretty much the fastest kid he's ever seen."

Her dad clears his throat. "And the most honest and humble."

"Well, it was something like that. Will you come see me?"

"Of course." I have to raise my voice to be heard over Jack, whose singing is getting louder to cover the fact that his backward counting's a bit rocky. Pretty sure we skipped from fifty-nine to forty-eight—not that anyone's going to point it out.

Holly pulls out a book and I envy her ability to read without getting carsick. I can't even respond to Mae's **We miss you!!!!!** texts without turning green. Jack must be the same, because there's no books in his bag and Mrs. Kahale spent the first five minutes of the drive coaxing him into taking a chewable Dramamine.

He sings his way through the thirties twice and makes it all the way down to nineteen before Mr. Kahale—who began the song in the first place—calls "Pause" from the driver's seat. "No more juice boxes. That's enough juice boxes for forever."

"But I'm almost done," Jack protests.

"Save the rest for the drive home. All this talk of juice is making me have to pee."

"I have to pee," says Jack. "Really, really bad."

His mom groans and his dad puts on his blinker. "Hang on, bud, I'm looking for a place to stop."

This will be our third bathroom break in three hours, but Jack was such a nightmare to potty train that none of us are willing to risk an accident. As soon as we park at a McDonald's, I lean to unbuckle him, trying to ignore how Holly's booster digs into my other hip. Once he's out, I maneuver past his seat and over the tote bags and backpack straps that booby-trap the floor.

"You doing okay back there?" Mr. Kahale asks as I stretch beside the car. Mrs. Kahale has scooped up Jack and run into the restaurant. "Sorry there's not more room."

"It's fine." I roll my shoulders to work some of the tightness out of my back.

"Noelle, you've—" Holly dissolves into a fit of giggles. "You've got—" Her pointing finger waves wildly with her laughter. "It's—on your *butt!*"

I swipe a hand down the back of my leggings and several fish-shaped crackers take a dive toward the pavement. Fabulous. If only Wyatt could see me now—with crumb butt and milk dribbled down my shirt courtesy of Jack's "leak proof" cup. Holly spent the last thirty minutes braiding the right side of my hair and there's marker covering my left hand from holding Jack's coloring book steady while he scribbled across pictures of flying horses. Let me tell you, I am a catch.

"I think we owe you hazard pay," Mr. Kahale jokes as his wife returns with Jack. I offer a smile and open the car door—it feels good to move, but late afternoon Upstate New York temperatures are not friendly to those of us whose coats are buried in the trunk. Plus, it's going to take a minute for me to wedge myself back into position.

"I'd offer to switch seats with you, but"—Mrs. Kahale gestures to her hips—"I don't think I'd fit."

"It's fine," I say as Mr. Kahale gives her a playful squeeze and she kisses his cheek. They are—as Coco would say—#RelationshipGoals.

Even if Holly's squealing, "Ew, gross!"

"Tell me a joke," Jack demands as I buckle him. The clasps are sticky with juice and furry from the ratty monkey that's his current favorite. Jack's loyalties to stuffed animals are fierce but fickle. Tomorrow, the monkey could be out and Sir Flames-a-Lot, the stuffed dragon, could be back in.

"Say please," his mother prompts as I rescue Mr. Bananas from the floor.

"Joke, please."

I don't normally babysit with an audience, and it's made this whole drive weird. Like, am I in charge of the kids right now—or are they? Who handles discipline? Because the ten minutes where Mr. Bananas was using my nose as a diving board were not my favorite, but his parents seemed to think it was cute.

I'm so aware of every goofy thing I do or say and wonder how long it will be until Mr. and Mrs. Kahale regret bringing me—because it's day one and I'm already sick of every joke I know.

"Knock, knock."

"Who's there," Jack bellows.

"Cargo." My voice is an exaggerated whisper, but Jack doesn't get the hint.

He yells, "Cargo, who?" with Holly joining in, so their voices are in stereo.

"Cargo beep beep."

They laugh uproariously, and Holly says, "Mom. Hey, Mom! Knock, knock."

I stifle a groan. Jack's going to want to tell it too—probably to both parents individually and then back to me. And I honestly don't think I can handle another four rounds of "beep beep" directly in my ear.

I wonder what movie the girls are watching. Autumn always picks *White Christmas* and I stick with *Elf*, but Mae and Coco are wild cards. Mae finds ones set in cool locations, and Coco chooses whatever new release is getting the most buzz. I bet they'd be more sympathetic about me missing break if I took a selfie right now, because despite my promise that this trip has *nothing* to do with Wyatt, that he won't even be here—I checked again with Holly on the sly; he's spending

Christmas in Arlington with his mom—they've been fixated on him ever since Mae revealed my crush.

"You know, when I made that joke about this year being less Santa, more mistletoe, I meant, like, Mae and the guy from our English class," Coco had said between bites of her omelet.

I'd been so annoyed they wouldn't name "the guy from their English class" that I *almost* revealed Coco's infatuation with Booker Primavera in retaliation. But if Mae hasn't picked up on it after *years* of Coco not-so-subtly pining for her brother, I'm not going to be the one to draw attention to the elephant-sized crush in the room. Though *I* wish I was in the room with the three of them right now.

I risk carsickness to send a group text. **Miss you too!**

"Hey, Noelle." Jack hits my knee with his monkey. "Knock, knock."

"I have a better idea," Mrs. Kahale interrupts. "Or, at least an idea I know *Noelle* will enjoy more."

If I had room to move, her comment would've made me squirm, because I'm not here for them to entertain me. They're literally paying me to do the opposite—even if that means tolerating hours of jokes repeated by kids who forgot to pack their indoor voices. And if I need a reminder why this is worth it, I've got it in my in-box: a confirmation of my audition time slot. In three weeks, I'll be trying out for Beacon.

But when do I tell Dad about it? Will he even care? He's

seemed *more* cheerful since banishing me for Christmas. And will I get in? Why does Mrs. Kahale's smile pop goose bumps up my arms?

At least one of those questions has an easy answer— apparently I hit the temperature controls on the console with my knee. No thank you, air conditioner, you are not needed today.

"What is it?" Jack asks.

"I ordered a copy of Wyatt's show—don't you think Noelle will want to see it?"

"What? Why?" The tiny space between their car seats isn't big enough for all my panic. It's bad enough my friends now know about my crush, but *the Kahales too?*! I'm three seconds from climbing out the sunroof to escape my humiliation. I haven't been subtle when talking to Jack and Holly, but kids are oblivious, right? *Right?*

"Because it's *Beacon*." Mrs. Kahale looks confused. "But if you don't want to—"

"No, I do!" Relief comes with a fine sheen of sweat. I nudge the console with my knee: *Sorry, air-conditioning, I do need your services after all.* Ballet. Not the boy. Duh. Especially since she knows about my audition. After I left the diner with the girls, she'd been my first call. The only other person I'd told. "I'm excited. This is great."

"Okay, then." Mrs. Kahale taps a few buttons and video begins playing on the built-in screens. Jack and Holly— who'd been playing a game of "toss the goldfish" over my head—freeze and orient toward the overture. And I know all the guidelines about "limiting screen time"—but, seriously? If them behaving like this was an option, why didn't we hit Play two states ago?

Not that I'm any better. I doubt I'd notice if they played catch with my phone or tug-of-war with my shirt. My breath catches as the Stahlbaum family steps onstage and I lean on Jack's cupholder to get closer to the screen. The music swells to the famous march as the party guests arrive and I'm no longer in the car but in the audience, lost in the sound of the live orchestra, the choreography, the dancers, the story they're telling together.

I'm rapt. And not just because I'm looking for Wyatt in each dancer who appears but because *this* is ballet. This is what I want, and it's so far from where I am. It's a form of beauty and magic that makes my eyes fill with tears when the beloved Nutcracker is broken. I'm openmouthed at the costumes and set changes.

For a moment I wonder if Wyatt and his sister played the same part this year—because the soldiers and mice look like young teens. There's no one Jack's age in Beacon's production; even the youngest partygoers are older than Holly. The leads are all played by members of Beacon's company, not their students. But I'd recognize Wyatt even through stage paint and costumes. He's not in the first act.

As the second act opens, the line between the upper-level students and the professionals begins to be less clear. I'm pretty sure the divertissement section, with its dances about food and flowers, is a mix of soloists, members of the corps, apprentices, and a few advanced students.

When the French dance—les Mirlitons, a.k.a. "marzipan"—begins, I spot Wyatt even before Holly yells his name. He's the dancer between two tutus in the bouncy pas de trois. The first section is an exercise in synchronicity. Wyatt supporting the women in lifts and turns—after which each dancer takes a turn in the spotlight. I'm holding my breath for his solo. He *owns* the stage, garnering a round of applause for a series of endless, impossibly high entrechat quatre before the song ends. I wish I could explain the way watching him dance makes me feel; I may never have met Wyatt, but I know so much about him from the way he moves.

After Wyatt exits the stage, I sigh and lean farther onto Jack's car seat—only then realizing he's asleep. On my other side, Holly is playing something on her tablet. Mrs. Kahale catches my eye and mouths "peace and quiet"—I give her a quick smile before returning my attention to the screen. The Sugar Plum Fairy is coming up. I know her performance will be far above my skill level—but, someday.

"Snow!" Holly points out the window. "First snow! I win."

"It's a contest we have," Mr. Kahale explains. "Every drive up, the first person to find snow on the ground wins. It gets less competitive as the winter continues. Sometimes you 'win' before we leave our driveway. But you got it, Holls! And we're only an hour away."

Every muscle in my body protests that an hour sounds like forever. But it's when we're *five minutes* away—right as Mrs. Kahale says, "If you look out your window, you can see Mount Kringle"—that the true fun happens.

Jack wakes with a start, mumbles, "My belly hurts."

Before I even have time to say, "I'm sorry, bud," or rub his back, he leans over the side of his car seat and pukes. All over himself and me.

Babysitting Tip 7:

Asking questions isn't a sign of weakness;
it shows maturity. If you're not sure, call or
text the parents!

The car swerves slightly when Mr. Kahale realizes the vomit-fest happening behind him. "Hang on, Jack! We'll be there in three minutes."

I'm pretty sure his wife catches the incredulous look I aim at the back of his head, *Hang on, Jack?* Every snack he'd eaten on the drive and failed to *hang on to* is splashed down the front of my shirt and pooling in my lap. Pretty sure I'm ruined on Goldfish crackers and grape juice for life.

I sit frozen as Mrs. Kahale roots in her purse, murmuring a stream of apologies and sympathy. She pulls out a half-empty travel pack of wipes, which, yeah, that isn't going to make a dent in the puke soup I'm swimming in.

Holly alternates between gagging and telling me how gross it is—I guess in case I don't already know? Jack is crying. I'm not sure whose reaction I want to copy. Both? Adding my own special notes of panic and regret to the chorus?

"Hang on. I'll roll down the windows," Mr. Kahale says. There's a slight improvement in the smell, but the freezing air on my vomit-wet skin isn't a fun feeling either.

Mrs. Kahale dumps her soda outside, then passes me the cup. "Can you just, kinda . . . scoop it in here? I am so sorry, Noelle."

Scooping—not so much. Not with the windy road we're traveling. Then the car stops. Mr. Kahale backs into a driveway. I envy the adults and Holly the super-speed with which they exit the vehicle.

"What an absolute mess," Mr. Kahale says as he extracts Jack. "Noelle, I'm going to ask you to stay put a minute while I take out this car seat. Then maybe you can just slide out?"

Sure. I'll just sit and wait. Keep marinating in the puke. I mean, he's not wrong—it's the best method for containing the disaster—but I want to launch myself out of the SUV and into the closest shower. I don't care if that makes me a vomit-flinging tornado.

I take a deep breath to calm down, then smell myself and regret it.

Once I'm finally outside—and sliding across the leather back seat meant going right through another puddle, so now my butt's wet too—I do a sort of shake-off on the driveway. Mrs. Kahale hurries over with large bath towels she ran to get from the cabin, and Mr. Kahale says, "I'll take the kids inside and get them clean."

"Do you want to take off your clothes out here and wrap up?" Mrs. Kahale suggests once they're gone. "I'll throw them right in the wash."

Stripping down in ten-degree temperatures on a gravel driveway between an SUV and a forest isn't my idea of fun. "I guess?"

"Oh, Noelle, it's in your hair." Mrs. Kahale clucks. She's gone full maternal, holding out the towel, offering a hand for balance as I shimmy out of my leggings, then tucking my boots beneath my feet so that I don't put them down on the snowy ground. She keeps my hair out of the way as I peel off the wet shirt, then wraps me in a towel like a little kid fresh out of a bath.

It's been so long since someone mothered me like this—six years. My eyes fill as I fight off memories of times I'd gotten sick and Mom had been there with cool fingers on my forehead, a warm mug of mint tea, snuggles, and dryer-fresh blankets.

"I'm so sorry," Mrs. Kahale says again. "This isn't how I wanted to start the trip. I promise the rest will be better. Take as long and hot of a shower as you want. I'll have Nick dig your bag out of the trunk and I'll set it right outside your bathroom. We can do a tour afterward—or if you just want to go straight to bed, everything can wait until the morning."

I don't answer because we've crunched around the car and their house is visible. I stop, openmouthed to stare. "I thought you said it was a cabin?"

I'd been picturing something Jack could build with Lincoln Logs, but this belongs on the cover of *Architectural Digest*. Which isn't to say there aren't logs—there are, lots of them. Forests worth. The structure seems to be all logs and glass, and light glows out from the huge windows, illuminating pristine snow and pine trees and decks for days.

"You own this too?" I want to swallow the words as soon as they're out, but come on. Their house back in Juncture is huge and gorgeous—how many rock-star homes can one family have?

Mrs. Kahale laughs—maybe a little uncomfortably—and opens the front door. "I'll show you around after you're clean."

Right, showering. Since I've moved from shivering to quaking, I don't protest—just pile my boots by the others' and follow her across wide plank floors—covered in the plushest throw rugs my bare feet have ever enjoyed—through a bedroom and into the attached bathroom.

I just get glimpses, impressions—airy space and lots of golden wood. But the bathroom is stone and glass. It has two sinks and two doors. I lock both, wondering how to use all the fancy shower settings and if this is their bathroom I'm defiling, but I'm too cold and smelly to care.

My bag is right outside one of the doors when I'm done, and I quickly pull on sweats. I'd given my bra a much-needed scrub too. I drape it from the showerhead so it doesn't drip on the floor and pad out of the bathroom in socks, holding my bag, since I'm not sure which room is mine. It falls from my fingers as I hit the main room. "Wow."

"It's pretty great, huh?" Mr. Kahale stands from where he'd been crouched by the fireplace, a beer in one hand.

My eyes drop to him, and he's gesturing wide—which, phew. Because *my* wow had been inspired by the huge portrait of five people in snowsuits hanging above the mantel. Specifically, the person on the left—helmet in his hands, ski goggles on the top of his head, lips full and slightly parted—

Yeah, my "wow" had been about Wyatt, but if his dad wants to assume it's about the house, I'm very cool with that. Now that I take it in, the house is pretty dang wow too.

Mr. Kahale flips a switch on the side of the mantel, and a fire roars to life, making the room impossibly more picturesque. I'm already daydreaming about doing stretches on the rug in front of the fire. "Pizza should be here soon. Ginger's getting the kids in pajamas."

I nod and spin slowly. I was definitely right about the logs—they're everywhere, in both the furniture and the architecture. There are huge beams that cross the soaring ceilings above the family and dining rooms. These flow into a kitchen with wood cabinets, stainless steel appliances, and stone countertops. The wall opposite the kitchen is all fireplace—rough-hewn rocks that climb from floor to ceiling. The whole back wall is windows, except for where there's glass doors to a deck. I'm pretty sure that's a hot tub.

On the far side of the kitchen is a set of open-backed

stairs that lead to a lofted seating area overlooking the living room. Beyond that is a set of double doors.

"Our bedroom's up there," Mr. Kahale says, following my gaze. "And the kids share a bunk room down that hallway." He points the way I came. "I think Ginger showed you the guest room where you'll be sleeping—it's got the bear picture above the bed."

"Oh, thanks." I didn't notice a bear picture, but at least that means I didn't leave my bra to dry in someone else's bathroom.

"Can I get you anything?" he asks. "Cherry seltzer, right?"

I nod and we hear Jack and Holly before we see them, excited footsteps stampeding our way. "Noelle!" they screech like they haven't seen me in days. "Want to see our room? Can she tuck us in? Please, Momma, please?"

A knock on the door interrupts—and all that excitement they'd just shown me? I'm a bit insulted when they show the same level for the delivery guy. "Pizza! Pizza!"

"Let's eat," Mrs. Kahale says. "Then I'll show you around."

Back in Juncture, there's times I've almost felt part of this family—like the money they give me for hanging out is just a very generous allowance. That illusion is shattered here. There's so many things I should probably tell them: I don't like pepperoni on my pizza; I can't take the kids in the hot tub, because I didn't pack a swimsuit for a ski trip to a "cabin." And there's things I should ask: Will you show me how to work the TV? What's past the bathroom's other door?

Is there any orange juice coming in the groceries you're having delivered tomorrow? How early do the kids wake up? When should I? Can I borrow some toothpaste?

The toothpaste I end up borrowing from Holly and Jack as I tuck them in. Mr. and Mrs. Kahale tell me a half dozen times that I don't have to. But Jack is insistent and . . . isn't that why they brought me? Regardless, after my fifth reassurance, they fill glasses of wine and retreat to their private balcony. I follow the kids down the hall, where I brush my teeth with something called "Sparkle Berry" and read three books, sing two songs, and tuck them into the coolest bunk beds I've ever seen.

There are two pairs of them. Holly sleeps top in one, and Jack bottom of the other. They flank a set of stairs that's built into the wall for access to both top bunks. Each bed has its own bookshelf, reading lanterns, and thick, red velvet curtain for privacy. Jack's shelf is full of stuffed animals and his lantern has a dimmer bulb.

"Leave it on," he tells me as I adjust his blanket and wipe toothpaste off his chin.

"I'll see you tomorrow, goofballs," I say. "Sweet dreams."

I stick my head in my bedroom as I pass; yup, there's a bear picture. I'm ready to climb under the purple covers and sleep, but the getting-paid part of me feels like I should report that the kids are down and say good night. I wander back out, immediately feeling awkward when I realize Mr. and Mrs. Kahale haven't come downstairs.

So I scrape pizza crusts into the trash can (where they bury the napkin I used to hide the pepperonis I picked off mine) and load the dishwasher.

I text Dad and try vidcalling Mae, but she doesn't answer. They've got to be done with their movie marathon by now—I want to know their picks and what I missed. And if I made the wrong choice, because it feels weird to be standing solo in the Kahales' living room. Would it be weirder if they came out while I was stretching?

Maybe. So I give a longing look at the rug, flip off the fireplace, and go get in bed. My mouth still tastes like Sparkle Berry toothpaste and the logs that cross the bedroom's ceiling look too heavy to be hanging above my head. And too far away. I'm used to the close corners of my apartment, the dance poster I can reach up and touch, the side table squeezed between my bed and the wall, where I charge my phone and keep a glass of water. Here I have to roll to the edge of the mattress and stretch to reach my phone. And since I'm rolling over, I might as well keep going—get up and stretch, dance, until my mind quiets. *If* it quiets.

The cabin is stunning, and there's no doubt this room is designed with soft things to balance the rugged logs—there's a faux-fur rug, a velvet overstuffed chair, and even the bed, with its flannel sheets, crushed velvet duvet, and piles of cozy throw blankets, is like sinking into a cloud.

But I feel a bit swallowed up by it all. Uncertain about where I stand or what I'm supposed to do. I pause mid grand battement and lower my left leg, feeling the stretch through my hips ebb. Was putting the kids to bed enough? Did I earn my paycheck today?

And tomorrow, Christmas Eve Eve, what will that be like here? What will it be like back in Juncture? Will Dad do anything but work if I'm not there to interrupt? Will my friends do the gingerbread house contest without me?

It's a long night. An early morning. This house sounds different, settles different. I startle awake because of a strange noise from beyond the door to the deck. It could've been a bird, or snow falling off a tree branch, or a bear, wolf, coyote—whatever people-eating nature lives up here. Once my brain starts making that list, I'm up for good.

Not to brag, but I'm a sleepover expert. I know what to do in each of the girls' houses. Autumn wakes up early and Mae sleeps in. Coco is a big fan of an all-day doze if she doesn't have morning practice. I know whose parents like coffee, and who's chatty or silent before their first cup.

I don't know any of that here. Not when Holly or Jack wake, nor what they're allowed to do or eat. Not if I should attempt to set up the coffeemaker, if there's any food in the fridge, or how to work the TV in my room if I wanted to watch anything before they wake up.

So I'll do what I always do when I'm stressed: dance. I tiptoe out of the bedroom in my socks and the sweats I slept in. My back and hip flexors are still furious about yesterday's squashed drive, so I start by stretching them, then move toward the dining table. I use the back of a chair as a substitute barre and do some simple progressions to warm up. Plié, relevé, passé; plié, relevé, passé. I've moved to single-leg relevés and am holding the position on the ball of one foot, when a knock on the door makes me stumble—almost Heimliching myself on the back of the chair.

But I can't even cough or sputter—because what if the person knocking *hears me?* If I don't feel comfortable opening the *fridge*, I definitely don't think I should answer the door.

I drop to a crouch and creep closer to it. It's solid wood—no peephole—and I can't see anything when I peek out the side window. My prayers that it was a tree branch or squirrel go unanswered, because the knock comes again—louder this time. Five distinct raps, followed by a muffled, "Hello? Anyone awake?"

In movies, characters hear through doors by pressing an ear to them. I've never needed to, because the apartment walls are paper thin; I can hear every time Dad bangs his knee on the filing cabinet and curses. I shift to a stand and try it out. It sorta works? I hear muttering and the sound of a ringing cell set to speakerphone. Mr. Kahale's voice mail picks up. I didn't hear any ringing from inside the house, so either the bedroom doors are thick or he has it set to silent. There's a curse from outside and I jump when the knocking begins again—directly against where I'm resting my ear.

It has to be the groceries Mrs. Kahale said were being delivered this morning. She'd raved about the convenience of getting the ingredients for Christmas dinner without having to brave the crowded stores. I assumed she meant at a reasonable hour. Though if they need milk for coffee and cereal, then why not seven a.m.? And what if the delivery guy leaves and it's my fault there's no food? Not just milk, but no ham, or turkey, or whatever their holiday meal is.

Noelle Partridge, starring in *The Babysitter Who Ruined Christmas*. Ugh. I have to open the door. Either that or go hide in my room and pretend I was asleep. I glance over my shoulder and consider it. Because there'd be no excuse for being awake and not answering, right?

There's another round of knocking. I kinda admire this delivery person's tenacity, and if they come bearing orange juice, maybe it will even be worth the panic. I take a deep breath and flip the dead bolt, spin the regular lock, then twist the knob.

I pull the door open, but it's not the sudden rush of subarctic air that steals the breath from my lungs. It's the person on the doorstep.

He's standing beside a suitcase, facing away from me—staring up the driveway at an idling car with a cell phone pressed to his ear. "Come on. Come on. Pick up."

I gasp or squeak—make some sound alerting him to my presence, and he waves to the car, which leaves. He drops his hand and his broad shoulders drop too. I mean, I can't really see that they're broad through the puff of his down jacket, but I've practically got an advanced degree in knowing the lines beneath it.

"Surprise! Merry Christmas!" He spins with an expectant smile on his face. It crumples when he sees me. His voice doesn't sound the way I imagined—all those times I've day-dreamed him saying hello, complimenting my dancing, telling me I'm gorgeous. It's deeper, rougher, and if we're being honest . . . hotter. His eyes are throwing some heat too—but not the smoldering kind. This is straight-up angry accusation. His gaze darts to the number on the side of the cabin, then over my shoulder to the interior. "Who are you? And why are you in my dad's house?"

I can't remember my own name, but I certainly know his. My voice squeaks as I say it. "Wyatt!"

Babysitting Tip 8:

Kids feel safer when they know who's in charge.
So the first time you meet a new kiddo-client, make
sure you establish clear rules.
And never let them see you sweat.

A t first I think the beeping is my alarm clock interrupting the world's best dream. Because I must be dreaming. So I ignore it, refusing to wake up. Wyatt! Wyatt Kahale! The dream version is even more handsome than his pictures. He's also a lot more scowly. Not sure why my subconscious is giving me my fantasy guy but having him glare murder at me.

More beeps. A triple chime. I don't remember my phone having that setting. Wyatt looks past me to the wall. A second triple beep. This one louder.

He points from me to . . . the security alarm! "Are you going to enter the code?"

"I—I don't know it." Three beeps. Faster. Louder. I glance at the stairs leading to the Kahales' bedroom, doubting this is the alarm they want waking them up on their first day of vacation. "Don't you?"

"Dad changes it every year." He pushes into the house and studies the keypad. "Why would you open the door without turning the alarm off?"

"Because you were about to wake everyone up!" Also, because I didn't notice the alarm existed, but he doesn't need to know that.

The beeps are gone. Replaced by a full volume, constant blare and a mechanical voice saying, "Intruder. Leave immediately." We're both wincing, covering our ears. Even still, I can hear him shout, "Yeah, because this isn't going to wake them up?"

I attempt a glare through my wince. "Well, technically, there is an intruder . . ."

He goes stiff at my words, but I don't have time to analyze that because there's new kinds of commotion. Bedroom doors being flung open. A phone ringing.

"Wyatt! Wyatt!" Holly and Jack are sleepy-eyed, bedheaded, leaping hugs.

And there's his smile as he returns them. "Hey, fam."

It slips from his face as Mr. Kahale hangs leans over the railing of the loft and frowns down at the chaos. "What's going on?"

"Wyatt!" Holly points like her dad can't see him. "Santa *is* real! It's a Christmas miracle!"

Mrs. Kahale runs down the stairs with her bathrobe streaming behind her. She plucks a phone from the wall by the fridge. "Yes, this is Ginger Kahale." She plugs one ear with her free hand and shouts to confirm the address and give a passcode.

Holly and Jack are still climbing Wyatt like he's a jungle gym, but he barely acknowledges them. His wary eyes are glued on his dad's progress down the stairs.

The alarms cuts off so suddenly the silence feels as sharp as the blare it replaced.

"Yes, yes," Mrs. Kahale is saying into the phone. "Our babysitter opened the door. Yes, I will make sure to tell her. Yes, I understand—"

"Wyatt?" Mr. Kahale pauses a few feet from his son. Wyatt has curved his arms around Holly's and Jack's shoulders. They're squirming like happy puppies in his embrace, but from my vantage point it looks like they're being used as human shields. His posture stiffens as his dad asks, "What are you doing here?"

"I wanted to surprise you." The chill that dances up my spine isn't because the door is still open, Wyatt's stuff on the welcome mat. His tone warps the punctuation on his sentence—instead of an exclamation point, it's a question mark.

"Mission accomplished," says Mr. Kahale. "How did you get here? Does your mother know where you are?"

"A plane, a bus, and an Uber," he answers. "And, yeah. Mom knows."

There's a look exchanged between the two of them. One that goes over Holly's and Jack's heads but tightens my throat.

Mr. Kahale gives a brief nod at the same time his knuckles go white around his cell phone. And then his grin is sincere, his voice gruff as he pushes through his younger kids to engulf his son in a hug. "This is the best surprise."

The pause before Wyatt lets go of Holly and Jack is barely noticeable; then he's hugging his dad back. I have to look away from the sheer relief on his face, because there's no way he meant for that to be public. And because the whole exchange makes my chest ache. I want my own dad, the one of last summer, last spring, the one who jokingly threatened to make *Team Partridge* shirts to wear to my recitals and middle school graduation.

"Come on, let's get your stuff." Mr. Kahale releases him from a hug, only to clap a hand on Wyatt's back and give him a playful shake as he picks up the suitcase. "I can't believe you're here—but I'm sure the Uber bill will be a pretty big confirmation. Everything went okay? No problems in transit?"

Wyatt shakes his head. "It was fine."

The kids are dancing around. Wait, that's not Jack's excitement dance; it's I-have-to-pee. I shepherd him to the bathroom as Mr. Kahale continues to narrate his surprise. "I can't believe we get you for Christmas." He falters. "You are staying for Christmas, right? How long can we keep you—"

I pause in the bathroom doorway, one more person holding their breath for his answer.

Wyatt has a strange look on his face as he bends over his backpack. "Yeah, I'm staying," and I wonder if I'm the only one whose radar is on red alert. There's more to this story.

"Noelle, my zipper is stuck!" Jack is jumping up and down by the toilet. Since tinkle waits for no man and Wyatt's apparently not going anywhere for a few days, I tear my eyes from him and pivot toward the potty.

By the time Jack's done, Mrs. Kahale has finished her call and is setting the table. Maybe I'm supposed to head there and help, but I drift toward where Wyatt, Holly, and their dad are huddled around the security alarm. I tell myself it's because if Mr. Kahale is giving lessons on disarming it, I should hear them too. That's a totally valid, totally logical excuse. It has nothing to do with the fact that Wyatt's flung his coat over a chair and that underneath he's wearing a black sweater that showcases acres of toned back between broad shoulders. I swear I'm about to make my presence known, to ask about the code, when Wyatt speaks first.

"Why did you bring a *babysitter*?"

I stop short.

"Right?" Holly props her hands on her hips and, *ouch*! That's the last time I let her braid my hair. "Because I'm not a baby. I keep telling them they need to find another word for Noelle. 'Kid-sitter' or 'big friend' or something."

Okay, well that's adorable. Fine, she can keep practicing Elsa-looks on my head.

"No, I mean, why is she even here? And now that I am, should we send her home?" Wyatt has his phone out. Is he already looking up flights? "Holls, is this the one you say always asks about me?"

The question falls into dead space because clearly I've died from embarrassment or need to murder a less-oblivious-than-I-thought eight-year-old. Also because Holly's noticed me and done some sloppy, giggly spins to my side.

But Wyatt's typing and doesn't see me. "There. Mom knows I'm alive—or she will, once she wakes up."

When he lowers his phone and registers that I'm stand-ing beside his sister, he looks just about as panicked as his dad, who's been clearing his throat and searching for a way to make this less awkward. Since they both seem to be at a loss, I step forward and hold out my hand.

"Hi, I'm Noelle." Wyatt doesn't move, so I add, "Holly and Jack talk about you a lot. It's nice to meet you."

He looks at his dad, across the room to his stepmom, at Jack sitting on the kitchen counter passing his mom silver-ware, and Holly hanging on to one of my hands with both of hers as she slides her socks around the hardwood floor. He doesn't look directly at me. "I'm Wyatt. I guess you're joining us for Christmas."

"That was the plan." I turn to Mr. Kahale. Am I headed for an Uber, a bus, and a plane? If so, it's a good thing I've barely unpacked.

"It's still the plan." He faces Wyatt and says firmly, "Noelle is our guest and wonderful with Holly and Jack."

Wyatt's raised eyebrows have a whole incredulous conversation. And instead of communicating *"Are you the dance partner I've spent my whole life searching for?"* they say things like "I hate this plan." And "You pay your 'guests'?" and "I don't want her here."

But he doesn't voice any of this. He just turns and stares at me until his scrutiny is interrupted by another knock on the door.

"Did you bring a friend?" Holly asks, but I don't think he hears her. He's too busy giving me a smug smile as he turns and enters a passcode on the keypad—hitting each button with exaggerated slowness so that I can catch it—before he opens the door.

The dang groceries. I cross my arms. He was supposed to be groceries, and right now I like the bunch of bananas at the top of one of the green reusable bags more than I like the boy carrying it.

"I wish he'd been orange juice," I mutter to myself as I pick up a bag from the foyer to take to the kitchen. But either I don't mutter as quietly as I thought or the acoustics in here are unreal, because Wyatt snorts as he approaches for a second trip.

"Pretty sure I deserve that, but c'mon, aim higher. I'm at least"—he glances in his bag—"filets or the good ice cream." He waggles his eyebrows at me and pivots.

I'm left with juice and burning cheeks. I huff. This is not how Wyatt's supposed to behave. It's not who he's supposed to be.

Except . . . he endured a plane/bus/Uber all before seven a.m., so who knows how early he got up. He's been dancing six performances a week since Thanksgiving. And his big surprise was ruined by a stranger and a security alarm. Maybe he's allowed to be a little snippy.

And he's *Wyatt*. Wyatt, who's currently giving Holly a piggyback ride so she can deliver a box of Cap'n Crunch to the cabinet in style. She's squealing and laughing and Jack's demanding his own turn—and getting a trot around the living room's coffee table. Wyatt joins in when Jack picks up right where he left off yesterday: "Nineteen grape juice boxes on the wall . . ."

Mr. Kahale laughs. "How about fewer juice boxes and more . . . waffles!"

It's the perfect cinematic family moment, but it's not my family. I'm still standing by the door.

"Noelle," calls Mrs. Kahale over the kids' cheers. "Do you see eggs over there? I know I ordered some."

I scan the bags. "Got 'em." And thank goodness for having a purpose, because I don't know how I could've intruded on their scene without one.

Mrs. Kahale trades me a bright smile for the carton. "Good morning, sweetie. I promise they're not all quite this chaotic."

The kids do waffle victory dances and Wyatt disappears somewhere with his bags while I help Mrs. Kahale sort the groceries and Mr. Kahale mans the waffle iron. It turns out that teamwork does make the dream work, and I'm so glad to be included on this one, because we're soon sitting down with mouths full of the fluffiest waffles and fresh syrup. We're all smiling around bites and *mmmm*s.

Wyatt lifts his glass toward me. "Is it safe to ask for the OJ, or—"

I need the rest of the sentence to figure out if he's amused or antagonistic, but he just raises his eyebrows and waits.

On the one hand, we both like orange juice, so clearly we're soulmates, but on the other . . . is he *teasing* me? I tighten my fingers around the OJ and force myself to take a deep, calming breath. Maybe he gets hangry? Like Holly. In which case should I hold pre-waffle crankiness against him? Hmm.

When it comes to head games played by her swim meet competitors, Coco swears by "Kill 'em with kindness"; maybe it'll work for me. I pair the juice with my brightest smile, and he's so busy blinking at me that he doesn't move to take the carton. I'm debating whether I should pour it for him or just set it down and break eye contact—when there's another knock on the door.

Mrs. Kahale rubs her hands together. "Well, Wyatt, you're not the only surprise today."

"Who else is coming?" Holly asks.

"Just a few of Santa's helpers." Her mom opens the door to reveal two men carrying an enormous Christmas tree.

They do a sort of acrobatics as they maneuver out of their snowy boots without dropping their cargo, but despite this feat, I'm unimpressed. Christmas trees aren't like pizzas. They're not meant to be ordered and delivered in thirty minutes or less. Trees are personal. Half the fun is circling each contender to look for bare spots and debating the options. I like short, fat trees with full branches. Dad likes them taller, leaner, with plenty of space for ornaments. We stand in the grove at the tree farm negotiating pine versus spruce until it's our cold noses that force the decision. Or, at least we did every year before this one.

My sigh draws Wyatt's curious glance, but I look away. This isn't my tree; my opinion isn't needed.

Though I've got to admit, whoever was in charge of the Kahales' tree chose well. It's enormous; once they set it into the stand by the windows, it's got to be at least twelve feet of lush, fragrant fir. In less time than it takes Dad and me to get ours straight—("A little left. No, a little right—too much."—until I'm crawling out from underneath the tree with needles in my hair and a stomach that hurts from laughter)—these men have it watered, draped with the tree-skirt, and even vacuumed to pick up any stray needles. They do all this while we sit and eat waffles. I feel weird, spoiled. And a little shell-shocked when I see Mr. Kahale slip them each a hundred-dollar bill as a tip.

Along with the tree, they'd delivered several cardboard boxes to the kitchen and stacked them beside the rice cooker. I assume these are ornaments until Mrs. Kahale says, "We need the tree to warm and settle before we decorate, but in the meantime, I've got another project for us." She carefully carries one of the boxes over to the table and opens the top.

I'm standing back, letting the kids get first peek, but when Holly gasps, "Gingerbread houses!" I practically knock her over so I can see. I end up pressed against one of Wyatt's biceps. Which isn't a bad place to be—at least not in my opinion.

He, however, jerks away like he's burned, or like I still smell of vomit, but I'm too excited to be insulted. Too busy blinking back grateful tears as Mrs. Kahale says, "A little birdie told us it was someone's favorite tradition."

I let Mr. Kahale explain the idiom to the kids as I beam at her. "My dad?"

"No. Mae."

Not Dad. Her answer twists my stomach. I wanted it to be him. I wanted him to make *some* sort of effort. "Oh. I forgot she's sat for you too."

Mrs. Kahale smiles. "I may have called her for reconnaissance on how to make the holiday special for you."

I'm not sure how to react to these people who put more effort into my holiday happiness than my father. I'm not family, but I'm more than an employee. Mr. Kahale said "guest," but that doesn't quite fit. And while this might not be *my* version of Christmas, the smell from the tree is starting to permeate and it's undeniably festive. "For me?"

I'm pretty sure Wyatt asked a similar "*for her?*" under his breath, but it gets lost beneath simultaneous "I don't think so, mister!" and "Gumdrops aren't breakfast!" aimed at Jack.

He releases a handful of candy back into the box, which is loaded with every conceivable gingerbread house treat. "After?" Jack asks. "We'll eat it then?"

"We'll see," says Mrs. Kahale before turning to me. "So tell us how this works. I got the deluxe kits with pieces and frosting and decorations. Where do we start?"

There are five sets of eyes on me, and maybe I should be self-conscious that one of them is Wyatt's, but we're talking *gingerbread houses*. Christmas trumps crushes. "We'll want to assemble the houses, then let them set for at least a half-hour. Otherwise they'll collapse when we decorate."

Back home we always build them, then challenge the Primavera twins to a snowball fight—outside if the weather cooperates, but they also have a bin of these indoor pompom ones we can pummel each other with in their rec room. Once Booker and Hudson have thoroughly trounced us, we return to the Primaveras' kitchen to decorate. The twins always agree to be Dad's sous-judges in exchange for the leftover candy.

"Half-hour for structural integrity, got it," says Mr. Kahale. "So, let's build houses, then grab showers and get dressed before we decorate. Then get Holls to her race."

The kids are bouncing—and Mrs. Kahale is smartly removing the bags and tubs of candy and placing them out of reach. "I bought three—I figured that Holly and Jack would probably need help and partner with us, but—"

Her eyes shoot to Wyatt as mine find the floor, but I'm peeking sideways through my hair to see his reaction.

It's a shrug. I mean, I'm not sure what I expect. A grand jeté in delight as he begs to be my partner? I certainly wouldn't complain about that, but his actual response—"I know nothing about gingerbread houses. I'll skip it"—is borderline grinchy.

"Oh, c'mon, bud," says his dad. "I'm sure Noelle can teach you a thing or two. Plus then we've got even teams, because if I remember right, this is supposed to be a competition."

Wyatt's jaw clenches as he glances at me, but instead of looking away, I stare back and hold out a pastry bag of frosting. "It's sugar, water, egg whites, and cream of tartar—I'm pretty sure you can handle it."

"Fine." He grabs the icing from my hand a little too zealously. The protective tip pops off and a stream of frosting shoots out—much to the delight of Jack.

"Don't eat that!" I say as I wipe it up with one of the paper towels I'd wet in anticipation. Then I tell his big brother, "I won't even blame you if we lose."

There are four other people in this kitchen. At least I think there are—but they could've all left and I doubt Wyatt or I would've noticed. He's staring at me so intently, eyes dark, brows furrowed. I don't know what he's looking for, but I raise my eyebrows in challenge. I may not have been part of his big surprise plan, but I'm here and I'm dang good at gingerbread—I've won the contest three of the last five years. And Wyatt may be Wyatt, but he's about to enter my domain. Where I rule with a candy cane scepter and a fondant-and-gumdrop crown.

Wyatt's voice is deeper as he lifts his chin in acknowledgment. "I never lose."

"Okay, then!" Mr. Kahale claps a hand on each of our shoulders. "I guess it's game on."

Babysitting Tip 9:

Just because their parents are paying you,
doesn't mean you have to let them win.
Losing is character-building for kids,
so let your Candy Land prowess shine.

"Wait! We need music," I say as everyone's unboxing frosting and flat slabs of gingerbread. I pull out my phone and smugly cue up the *perfect* playlist—one that every person here will know and appreciate: *The Nutcracker* score.

Jack starts humming, Holly's bopping, but Wyatt cuts in. "Nope. If I have to hear that one more time—"

I gasp. "Sacrilege."

He shrugs. "You try listening to it every day for months. You'll get pretty sick of it too."

I look down at myself. So, fine, I'm not dressed as a bunhead at the moment. I'm in joggers and a slouchy shirt, not a leotard and pointe shoes. Still, it's not *un*-obvious I'm a dancer. I've had strangers on the street recognize it from the turnout in my walk and stance. I may or may not shift my feet into first position before responding. "That's never happening."

"Guess your attention span is longer than mine," he says easily. "I'm still vetoing it. Pick something else."

Pick something else? Like it's no big deal. Like *Nut-cracker* isn't one of the highlights of my year and I didn't watch him defy gravity during his solo. There are five pairs of eyes on me, four concerned and one indifferent. And something Coco said at the diner is rolling through my head like crashing waves: *"Maybe this ski trip will be good for Noelle. I love Christmas and our traditions—but you've gotten a little intense about them and it's not as fun anymore."*

Fine. I'll dial down the intensity. Prove to Coco I can be flexible. I execute the stiffest shrug in the history of shoulder movements. "Sure. Why don't you pick the music, then. Something festive and—"

"I've got it," he says.

"I've got it." He says the same words ten minutes and three different versions of "Little Drummer Boy" later, as he slides the last piece of gingerbread into place. It's the opposite side of the roof from the one I'm currently anchoring.

"Don't let go," I say. "It needs to set."

"I've got it," he repeats. "Since you told me the same

thing for each of the sides, I think I've really, truly got it by now."

"Figured it was worth checking," I shoot back, nodding toward his phone. "Because clearly you like repetition."

His mouth tightens, but I'm pretty sure it's because he's fighting back a smile.

Fine, I'm being bossy, but I do have a lot of experience with this. Also, usually when I'm giving directions, I'm giving them to people who are eleven and under.

"This cover's a classic," he says.

"Please tell me the playlist isn't endless 'rum pah pum pum,'" I say, just as Holly and Jack join in with an enthusiastic chorus, the latter flinging frosting from the tips of his fingers as he air drums.

"Wait and see."

"I don't think I can handle any more surprises today." I say it sarcastically, but the words echo in a hollow place in my chest. These gingerbread houses were so kind, and Holly and frosting-covered Jack are adorable with them, but none of this is the same. The kits are too fancy, Coco's not turning frosting-making into a science experiment, Mae's not looking up European castles to try and replicate, there's no Autumn with her protractor, checking that her walls meet at right angles. The soundtrack is wrong, the setting is wrong. And Wyatt—he's here, he's gorgeous, but he's not what I expected. He's wrong too.

It's possible we're having a stare down. It's possible it's

happening in front of his family—my employers. It's possible that his hand moved and my thumb is now touching his as we hold our sides of the roof together. And it's a thousand percent certain that my entire awareness is split between his brown eyes and the millimeters of my skin that are pressed against his. His gaze is cool, but that place where our fingerprints are meeting is so very, very hot. It's possible the frosting might melt, the gingerbread might toast, the—

"Help! Noelle!"

Wyatt jerks his chin to point to his sister as I register the sound of Holly's distress. She sniffles. "It won't stop collapsing. Mom's doing it all wrong."

Wyatt brushes my hand out of the way and assumes responsibility for both halves of our roof, and I take in the chaos on the other trays. Jack and Mr. Kahale's house is standing—but doing so at all sorts of improbable angles. Holly and Mrs. Kahale's is a frosting-covered heap on their circular piece of gold cardboard.

"Maybe I should've gone with the preassembled ones," Mrs. Kahale says.

"Hang on," I call over my shoulder. "I've got the perfect thing to fix this in my bag." I'd packed the babysitting essentials, and no babysitter worth her weight in face paint or fort-making skills goes anywhere without baby wipes and a hot glue gun.

Wyatt's studying me again as I reappear with the magic tools, but I don't have time to interpret his gaze; I've got work to do. I plug in the gun and distribute wipes. "Take off all the frosting, we're going to use a shortcut and hot glue it."

"That'll work?" asks Mr. Kahale at the same time Holly says, "Isn't that cheating?"

"My friend Coco makes our frosting," I tell them. "Some years it's cement—other years it turns out like slime. We've learned to have a backup plan." I dig through their rubble, setting the house pieces to the side so I can wipe down the cardboard.

"Noelle, you are a wonder. As usual, I don't know what we'd do without you," says Mrs. Kahale when I've got the first three walls of their house standing.

I glance over at my work space, but Wyatt is gone. Some point mid-salvage he'd ducked out of the room, leaving behind a perfectly built house and his phone—where the playlist has switched to versions of "Twelve Days of Christmas."

I rub the tip of my thumb, still remembering what it felt like pressed to his. We might not have *twelve*, but this is the first day of *our* Christmas and I'm going to use however long we have to figure out if he's the "true love" I'd imagined . . . or more annoying than eleven pipers piping and four calling birds combined.

So once the others' houses are stabilized and we're on our frosting-setting break, I dive for my phone: I need my best friend.

Mae answers first ring. "Hey! How is it? Sorry I missed your call last night. *Booker!*"

She says her brother's name like it's a full explanation. And it kinda is. "It's okay, but you'll never . . . Mae, it's—I—he—"

"Um, breathe," she instructs. "You sound like that time you couldn't find your name on the recital casting list because you didn't realize there was a second page. What's going on?"

"Wyatt." I cup my hand around the receiver and whisper, like in this big room all by myself, someone might overhear me. Then, thinking better of it—and my tendency to turn on speakerphone with my cheek, I shove my earbuds in. Normally I practice while on the phone—not wild choreography, but at least adagio work—this time I flop on the bed.

"What about him? Did the kids tell you another cute story? I swear, someday you're going to meet this dude and it's going to be the weirdest thing because you'll be ready to write his biography and he'll be like 'Hi, nice to meet you.'"

"You're kinda psychic," I say, and cover my eyes with a pillow. "Because, *surprise*—he's here. And it's weird. But he definitely doesn't think it was nice to meet me."

"What?" Mae's screech makes me wince. "Tell me everything!"

I give her a thirty-second summary of the security alarm disaster—but then I falter, because I don't know how to describe what I don't understand. Is he hostile, hangry, or just still processing the fact that *I'm* here—the same way I'm trying to wrap my head around him? And at least I already knew he existed . . . Though from his question—*Holls, is this the one you say always asks about me?*—apparently he's heard about me too. Did he feel the gingerbread house sparks? Or would he chalk them up to a sugar high from maple syrup and the nonpareils I totally caught him sneaking from the decorations?

I press the pillow tighter to my eyes and adjust the headphone wire so it's not strangling me. We were supposed to meet at Beacon. He was supposed to see me in the halls at my audition and be so intrigued that he snuck in to watch—then be so blown away that we'd be the It Couple before my acceptance letter arrived.

He keeps doing this wrong, messing things up, not being the person I want him to be. And despite all that—"I don't know how it's possible, Mae, but Wyatt's even cuter than his photos. He's got shoulders for days. His hair's a little longer, but in a good way. And his cheekbones! But it's his eyes—" I squeeze mine tighter, remembering how it felt to lock gazes as we both held the gingerbread roof.

"Shocker—I've got *ears* too. Not sure if they're 'cuter' than in pictures, but they work a lot better."

My eyes fly open as I fling myself upright, launching the pillow across the room and yanking the earbuds from my phone as it falls from the bed. The cord dangles uselessly and Mae's barely audible voice comes from the carpet. "Noelle? Noelle?"

Because she isn't the one who'd commented on his ears—she's way more likely to ask about abs. *Wyatt* is standing in the doorway between my room and the bathroom, wearing a scowl so fierce it could melt the snow on the deck outside—which would be sort of helpful, since I'm considering making my barefoot escape out that back door.

"Don't objectify me."

I've still got earbuds dangling from one ear, wrapped around my neck. Mae's still calling out from the carpet, and my heart is beating faster than the steps in a petit allegro. As much as I want to protest his accusations—*I can't.* I was literally just admiring him piece-by-piece.

But . . . I was also having a *private* conversation. His ears may work fine, but they were eavesdropping. I'm still mortified—I'll likely be mortified about this forever—but my embarrassment is growing burnt edges, scorched by my kindling anger.

I stand and cross my arms—then uncross them when it tugs on the wire still leading to my ear. "Why are you in my room? Without *knocking.*"

He holds up his hands. "Whoa. Take it easy there, Sparkle Queen. The door to the bathroom was open. And I did knock."

Oh, right. I'd had my head under a pillow. But, wait, *sparkle queen?* I follow his gaze to the bedazzled phone case on the rug. That name spelled out in rhinestones above a crown. "It was a gift from a babysitting client." And while it wasn't *me* at all, it felt rude not to use it.

"Whatever. I was coming to ask if you wanted first shower, but forget it."

Oh. *Oh.* My eyes go wide as I eye the doorway behind him. *His* is the bedroom on the other side of the bathroom's far door. *He* is the one I'll be sharing it with. Fan-flipping-tastic.

But I didn't cry after yesterday's puke-deluge, and I'm not going to now. I keep my chin up and meet his eyes—they really are as pretty as I was going to tell Mae, even when they're narrowed with annoyance. "Go ahead and take first shower," I say with all the meager sparkle queen dignity I can manage, "but save me some hot water."

I hear his laughter echoing even after he shuts the door, so I take my phone outside to the deck.

"Tell me that really happened." Mae is giggling uncontrollably. "Actually, can you call back and retell all that when Coco and Autumn get here for houses? There's no way they'll believe me."

"I hate you," I tell her, my teeth chattering from the cold.

"That's fair." She's fighting to tamp down laughter. "Sorry, sorry. But, oh my gosh, Noelle, I think I just became a Wyatt fan."

Great that she approves of him, but he absolutely doesn't approve of me. Not sure I blame him, and I'm *really* not sure how I'm ever going to face him again. Because, if what he overheard wasn't bad enough, there's *more* humiliation waiting in the bathroom when it's my turn to shower. It takes the form of a bright red bra. One I'd left dangling from the showerhead to dry after I rinsed off Jack's vomit. One that's now hanging from the towel rack.

I'm not sure what else he could've done with it: Drop it on the floor? Shower with it dangling behind his head? But seeing it—knowing he had to move it? It no longer matters if he used all the hot water—I need an icy shower to cool my scorching blush.

This is going to be the weirdest week of my life. But I don't have long to dwell on it, because it's already been close to a half hour, which is twenty-seven minutes longer than Holly and Jack are capable of waiting.

I tell myself it doesn't matter that he saw my bra, or what he overheard, or that he won't listen to *The Nutcracker*, or that he didn't fall in insta-love and beg me to come to Beacon and be his permanent pas de deux partner. Right now, we have a gingerbread house contest to win.

Mae said if I sent pictures, I could be a proxy entrant. This ups the stakes—I've got a winning streak to continue and a novice as a partner.

But I'm not worried. You can't get as far as Wyatt and I have in ballet without being detail-oriented, precise . . . and monstrously competitive.

We're going to crush it.

Or, as the case ends up being—we're going to stand as far apart as is physically possible while working on the same small house, avoid making eye contact, and argue over everything. Or not *argue*, because we're not actually talk-ing. This is pro-level passive-aggressiveness, where one of us places something—thoughtfully, purposefully—and the other partner recklessly removes or moves it.

I let it go when he peels off the chocolate bar door and repositions the gingerbread tree, but who objects to fon-dant on the roof? Wyatt, that's who! Fondant is Gingerbread House 101. It wasn't like I was going to roll the smooth green sheet across the slants, trim it to size, and call it a day. I fully intended to add precise scallops in royal icing, then festoon each scale-shaped tile with a tiny red candy; but as I'm fin-ishing my first row of scallops, Wyatt takes the paring knife and slices the fondant off the other side.

"I'm planning something different," he says when I squawk in protest.

"*You're* planning?" Because last time I checked, *I* was the one who'd actually drawn up plans for a house. Unfor-tunately it's in my Christmas Extravaganza notebook back in PA, but I'd had a plan: Snowman Wonderland. I remem-ber enough to know it's going to be epic—if I can just get this guy (who I can only look at from the wrists down) to cooperate. But, ugh, what if he tells his parents about the conversation he eavesdropped? I grit my teeth. "What is *your* plan?"

"How about you take your half, and I'll do mine." He picks up the frosting and pipes it along the roof's ridge line. "There. Do whatever you want on your side."

I narrow my eyes. "Fine."

My side will be neat and classic: a candy cane–edged door, crushed wintergreen mints on the trees, a gleaming skating pond made from clear sprinkles, complete with snowmen skaters.

His side apparently involves . . . *power tools?* He disappears for a minute, then returns with a cordless drill, telling his family, "You can't object to my using this since you got hot glue."

I hold up a hand. "Wait, am *I* allowed to object?" But he pretends he can't hear me over the whir of the motor.

And then he *drills a hole in his side of the roof.*

I bite through the wintergreen mint I'd been sucking on, mashing my teeth painfully into my tongue. I can't—I can't even believe he just—

Fine. Whatever. I'll send Mae photos of *my* half. And I'll keep my eyes on this side too—I disown the other half of the property. But my hand shakes around the paring knife as I cut slices from a green gumdrop to make a wreath for my door, because is that . . . *cereal?* Why does he have the box of Life? It better be for a mid-construction snack.

And he's cutting—he's cutting his door into pieces?

I'm about to say something when the song finally changes. Based off his family's cheers, I'm not the only one thrilled we're done with "Deck the Halls." Except, this new song about a "bright, Hawaiian Christmas"—I don't know it. I mean, obviously I've heard it before, but I don't have it memorized. The Kahales are singing it with gusto, interjecting with bits of shared memories from past trips.

"You guys weren't born yet, but I wish you could've seen your mom's face the first time she tried poi." Wyatt grins at Mrs. Kahale as Jack and Holly turn, expecting her to re-create it.

She makes an exaggerated grimace, barely holding it before dissolving into laugh. "It's an acquired taste. I love it now."

Yeah, I have no idea what poi is, but should I chime in with similar stories from the Primaveras' Feast of the Seven Fishes? Or not interrupt and focus on learning the song's words?

By the third version, I've got "Mele Kalikimaka" pretty much down. By version six, I'm ready to never hear it again.

And even though I'm simply *not* having a "Wonderful Christmastime," I inwardly cheer when the song changes to Sir Paul McCartney. Though I must give some not-so-inward sign of relief, because I catch Wyatt's smirk.

I huff and turn my back on him, facing Jack, who's stuck his frosting-sticky hands into the red sprinkles and is now waving them around like red gloves—making Holly shriek as he pretends he's going to poke her.

Eh, let's be real, he's *going* to poke her.

"Jackster," I say, interrupting their battle. "Tell me about your house! I love"—I point to globs of icing with gumballs peeking through—"this. Did you make it?"

"That's the garbage dump," he says, which earns him a hug, sprinkle hands and all—because of course this trash-truck-loving kiddo would include a dump on his house. "Are we done yet?"

"Not quite," says Mr. Kahale. "I thought you were going to help me with the windows?"

It seems clear that Wyatt's siblings' attitudes about gingerbread houses are starting to mirror mine about his playlist. We're all *over it*. Right on cue, Jack whines, "*Ugh*. Can't we be done?"

Mrs. Kahale bargains for "ten more minutes" and sets a timer. I buckle down, ignoring the sticky urchin to my left and his brooding brother to my right. When the timer goes off, it'll be time for the big unveiling, which includes seeing not only the others' houses but the other half of my own.

I mean, I've peeked, but not extensively. I couldn't see the whole of his side. Or the hole *in* his side—which it turns out was to create a chimney from his hacked-up door and windows. Emerging from it is a foil-wrapped chocolate Santa. The cereal became roof tiles. Which, fine, they look cool . . . If you like a brown-on-brown, not-festive color scheme. Which I guess he does, since he's also striped the side of his house with pretzel rods to replicate the look of logs on a cabin. He's built an impressive deck out the same rod and frosting construction.

And while his decorations are minimal, he's created a

mountain—with another foil-wrapped chocolate posed on candy cane skis with pretzel rod poles.

"There can't be two Santas," protests his sister. Her house, unsurprisingly, is draped in garland after garland of green fondant with red hots garnish—holly everywhere. They've spelled out J O Y with white Good & Plenty and used the pink ones as window shutters.

And Jack's—well, his dad tried. But most of his piping and decorations were buried when Jack squeezed the frosting bag above the whole house—claiming he was adding "snow."

"So . . ." Mr. Kahale says slowly, "since there's really only one contender, do we judge the halves of yours separately?"

I can feel Wyatt's eyes on me. I straighten my shoulders but refuse to look over.

"What do you mean 'only one contender'?" Holly asks— well, it's less of a question and more of a dare mixed with a threat.

I put a hand on her shoulder. "We don't need a winner. It's better if it's just for fun." My words aren't altruistic. I'm not being a good babysitter—I'm being a bad loser. Because I don't know which way the votes would swing and I doubt my ego could gracefully handle being beaten by a first-time builder who ignored all my suggestions and broke all the rules but still managed to pull off something awesome.

A power drill? I'm undecided if it's creative or cheating, but I'll be attempting to use one on my house next year.

"You said it was a contest," protests Holly. "I want—"

"Wait, I thought someone had a ski race this after-noon? Am I going to get to see all this speed you keep telling me about?"

It sounds like something I'd say, but those words don't come from my mouth. It's not my elbow that my favorite show-off links her skinny arm through after jumping out of her seat so quickly she overturns a tub of peppermints and almost flips her house. *I'm* not the person who defuses this situation.

That'd be Wyatt.

I already know he outranks me in ballet, but is it possible he just beat me in building *and* babysitting too?

I narrow my eyes at the retreating back of the guy being dragged away by *my* favorite eight-year-old. It stings to remind myself that his claim is stronger. I'm just the sitter. She's his *sister.*

Babysitting Tip 10:
Not everything's a competition.
You don't have to be the favorite.

"**M**y team check-in starts at one and you need to feed me before." Holly—the same girl who leaves a trail of clothing through her house at bedtime and loses her library books twice daily—pulls out a checklist to make sure she has all her gear. A *checklist*!

And *holy snowflakes*, skiing requires a lot of gear. A helmet. Socks. More socks. Glove and glove liners. Goggles. Long underwear. Sunblock. ChapStick. Hand warmers. Neck warmer. Another neck warmer. Hat. Water bottle. Boots—ski and regular. Mouthguard. Something called a "spine protector"—which, yeah, I knew this wasn't safe. Parka. Pants. Poles. Skis.

After lining it all up on the floor, she scarfs down a grilled cheese sandwich, packs some of the gear into her duffel, and dons the rest.

While she's doing her whole body-snatched organized person thing, Wyatt's dragging his own gear out of the foyer closet and looking it over. I have no idea what he's looking for, but I understand the part where he winces as he tries to ease his foot into a boot. "Yeah, these aren't going to work."

His father chuckles. "Well, if you could just stop your feet from growing, we wouldn't have this problem."

Wyatt makes that universal grumbly noise—the one that means *I hear and acknowledge your dad-joke, but I'm not encouraging it.*

Mr. Kahale claps a hand on his shoulder. "If you're ready, Big Foot, come with Holls and me and we'll rent you a pair before the race."

"We're not all going together?" Mrs. Kahale and Jack and I are sitting at the table, taking a more leisurely approach to lunch—meaning we're stopping to chew. I thought the plan was for us *all* to head over so they could show me around the lodge—point out where to drop the kids off—and the best place to buy cocoa, which I'd sip by some cozy fireplace until their lessons were done.

Mrs. Kahale shakes her head. "They've got to get Holly checked in; we'll take the shuttle over later."

"Unless you want to come along and get a set of rentals?" Mr. Kahale asks as he zips his coat. "We're happy to sign you up for lessons."

I shake my head. "No, thanks. Strictly an indoor sports person." But I'm biting back questions I want to scream at the guy who's slinging skis over his shoulder—*How can you strap those to your precious feet and hurl your body down a mountain? There's no way Beacon allows it!* One wrong turn on the slopes and he's trading dance class for physical therapy. How can he be taking such a pointless risk?

I glance around, but no one else is giving Wyatt you're-an-idiot looks, so maybe I should neutralize my expression? Because based on his narrowed eyes, he definitely noticed. *Whoops.*

As soon as the front door shuts, Jack pushes out his chair and declares that he doesn't want to ski today. He doesn't want to ski *ever*: "I'm an indoor sports person, like Noelle."

Man, I love this kid . . . But it's possible this isn't the influence the Kahales want me having.

"Let's compromise," his mom says after a contemplative pause where she nibbles his crusts. "You can skip lessons today, but I want no whining the rest of the week." She has to raise her voice over his cheering. "And we still have to go to the lodge later to show Noelle around."

"Deal!" Jack grasps my hand and I hope his mom knows she's dreaming about the "no whining" part. "Now let's play."

Mrs. Kahale waves her dish towel to get his attention. "Not so fast. If you're skipping lessons, you're helping me decorate."

This is where I prove my worth as a sitter—because Jack's reluctance fades in the face of my enthusiasm. We're not doing the tree, obviously, but there's garlands to wrap around the banisters, holly boughs to hang above the fireplace. Stocking hangers, snowmen, angels, candles . . . and mistletoe.

I'd been whirling like one of the nine ladies dancing, decorating like an elf sugar-high on eggnog and peppermint bark—but now I falter as Coco's words play in my head. *"Maybe this year will be less sitting-on-Santa's-lap and more meeting-someone-under-the-mistletoe."* Or maybe I can hide this plant in the box I unpacked the nativity set from?

"That's the kissing ball!" Jack appears at my elbow—his voice extra loud and his mouth puckered up. He smacks a wet one on my elbow as Mrs. Kahale smiles and drags a chair from the kitchen to the overhang below the loft.

"The nail for that is over here. I apologize in advance if we embarrass you with PDAs—Holly and Jack are way too into catching Nick and me beneath it."

I force myself to laugh. "It's fine." It's totally fine—as long as Wyatt never learns of the times I've daydreamed about him plus me and this plant. Subject change! "Um, when do we leave for Holly's race?"

Mrs. Kahale climbs off the chair. "Nick texted. We're uninvited. The speedster doesn't want a certain attention-seeker to monopolize Wyatt."

I'm a breath from hyperventilating when she laughs and adds, "Families, huh?" and I realize she means *Jack*, not me.

My laugh is awkward and she pauses from shooing that "attention-seeker" to his room for a nap. "Are you okay? Have you talked to your dad?" If she means *about* Beacon, then the answer is no. If she means in general, well, still no, except for a few texts.

"I'm going to call him now, unless you need me?" I'm half hoping she gives me an excuse, but she scoops up Jack and waves me off. "Tell him we say hi."

Miraculously Dad answers, barking, "Timothy Partridge," in his business voice, so it's clear mine isn't the phone call he's expecting, but he stays on the line anyway.

I'm too choked up to talk after, "It's really pretty here," "I miss you," and "They bought me a gingerbread house kit," but Dad fills the silence with a story I've never heard before. About a time he and Mom went skiing and a lock of her hair kept blowing in her face on the lift. While tucking it back under her helmet, he dropped one of his gloves. "It was a very cold ride down for my left hand."

I laugh until I snort, and he says, "She did that too. You sound so much like her when you do it." Now I'm choking up again—until he adds. "I always saw you more as a snowboarder."

"What?" I sputter. "Snowboarder? I'm not going any closer to the mountain than I have to for babysitting duties, thank you very much."

"Where's your sense of adventure, kiddo?" he teases. "You're only young once, and fourteen-year-old bones heal pretty quick."

I know he's not serious, but he's bull's-eyed my

objection—broken bones means no Beacon audition. Not that he knows about it . . .

"Um, Dad?" This feels like the right time to tell him. It's the closest we've been to Team Partridge in ages—which is why I hesitate. On the one hand, I'll need a ride to the audition, and with how busy he's been, I should get on his schedule ASAP, but on the other, if there's a possibility we can fix things, do I even want to go? I mean, at least not *right* now. I don't have to start midyear, I could—

"That's my other line, kiddo. I've got to click over. Good talking to you. I love you."

He's gone and I'm left holding my phone, almost wishing he hadn't picked up, because I'm lonelier than before. And what I want to do is pout, dance, or call Mae, ideally do all three at once, but I can't because I'm getting *paid*—and I can hear Jack vrooming a vehicle around the living room. Which means the nap didn't happen and I need to pull it together so we can head to the lodge.

I take several deep breaths and turn to my suitcase. I don't own any clothing with the word "snow" in it. My winter jacket is a red toboggan coat, my gloves, hat, and scarf are mostly decorative—they have ruffles instead of liners. This is fine for today's tour of Kringle, but I borrowed snow gear from the Primaveras too. Mae's too short, so it's Rachel's coat and pants taking up space in my bag. Like so much of her clothing, they're rainbow striped. I'm going to look like a walking

Pride flag—but, as she'd pointed out, "There's zero chance those kids will lose sight of you in the snow."

Yeah, I'm less worried about *me* getting lost and more about Jack wandering off to do whatever's the ski equivalent of petting every dog you see. I'm worried about *a lot* of things as we take the shuttle to Kringle Village. There's so much to absorb: the route to the shuttle stop, how skis are stored in racks along the bus's side, how Jack taps his sleeve on a touchscreen as we board. Mrs. Kahale does too. Then she passes me a "Kringle Card" that I fumble against the machine.

"That works as a bus pass as well as a credit card anywhere in Kringle. Charge anything you or the kids need, but keep it safe."

I tuck it in the pocket on the back of my phone case, a little overwhelmed by the responsibility. And a lot overwhelmed by the passing scenery. Narrow steepled churches. Clapboard houses. Front porches. Snow on pines and parking lots and signs that makes even the Food Mart and 7-Eleven look festive. Jack bounces beside me as I recite joke after joke for him to turn and parrot to his mom.

But when we step off the bus at Kringle Village, it's a good thing he's holding on to his mom, because I forget all about him. "Oh my, garland. It's—it's—"

I'd been picturing something piney and snowy and pretty, but apparently my imagination isn't that great, because I wasn't prepared for a whole village of quaint buildings. Of soaring arches, balconies, peaks, and lights strung between rooflines—not just strands, but large orbs and snowflakes. It's all against a backdrop of mountain majesty that feels like nature showing off. I peel my eyes away and find Mrs. Kahale. "We have to stay until after dark so it's all lit up! I mean, can we? Please."

"If Holly and co aren't too tired, I was thinking we'd stay for the tree lighting." She points across an ice-skating rink—an ice-skating rink!—to the world's most perfect tree. I may squeal and do a happy dance. Fine, I do. And Jack copies me.

The sidewalks meander around shops and restaurants all in the same golden wood and glass style. All of their roofs, different heights and shapes, are tiled in the same manner. I blink as I take it all in. "Wyatt made Kringle on the ginger-bread house."

She nods. "I thought that was so clever."

Clever. Talented. Gorgeous. It feels a bit unfair.

"Hey, big guy!"

Apparently I need to stop even *thinking* Wyatt's name, because there's something about the Vermont air and my thoughts that summon him.

Though, when he's scooping up his brother and asking, "You gonna hit the slopes with me? Show me your skills? Where are your skis?" and tickling Jack as he pretends to search for the skis we didn't bring—yeah, I've got no complaints about Vermont's magic.

Jack is laughing and stealing Wyatt's sunglasses. For the first time, he's interested in skiing. "You'll stay with me? Let me go first?"

"Of course," Wyatt says with an exaggerated scoff. "Who else is going to show me how to do it?"

"Okay, maybe another day," says Jack as Wyatt sets him down. "We're showing Noelle around."

Jack doesn't let go of his brother's hand, but reaches for mine too, and that's just one degree of separation from Wyatt. We're practically hand-holding by proxy. My face still feels all soft and smiley from watching their tickling show when Wyatt catches my eye above Jack's head and asks, "What do you think of Kringle?"

"I think you should've won the gingerbread contest."

He laughs. Not the goofing around laughs I've heard so far. This one is loud and wild, like I've caught him off guard and delighted him. It makes my cheeks flush and my pulse dance.

Mrs. Kahale offers commentary as she leads us down the path, pointing out a coffee kiosk, a fancy boutique, a real estate office, skate rentals, and a store that sells Adirondack chairs.

And I hear her—sorta—but I'm caught in the scent of snow and pine and fire pits that must be crackling somewhere out of sight. I'm dizzy tracking all the cords of lights that will be so dazzling later. And Wyatt. I'm inundated with the awareness of him, just one small person away from me.

He's chatting about squirrels or something with Jack, but when he glances sideways at me there's a zing in each connection, a lengthening of each look.

"This is where you'll be spending most of your time," says Mrs. Kahale, pausing outside a large building labeled THISTLE LODGE. "Holly and Nick should already be waiting inside—unless they're not, in which case Holly talked him into taking a victory run with her and we're going to be waiting awhile."

"So, basically, we'll be waiting?" I tease, because there's zero chance Holly didn't win or ask or that he said no. But that's fine with me. Bring on the cozy chairs and fireplaces!

Wyatt lets go of Jack to grab the door for a couple juggling their gear, and once they're through, it's our turn. I squeeze Jack's hand and suck in a huge breath as we step inside the large building—but then my face puckers.

It smells of sweat and fast-food restaurants. With a sprinkling of road salt as seasoning—which makes sense, because my feet are crunching in so much of it on the floor, mixed with puddles of melted snow.

It's loud—louder than the cafeteria it resembles in both smell and appearance: long, school-style tables and cheap molded chairs. They're covered in bags ranging from high-end duffels to the kind that go in kitchen trash cans. There are so many people. The sounds of a hundred conversations mixed with the clop of ski boots has me freezing at the edge of the red rubber mat inside the door.

My eyes are pinging everywhere: from video screens of trail maps and ski conditions to rows of garbage cans, to a tray return station and a snaking line for food, to . . . Wyatt. He's watching me, quirking an eyebrow, which means every ounce of my disappointment must be showing on my face.

I wipe it blank and turn to Mrs. Kahale, dutifully making mental notes as she walks me through where they normally leave their family's stuff—*unattended!* Where to line up for lunch, what Jack likes to eat, and then, crossing to a door on the far wall, we tromp back outside onto snow as she leads me to an area marked off by stakes topped with colored flags.

"I'm the blue group," Jack says glumly.

"This is where his class meets," she clarifies. "You'll get him all suited up, then drop him and pick him up here."

While I'm absorbing this, a guy in a blue jacket walks over, and whatever Jack's problem with lessons is, it isn't his instructor, because he flings himself at the dude.

"Okay, what gives?" Wyatt sidles up and asks. "When you walked in back there, you were pouting worse than Jack when he skips his nap."

I shrug and turn back to Jack, but he and his mom have followed the instructor to look at something on the small slope. "He doesn't really take naps anymore."

"Yeah, that's so not my point," says Wyatt. "Why the frown?" He stands there, one eyebrow raised, his mouth quirked, like he has an eternity to wait for me to crack.

And maybe he does, because the ski instructor's asking, "Who's there?" and I've armed Jack with lots of knock-knock ammunition.

"Fine," I huff. "I was picturing something with a few more fireplaces and fluffy couches and a few less decibels of noise." Clearly the lesson of today is *Noelle's fantasies are nothing like reality.*

"Ah." He nods, then calls, "Ginger, I'm taking Noelle to see Juniper Lodge." He waits for her thumbs-up and says, "C'mon. Fireplaces and fluffy couches are this way."

I follow him, achingly aware there isn't a small child separating us—that his arm brushed my shoulder as we dodge a raucous group. "Why are you doing this?"

By "this" I mean "being friendly," but that feels rude to ask. I'm pretty sure he infers it anyway, because he snorts. "If you'd rather stand outside and hear Jack's comedy show . . ."

"No, I'm good." My response is speedy, but my steps slow in admiration as the path curves past the skating rink. "That tree is amazing."

"It's pretty cool to see it lit up when you're coming down the mountain," says Wyatt.

My nose crinkles—won't be doing that! He heads past the crowds gathered for the lighting into a large building with balconies and chimneys galore.

"This is Juniper Lodge. It's got the spa, the hotel rooms, the kids and teen clubs, a couple bars and restaurants—and all the couches and fireplaces you could want." The doors open automatically and he gestures for me to go inside.

I pass through two sets of doors and into blissful quiet. There was a subtle sign outside for the SKI VALET and I'm not a hundred percent sure what that is, but if it means no clomping ski boots to disturb the tranquility, I'm all for it.

Because, holy frankincense! This place is jaw-dropping. The amount of garland puts Holly's gingerbread house to shame and—"That's—that's not a tree." It looked like one at first, a giant one decked with red bows. But, no. At the center of the lobby is a towering tower constructed from potted poinsettias.

The ceilings climb and the couches curve like commas, inviting private conversations or cozy reading. There are bare birch trees and lights and the quiet music of a piano drifting from somewhere past this lobby. Railings circle the upper part of the room, teasing a second floor and more places to tuck away. And fireplaces! Three! It's so perfect I want to spin around and take it all in.

So I do. First in a slow, flat-footed rotation, then an impromptu pirouette.

"Oh. You dance." Wyatt's words aren't a question, and they aren't excited. "Right. Your comment about *The Nutcracker*. Huh." His eyes narrow in new scrutiny.

Instead of answering, I plié, passé into a pirouette.

"Good turnout," Wyatt says, and I smile before realizing he's not done. "But your landing could use some work."

My smile fades. "I'm in boots!" I waggle one at him. If I had my pointe shoes, I'd show him landings. And extensions that would make him weep. En pointe, I'd be taller. I could look him in the eye, I could lean forward and bite at the smirk on his mouth. He's the perfect height for my pas de deux partner—his only flaw being that he looks like he'd rather trip me than lift me.

Wyatt gestures at his own snow boots, then lifts his eyebrows before rising to relevé and executing a perfect double pirouette.

"Ooh, dance off," says a woman sipping a cocktail on the closest sofa. I can't tell if she's holding a furry purse or a purse-sized dog. "Brava! More."

But one of us goes to Beacon and one of us only wishes she did. This wouldn't be a contest; it would be an ego stomp. Mine's already pretty squashed, thank you very much.

"Another time," says Wyatt. Not rudely, but firm—and there's something off in his expression, something guilty or wistful. It's how I imagine my face looked when I ignored a call from Miss Janet today, or each time I pick up my phone without listening to her voice mail. He leads me closer to the poinsettia tree. "So, will this do?"

"Are you kidding?" I bounce in my boots to stop myself from more impromptu dancing, then blush, realizing it probably makes me look like Jack pre-potty break. "It's amazing."

Wyatt's eyes don't follow the movements of my arms as I gesture at—well, everything. They're locked on my face, on my awe and excitement, which is getting harder to hold on to under his scrutiny. "Since we finally don't have an audience"—he's talking about his family, not the dance battle lady—"why are you here?"

"At the lodge?" I falter under the ferocity of his question; my interpretation makes no sense. He brought me? But the larger context doesn't either. "On this trip? Your parents hired me. I'm their babysitter."

He makes a grumbly sound that's hotter than the draft from the fireplace. Or, at least it would be if he weren't frowning. "Why did you say yes? What kind of person gives up Christmas? I thought maybe you were Jewish or didn't celebrate—but it's Hanukkah too and you seem to have an opinion on *everything* yuletide, and—"

"Excuse me?" He's not entirely wrong, but he doesn't get to mock my love of Christmas. I narrow my eyes. Who does he think he is? "I'll put some yule in your tide!"

Wyatt coughs. "Is that a threat . . . or a pickup line?" His eyes are bright, like he's trying not to laugh.

"No!" I gasp. "Neither."

"I have no idea what it means."

"Yeah, well, me neither!" But, fine, it sounds ridiculous. I sigh. "Look, I owe you an apology. The part of my private phone call you eavesdropped on must've been weird to hear. I wouldn't have said it if I knew you were listening."

His mouth quirks before he wrangles his expression back to stern. "That's your apology?"

I ignore him. "But we're both here and—"

The corners of his mouth go flat. "You should go home."

I take a step back to make room for his ego. "Because I said you were hot? I can't be the first person to point that out."

"What? No." He shakes his head. "It has nothing to do with that. I don't care what you tell your friends about me. You've got to know you're gorgeous too—that's not relevant—" Did he? Did he just call me *gorgeous?* Any thrill those words might inspire is quickly soured when he adds, "But I'm here now, so you can go."

"You know, only one of us was invited for Christmas." I fumble with the toggle buttons on my jacket. I want to blame overheating on the fireplace, but this is anger-sweat. "Spoiler: It wasn't *you.*"

His eyes go wide. It takes a few blinks for him to erase the hurt from his face. "Only one of us shares DNA with them—and, *spoiler*, that's not you. Given the choice between family and someone they have to pay, why would they even want you at Christmas?"

Those words hit like a punch. *Why would they even want me?* Who knows? Dad doesn't. But instead of retreating or crumpling, I clasp my fingers around my bracelet—*dance, play, family*—and step forward. "I know they're *your* family, but I also *know* your family." I'm standing closer to him than is comfortable, but he hasn't moved. "I spend more time with them than you do."

He flinches. It's so subtle that if I hadn't been totally invading his personal space, I wouldn't have noticed. It makes me soften my voice and step back. "I'm a good baby-sitter. I love Holly and Jack. So whatever secret evil motives you think I have, you're wrong. I'm not some South Pole elf, here to ruin Christmas."

He grips the back of his neck and kneads the muscles there. And even now, when I'm not sure if I should be furious or sympathetic, the action is still distractedly hot. "South Pole elf?" One side of his mouth hitches up. "I'm being a jerk. Sorry. I don't think you have secret evil motives."

Okay, that was a way better apology than mine. But it's not the whole story. He's hiding something. Instead of being nosy, I lift my eyebrows in my best saucy look. "I guess we'll just have to share them for Christmas. But, fair warning, I'm an only child. Sharing's not my forte."

And there it is, his laugh—wild and surprised. "Noted."

I let myself soak in this moment in this setting with this person. He's got more layers than the poinsettia tree, but at least one of them includes smiling at me like I'm irresistible and calling me gorgeous. It's a start.

"There you are!" We take steps away from each other as we turn toward his stepmom. She's red-cheeked and out of breath. "I left everyone at the tree lighting. I tried calling, but cell reception here can be spotty."

"We missed the tree lighting?" I wince at how shrill my

voice goes. Wyatt's eyes shoot to me, and I'm trying not to pout, but . . . *again?*

Mrs. Kahale's gaze sharpens as she takes in our position. Not standing as close as we were, but closer than two near-strangers should be. And did she see us bickering? She sounds concerned as she asks, "What were you two talking about?"

Playing possessive tug-of-war doesn't really sound professional, and there are zero answers on Wyatt's stony face, so I hunt for them in the poinsettias, the couches, and finally find one when I stare down at our feet. Our turned-out feet.

"Beacon," I lie. "I was asking about it."

"Oh!" Mrs. Kahale's face brightens. "You told Wyatt you're auditioning?"

His mouth drops open. "What?" In four shocked letters he's destroyed any hopes I had of audition advice—and tipped off Mrs. Kahale's suspicions again.

I'm insulted. Had he thought I was a balletomane? The dance world's equivalent of groupies. And nothing against them—the art needs them—but I want him to see me as an equal, not a fangirl. Yes, my boot pirouettes need work, but I'll be in Russian Pointes when I nail my audition and in the classes where I show him just how false his first impression was.

I grit my teeth. "Let's go see the tree." But once I storm outside, I can't bring myself to look at it. Wyatt is right at my elbow, and I can tell he wants my attention. I avoid his gaze by hugging his sister. "I hear you had a great race."

"Yeah." I love Holly's shrugging acceptance of her skills. "Did you have cocoa? We did."

"I can tell." I trace a line across my upper lip to indicate her chocolate mustache. She laughs.

"Let's head home," says Mr. Kahale, reaching for his wife's hand as Jack grasps Wyatt's. "I don't know about you all, but I'm starving."

Holly runs ahead to where her skis are leaning on a rack, leaving me beside Wyatt again. He points over his shoulder at the tree. "Did you get a chance to admire it or whatever?"

I shrug. "I can't believe we missed it. You don't understand." There's so much magic in that second between darkness and illumination. The whole world looks different when it's first lit up—and I swear I feel the glow in my chest as much as I see it on the snow and skin and smile of everyone who's around me. And sure the tree is grand and gorgeous now—but that's a totally different emotion. The first one feels participatory—hopeful. And now, it's just admiration.

"You're right, I don't," Wyatt says slowly. It's not a dismissal. He hasn't turned back to Jack and his nonstop narration about the five dogs he saw and their sweaters and antlers. It seems like he's asking to, but I'm still annoyed he wasn't immediately pro-Noelle-Beacon, and it's all so big and personal—I don't know how to begin.

"It's just . . . This is the second tree lighting I've missed this year. My hometown one was rained out and rescheduled for during *The Nutcracker*."

"Oh." He nods twice, then smiles. "Well, I've got some good news. They do the tree lighting every night from now until New Year's. You can see it another time."

The knit fabric of my gloves catches as I cross my fingers. Because . . . maybe? If the Kahales are here at just the right time on another day. If they're willing to wait, if no one needs a potty break. If I have a night off. Because while he was quick to point out that he's family and I'm paid, he doesn't seem to grasp the implications of that. My time's not my own. And while I know the Kahales would make this happen if I asked, it'd be a lot of work to get everyone loaded in the car to drive over for that one, perfect second.

I mean, even keeping Jack out of the snow on our short walk to the parking lot is a full-time job.

"Hey, Dad," Wyatt calls as we reach the edge of the sidewalk. "We're going to take the shuttle. I think Noelle needs more practice."

I bristle and open my mouth to squawk—I know how to ride a bus, thank you very much—but Wyatt says, "Trust me," under his breath, and for whatever reason, I do.

So when Mr. Kahale turns to me, I shrug. "It wouldn't hurt to do another trial run. This time with skis." I point to Wyatt's.

And the jerk actually hands me his. He doesn't laugh as I fumble carrying them or when I struggle to fit them into the rack on the shuttle, but he doesn't jump in to help either.

"I can't do it," I say, panicking that I'm holding up the bus.

He shakes his head. "You can. Lock the skis at the binding, then slide them straight in."

"Fine," I growl, and *fine*, he's right, that works. But by the time I board and collapse in the seat beside his, I'm stress-sweaty and annoyed.

I whirl on him, but he's grinning, not mocking. His sincere "Good job" makes me preen. He adds, "Also, you did *not* want to ride in the SUV. It smells like puke drenched in carpet cleaner. My God, the drive over was awful."

Oh. *Oh.* So maybe his shuttle motives were kind, after all. "At least you missed the fireworks show when it happened."

"I heard." He grimaces. "Which is why I figured you'd already suffered enough."

We don't shake hands or sign our names on some magical peace treaty, but just like back in Juniper Lodge—before the awkward mention of Beacon—there's something in our held gaze that makes me think we're on the same side again. I smile. "Thanks. Plus now I get out of bedtime. Last night they wouldn't let anyone but me tuck them in."

I'm not saying it to insult his parents. I'm not bragging that his siblings like me better—but my words tighten the skin around his eyes. "Maybe they'll wait up for us?"

"Not likely. Jack didn't nap and Holly crashes hard when she's tired. I bet they had to blast music to keep them awake on the drive."

His face tightens more. I'm definitely not imagining this. A minute ago he was relaxed, now he's tense and coiled, a crumbling smile barely clinging to his mouth. I know he doesn't get to see Holly and Jack that often, but is he really this upset about missing out on the battles of brushing and tucking?

"They'll be up early," I tell him. "Your mo—Mrs. Kahale—says they never sleep past seven."

"You really do know them." His voice reminds me of the music of *The Nutcracker*'s "Pas de Deux—Intrada," but before I can fully process why he sounds sad and wistful, he changes its tenor. It's the battle of the Mouse King, a challenge, when he adds, "So do I."

I study him, but he's looking out the window. And while I could write an instruction manual on his siblings, I only know Wyatt by his cover. He's a mystery, but so far all his pages are blank.

Babysitting Tip 11:
Beware of the power of puppy dog eyes and footie pj's.

It's still dark when I wake, but I'm not falling back asleep. Holly and Jack will get up soon, and I need to do *something* to earn the ridiculous salary the Kahales are paying me, even if it's just keeping the kids quiet so they can sleep in.

Wyatt is already sitting on the living room couch. He has his head tipped back and his eyes closed, but they fly open and he turns when I come in. His gaze darts past me to the hall before returning to my face. "They're still sleeping?"

It sounds like he wishes he could be, and I wonder if his reasons for coming out here are similar to mine. "I'm sure they'll be up any minute."

His eyes are on the hallway as he nods. "What are you going to do?"

"Stretch?" If I'm trying out for Beacon, I can't let myself get rusty. "You—*They* can join me." I chicken out from inviting him, because we haven't acknowledged what his step-mom revealed in the lodge—or his strange reaction to it.

His eyes scan my clothes. I'd changed from pajamas to leggings and a fitted long-sleeve shirt. "They'll do that?"

"Holly might tolerate it if I turn it into some sort of contest. But Jack, yeah. Definitely. He'll make it his own thing." These are offhand shrugging answers, but he's nodding, processing them like I'm giving him state secrets.

And when his siblings tumble down the hall, he's on his feet beside me, joining me in urging them to "shhhh." He heats up leftover waffles for Holly as Jack—just like I predicted—opts to dance with me. Wyatt watches me over the rim of his cup as we run around the couch on demi-pointe and jump between plies in first and second position. "You go to their dance school?" I nod and he adds, "You're good."

I'm caught between reactions—because I've heard Miss Janet's lectures on owning my talent versus false modesty, but it's equally awkward to say, "I know." Not that he can tell my true skills from bopping around with Jack.

I settle on "Thanks" but the word is blocky on my tongue. It's mixed with a desire to ask "Good enough for Beacon?" and to show off what I can really do.

While Wyatt and I are holding a stare down that consists of stiff nods and thoughts we're not sharing, Jack finds my phone. Our eye contact is broken by a blast of "Here Comes Santa Claus" that has us both whirling and shushing and him dropping the phone. By the time I extract it from under the couch—thankfully unbroken—and pause the song, the door to his parents' bedroom is opening. Wyatt slumps in his chair.

Mrs. Kahale leans over the railing in her curly, bedhead glory and smiles. "Merry Christmas Eve, my loves! We'll be right down."

From there the day goes in fast-forward: cooking, eating, coordinating schedules. Wyatt's phone rings mid-meal and he leaves to take the call.

"Noelle, will you think we're absolute heathens if we watch Christmas Eve service on TV?" I'd been tracking Wyatt's exit, so I'm a beat too slow to react, and Mr. Kahale elaborates, "The church in town is doing a candlelight thing—and real candles in a two-hundred-year-old building isn't something I feel pairs well with—" He jerks his chin toward Holly and Jack.

"Oh." I set down my orange juice. While I have memories of church, I haven't been there in six years. I don't know if it was Mom's thing and Dad just went along, or if he ever believed, but he doesn't since she died. Stepping back *in* a church for the first time since her funeral feels like way too much, but I have a sudden craving for the songs and ceremony of it. Filtered through the TV might be perfect. "I—I think that sounds good."

"Excellent," says Mrs. Kahale around a crisp bite of bacon. She holds her hand in front of her mouth as she chews and swallows. "Let's do showers, then tree, and a little downtime before church and dinner."

"I didn't hear anything about skiing," says Holly.

"If there's time," says Mr. Kahale.

It's all the incentive Holly needs to grab Jack and drag him to get dressed. Mrs. Kahale calls after, "And I don't want to see your bag dumped everywhere. Clothes go in your drawers, not on your floor."

I turn to exit too, but Mrs. Kahale says, "Noelle, could you come up with us for a second?"

I offer a chipper "Sure" in my best babysitter voice, but my insides are roiling as I follow them up the stairs. The balcony sitting room is gorgeous—cozy couch, patterned arm chairs, family photos, and the view of the room below and out the big windows is mind-blowing, but mine is already blown: *What did I mess up? Am I getting fired?*

Mrs. Kahale pats the couch beside her, but I hover by the stairs. "We just wanted to check in with you," she says. "See if you need anything, and how things are going."

I've instinctively curled my hand around the railing like it's a barre, and I let it take more of my weight. Does their concern mean I *haven't* messed up—or that they're giving themselves an opening to express their disappointment?

"I know you didn't expect Wyatt to be here when you asked me to come—so if that changes things"—I have to swallow before I force out the rest of the words—"I can go home. Take a bus, plane, whatever."

There's a tread on the stairs, a loud throat-clearing, and just the top of Wyatt's head can be seen from where he paused halfway up. "Save yourself! A bus or plane would be way more enjoyable than the puke mobile."

"Then it's a good thing you're flying home instead of driving with us," says his dad. Wyatt's down too many stairs for me to see his face, but he makes a soft sound of pain that's buried beneath Mr. Kahale's chuckle. "I'll have you know I aired out the car last night and sprayed it down. It's not as good as a detail, but there'll be no suffocating until we take it for one. Now, get out of here, Wyatt."

Wyatt raises his hands so that both palms are visible. "I'm going. I know. No kids allowed in Santa's workshop before Christmas. You'll notice I stayed on the stairs. I haven't peeked or seen any of my presents."

"Joke's on you," his dad says. "We mailed your presents. They're sitting at your mom's house."

"Speaking of Mom—" Wyatt's voice sounds bitter. "I came out to tell you she wants you to call her."

"Okay." Mr. Kahale's voice and face are carefully neutral. "Will do. Thanks, pal."

They wait until we hear a door close in the hallway before pulling a box from behind the couch. Ski boots. "Thank goodness for growing feet," says Mrs. Kahale. "He can't have nothing beneath the tree. Though I hope he's okay with a stocking that's full of glove warmers, ski socks, trail mix, and beef jerky. Because that's pretty much all I had time to grab from the general store while Nick was taking Jack to the bathroom."

I smile politely, but doesn't this sort of prove my point? Christmas is a *family* thing. They've got church and kids who believe in Santa and I saw their whole set of matching stockings when we were decorating yesterday. Wyatt has a place in these traditions—a red quilted stocking!—I don't.

"Noelle," Mr. Kahale says. "We don't want you to leave, but if you've changed your mind and want to go, we'll absolutely buy you a ticket and get you home as soon as we can. Have you?"

"No. But, Wyatt—"

He shakes his head. "Wyatt coming is a great surprise, and the kids adore him. But we hired you for a reason."

They exchange a look and it's Mrs. Kahale who leans forward and elaborates. "I think there's more to Wyatt's arrival than he's telling us. We've tried to talk to him, but he's a vault."

"And his mom is . . ." Mr. Kahale throws up his hands. "She's no help. We don't get to see him that often and I don't want to turn the whole holiday into me bugging him about what's going on, and him shutting down."

Mrs. Kahale pats his leg, but her concerned look is for me. "I know you don't know him—but he's normally not so . . . prickly? I don't think it's personal, but he wasn't welcoming to you yesterday. I can talk to him if that's making you feel—"

My panic is a series of fouetté turns churning up my thoughts. "No. It's totally fine. I mean, you don't need to talk to him. He's—we're good. Really."

"You're sure?" Mr. Kahale asks.

I realize I'm nodding too enthusiastically and rein it in. "I'm positive. He was super-helpful on the shuttle yesterday and great about showing me the lodge."

They exchange another look and Mrs. Kahale scoots forward in her seat. "Noelle, your keen insights are part of what makes you the best babysitter. You can tell when Holly's hangry; if Jack's acting up because he's bored or looking for attention."

"Thank you." I think that's a compliment, but I'm rubbing my Achilles with my other foot, not sure where this is headed.

"If you find out anything about what's happening with Wyatt, would you let us know? Hopefully he tells us—but in case this is a scenario like when you figured out Jack wouldn't wash his hands in the kitchen sink because of the garbage disposal . . ." I seriously doubt Wyatt's scared of an appliance, but she shrugs and finishes, "It'll make me feel better to know we have a woman on the inside."

Lots of clients have said things like, "She's a little sensitive today, see if she'll tell you why . . ." Or, "When he practices piano, can you tell him how great he sounds? He's getting discouraged." Even my friends' parents occasionally enlist me in subterfuge: Autumn's parents asking for help pulling off a surprise party, Coco's parents wondering if she's stressed about a race, Mae's parents wanting birthday present ideas.

This feels different—he's not a kid, he's not my friend. He's *Wyatt*.

And I have a huge collection of stories about him from his siblings, and a string of observations from the past day—tickle fights and piggybacks and calmly wiping up the juice Holly spilled this morning, despite him warning her to hold the cup. He's sweet with his dad and stepmom.

But I don't *know* him: why he didn't—*doesn't?*—want me here; why mentions of Beacon make him uneasy. I don't know the patterns behind his mood shifts or what makes him tense up.

And I'm pretty sure it's none of my business.

But I say, "Of course!"

It's the people-pleaser knee-jerk response I'd give to any babysitting client. It comes from the same part of me that says "Oh, I don't mind" when parents come home an hour late. Or when I discover I'm watching a family's kids plus three friends on a playdate. Or when I show up and they say, "Our plans got canceled. Sorry we forgot to call."

"Great," says Mr. Kahale. "Thanks, Noelle. You're the best."

My stomach is sour, because I don't love what I just compromised to get that praise. It leaves me impatient for my turn in the shower, so hopefully I can wash off how wrong and weird this feels. Yet it doesn't stop me from asking "Do you need help wrapping?" because I *need* to be useful, needed, and wanted here.

"No, we're all set. Thanks," says Mrs. Kahale. "We're just getting organized for now. We'll do the wrapping tonight behind those doors with some wine and that new Christmas movie about going on safari."

That's the movie Mae picked for our marathon, and I have

a pang of homesickness for them all as I head down the stairs. If I were home, we'd be wearing ugly Christmas sweaters, exchanging gifts. I'd be joining Mae's family for the Feast of the Seven Fishes. Then Dad and I would tell the stories of each of Mom's snow globes before I unwrapped the one she'd labeled with this year—and I'd add it to the collection. It's the lack of snow globe that breaks me—how could I have left it behind at home?—and I ugly cry in the shower.

I pull it together before I turn the water off. By the time I dry my hair and leave my room, my eyes aren't red, but Mrs. Kahale still gives me a quick side hug and says, "Have I mentioned we're so glad you're here?" as Wyatt, Mr. Kahale, and the kids troop in the front door with rosy cheeks and snow-dusted clothing.

"Best snowball fight ever," Jack says through chattering teeth.

"We were going to wait for you," says Holly, "but—"

I tap my chest. "Indoor sports girl. You made the right call."

Mrs. Kahale points to a row of mugs. "Come and get your cocoa, then it's on to ornaments."

Jack takes off like a disrobing tornado at the word "cocoa." I pick up his trail of clothes while he barters for "One more marshmallow."

Something white catches my eye on the boot tray as I'm retrieving his hat. I thought it was a wet sock, but it's not.

"Oh, hey! That's mine!" Wyatt tugs the crumpled envelope from my hand. He shoves it in his back pocket and his eyes flash to the kitchen, where marshmallow haggling continues. "It must've fallen from my coat. Thanks for finding it."

"Sure." I shrug and head toward the fireplace to spread Jack's wet clothes on the stone hearth. And maybe if I weren't so *aware* of Wyatt—of the changes in his posture and expression, or if I hadn't had that spy conversation with his parents, or if it had been any other mail, I would've forgotten.

But the envelope has a bright red logo. One I doodled on class notes, traced on brochures, and stared at online before I clicked Apply.

The letter is from Beacon, and it's addressed to his dad.

I'm not sure whether I should reassure him my lips are sealed or go report to his parents.

In the end, I do neither. It takes a half hour of cocoa, Christmas tunes, and ornaments before the tension truly leaves Wyatt's smile. I give him space as he picks up Holly and Jack to hang glittery snowflakes high in the branches. And while I think it loudly and frequently, I voice none of my mental comparisons to partnered lifts. Nor do I stare at the butt pocket of his jeans where the envelope's peeking out.

Mrs. Kahale tells me the history of each ornament as she unwraps it. The kids' handprints, a Venetian glass ball from their honeymoon, a set made from koa wood bought last spring break. I'm missing my own, nonexistent tree, my own memories—so while Wyatt's smile grows more genuine as Jack hangs candy canes from his ears, mine gets wobbly.

I excuse myself to get a drink, but as I'm opening my seltzer, I see red lights outside. "A package was just delivered."

I could kick myself as soon as I'm done saying it, because Jack is zooming to the window. "A *truck?* Where?" And what if it's a present? What if it's shipped in its original packaging and shows the toy inside? Rookie babysitter fail. I should've distracted the kids, not snagged their attention.

But Mrs. Kahale says, "Oh, phew!" as she scoops it off the welcome mat and clutches it to her chest. She nods at Mr. Kahale, who's snuck upstairs to retrieve a handful of gift bags, then beckons everyone to the couches. "Decoration break!"

Holly and Jack make quick work of their tissue paper. They pull out sets of green-and-white pajamas. They're not quite identical: Holly's have snowflakes and Jack's, snowmen, but they're coordinated. Mr. Kahale reveals a pair that matches Jack's print, only it's button-up-style versus long johns.

"We always have new Christmas pj's." Mrs. Kahale extends the package to Wyatt but doesn't let go. "I hope these are okay. I had them overnighted, but they didn't have the matching pair anymore. I had to make do with what they had in stock. We're wearing green and white this year . . . and these were green and white."

Behind her back, outside of his view, she crosses her

fingers, probably picturing all the photogenic treeside moments that depend on his reaction.

Wyatt tears open the top of the package and looks inside. His eyes widen and he sucks in a breath, but he smiles and says, "They're great. Totally great. Green and white. No worries."

He does not, however, hold them up. "Put them on now?" Jack asks, clambering into his brother's lap.

"*After* dinner," says his dad.

But Jack's not listening. He's peeking into the package. "I want a pair with animals too."

I sit up straighter. Did I hear that correctly? Judging by the way Mr. Kahale is trying not to chuckle, I think I might've. I ask, "Um, animals?"

Jack talks over me, pointing. "What does it say?"

"Fa La La La llama," Wyatt deadpans as he ruffles his brother's hair. "Sorry, little man, you'll have to eat a lot more vegetables before you grow tall enough to steal my clothes."

I catch his eye and the amusement there makes it harder to bite back a laugh. "Can I— Can I see?"

He dutifully holds them up, exclaiming, "Oh, look! It's a one-piece," as they unfurl into his lap.

"It was really last-minute," Mrs. Kahale says. "Maybe you could trade with your dad?"

"No. They're great." He grins reassuringly at her as Jack drapes the legs around his neck like a llama-print scarf. "Who doesn't want a . . . a . . ."

"Onesie?" I supply, before it's entirely too much and giggles explode out of me like a shaken soda.

Holly joins in too and then Wyatt, which seems to give his dad permission as well.

"You don't have to wear them," Mrs. Kahale says, reaching to unwind the earmuffed and booted llama print from around Jack's neck.

Wyatt grips the top half tighter. "You will pry these out of my dead hands. This family's wearing green-and-white Christmas pj's. I'm wearing green-and-white Christmas pj's. Really, it's no probllama."

Mrs. Kahale finally laughs, confiding, "If we'd been wearing blue, you would've had 'Happy Llamakkuh' ones."

Wyatt nods seriously, then tickles the squirmy guy in his lap. "Maybe next time. Feliz Llamadad, everyone."

I'm laughing so hard, I'm crying. Holly collapses into my lap in a snorty heap, knocking over the gift bag Mrs. Kahale gave me, spilling out my own pair of snowflake pj's. I mouth "thank you" to her between gasps.

Forget Santa and presents—I'm counting down the seconds until we're done with the gourmet dinner Mrs. Kahale had delivered and it's time for Wyatt to model his jammies.

"Showtime," he tells me with a shimmy as we enter our adjoining rooms. "Prepare yourself."

But, really, I don't think it's possible to prepare myself for Wyatt in a onesie. I mean, I've seen pictures of him in ballet tights, so it's not just the aesthetic. The more attractive thing—okay, the equally attractive thing—is his wink, his laughter, him clutching the pajamas to his chest and giving his stepmom a hug, saying, "Thank you. Really. Next year I'll give you more notice so we can all have matching animal one-piecers. I'm thinking otters."

I'm giggling as I change into my new pj's, which Mrs. Kahale totally didn't have to do, but the flannel snowflake print feels as warm as a hug. It hasn't been as weird as it should be to be an interloper on their traditions—but this is where it might get awkward. I'm hoping for all sorts of onesie antics to distract me from my mismatched, faded ballerina stocking being hung among their quilted monogrammed fanciness, to help me shake off the adrift feeling I got when my call home went to voice mail.

I pull my hair into a ponytail before heading back out. Wyatt's in the kitchen with his dad, bent over the table in a way that puts his butt on display—and I think it's for comedic effect, until I get close enough to hear their conversation.

"Your mom thinks you're not skiing this week."

Wyatt folds up the trail map he'd been studying. "I never said that."

Mr. Kahale blows out a breath. "She seems to think you're upset about your role in *The Nutcracker* and wanted a week away to clear your head."

I can't see Wyatt's face, but his expression makes his dad snort. "Right. Well, she sent me a meal plan and a list of workouts she got from your teachers—as well as links to videos. She wants me to oversee them and reassure her you won't step foot on the slopes."

"Dad—"

Mr. Kahale holds up a hand. "I deleted the email as soon as I saw Loaded Lodge Fries weren't on the menu. You know your mom's just trying to support your goals in her own way, but you're old enough to make your own choices regarding your body—whether or not to ski, what to eat, how often you work out."

Wyatt's voice is thick when he says, "Thank you."

His dad nods, "But I don't like lying. So not today or tomorrow, but sooner than later, we need to get on the phone together and hash this out."

Wyatt nods and they hug. "Anything else you want to tell me, bud?" Mr. Kahale's question isn't as casual as he thinks.

But neither is Wyatt's when he replies, "Nope. Nothing I can think of."

His dad turns to exit the kitchen and I'm about to be exposed as the least stealthy spy to ever wear snowflakes, so I step forward. "I didn't mean to eavesdrop. I was just"—I point to the fridge—"I wanted some juice."

"It's okay." Wyatt opens the cabinet and gets out two glasses, so I pour for us both. He pauses with the cup halfway to his mouth and glances toward where his dad's joined Holly on the couch. "My mom and I . . . We don't have a lot in common. The only thing we ever talk about is dance. I was home for maybe five hours before it got to be too much and I was looking up plane tickets to Vermont."

"What was your problem with your role in *The Nutcracker*?" I'm totally prying, but he was fantastic and I'm ready to tell him if he needs to hear it.

"I didn't have one," he says. "She did. Marzipan was a blast, but she'd be disappointed by any role but the cavalier."

I blink at him. "Beacon's a professional company. There's no way the male lead is going to anyone but the principal. Not that you don't know this." Because why am I explaining how his school works to him?

"In her mind, I'm the greatest thing that ever put on a pair of tights." He sets down his glass and shoves his hands in the pocket across the front of his pj's. In another context I'd make a joke about it, but right now, I just listen. "It's great that she believes in me or whatever—but except for when I'm performing, or posing for yet another set of dance pictures, she doesn't know what to do with me."

I flip through my mental scrapbook of the professional dance photographs at the Kahales' house. It's a lot. I'd assumed his school took that many. But now I'm realizing they're not from Beacon—that they represent something totally different for him.

I still have zero desire to throw *my* body down a mountain, but I'm suddenly glad *he* gets to. "It's good you've got this week with your dad."

He sucks in a huge breath but looks away. "A week. Yeah. Maybe." He exhales slowly as his eyes cut to mine. "Maybe longer."

There's a moment whenever Miss Janet's teaching new choreography when it stops being separate combinations and the pieces come together to make a dance. This feels like that—only instead of enchaînments, I'm connecting observations and facts: his arrival; his reaction to my audition; the envelope; his words just now . . .

"Are you . . . Do you want to *leave* Beacon?"

He rocks back, then takes two steps forward. We're close as partners in a pas de deux; close enough that he doesn't have to put any force behind his whisper. "They don't know. I haven't told them."

"The letter?" I ask.

He looks over his shoulder. "Spring tuition bill. I took it at Thanksgiving."

I nod, my thoughts spinning outward like a series of piqué turns—what he's said about his mom, their lack of common ground, her obsession with his career. *Maybe longer.* "And you want to live with your dad?"

He doesn't whisper this time, just nods.

"When are you going to tell them?" Maybe someday I'll learn to whisper in a way that doesn't make my voice sound judgy—it would certainly improve things in the wings of all ballet recitals—but that breakthrough isn't happening today and Wyatt flinches from my tone.

"Soon. But not on Christmas. I just—I need this trip to go well."

"Why wouldn't it?" I flick my eyes toward the ongoing couch-cuddle that belongs in a glossy advertisement. His family's practically perfect. Doesn't he realize how thrilled they'd be?

He touches my arm. "Promise you won't say anything before I do."

"I promise." But the sooner he tells, the sooner it's off my spy-conscience.

"Guys! Guys! Noelle and Wyatt are *under the kissing ball!*" Jack can barely get the words out between giggles. Everyone's eyes swing toward us, and I'm so aware of how close we're standing. That his hand is on my arm, heating my skin through my sleeve.

Mr. Kahale half stands from where they've been working on a letter to Santa. "What are you doing over there?"

Mrs. Kahale puts down her pen.

"I—I was complimenting his jammies," I stammer.

"Kiss! Kiss!" chants Jack.

"Stop it!" Holly elbows her brother. "They're planning a big surprise and you're going to ruin it."

Right now four-year-olds can take a time-out, but thank goodness for eight-year-olds! I seize that excuse like a life-line. "She's right!" I pull away from Wyatt's hand and raise a finger to my lips. "Please don't ask me any more questions." *Like, seriously, don't.* "You don't want to spoil our big Christmas surprise!"

Wyatt's eyebrows raise all sorts of doubt, so I kick his foot. He pulls on a smile. "Yeah, Dad. Don't spoil our surprise."

"You planned a surprise for us?" Mrs. Kahale glides over to give us a group hug. "Man, we are so spoiled this week with you both here. I'm not sure we're ever letting you go home."

Wyatt's eyes widen over her shoulder, so I laugh doubly loud to cover for his silence. But now we need a surprise and the day has already been full of them. *He wants to quit Beacon?* I'm not sure I can handle any more.

As we leave the kitchen to join the others, I give the mistletoe a wide berth. I know it's wishful thinking—it has to be wishful thinking—but for the second after Jack began demanding we lock lips, I swear Wyatt's eyes dropped to my mouth.

And maybe it was just to catch the promise I was making about keeping his secret—one that directly defies my agreement to spy on him for his parents—but it felt like *more*. And maybe it could be . . .

After all, what's Christmas without a few miracles?

Babysitting Tip 12:

No matter how much you hate mud pies, water balloons, or snowballs, sometimes you've got put on a happy face and get messy.

Our stockings have been hung by the chimney with care, letters to Santa have been signed and sealed. Cookies were plated, *The Night Before Christmas* was read, teeth brushed.

I bow out to call my dad while the eldest three Kahales cajole, coax, and threaten the youngest two—*"Santa won't come if you're not sleeping."*

Which I'm pretty sure is what my dad was doing—he sounds like I caught him mid-nap, yawning through his greeting.

"What'd you do today?" I wind the drawstring of my pj pants around my finger as I ask, but it's my throat that feels tight when he answers.

"Worked, mostly. Things are coming together. What were you up to?"

I feel like we're living in parallel time lines. It's *Christmas Eve.* I was Christmas Eve'ing. I don't care that things are "coming together"; I care that *we* aren't together and that *he* doesn't seem bothered by that. While I may be dressed like I belong on Team Kahale, I'm not truly a member. But Team Partridge isn't playing—doesn't seem to remember it's a team.

Dad yawns through five minutes of small talk before saying, "Well, Merry Christmas, kiddo. We'll chat tomorrow. Love you."

I have to leave my room after saying "you too," because I don't want to be shut in with my thoughts. I want juice and noise, distraction. Maybe I should go rile Jack up, just to have someone who'll chatterbox at me. But Wyatt and Mrs. and Mr. Kahale are easing the door to the kids' bedroom shut—looking a bit haggard from the effort. "Everyone down?"

Mrs. Kahale rocks a hand back and forth. "They're not quite to visions of sugar plums, but close enough."

"How about you two?" Mr. Kahale rubs his hands together. "You all set? Need anything for your 'big surprise'?"

Oh, frankincense, I'd forgotten about that. "Actually . . ."

"Only for you to get out of here so we can get to work." Wyatt is leaning against a doorframe like a catalog model, all smiles and charm. I don't know if he'd be advertising for onesies or cabins, but whatever he's selling, I'll buy eight.

"We're going. We're going." His dad raises both hands—one of which has a roll of clear tape looped over his thumb—and takes an exaggerated step backward. "We can tell where we're not wanted."

Mrs. Kahale rolls her eyes at his cheeky smile—which is so much like the one on Wyatt's face right now. "Don't worry, we have plenty of elf business to keep us busy. We'll stay out of your hair." She follows her husband up the stairs, calling down in a whisper, "There's cookies and eggnog in the kitchen—help yourselves."

Wyatt makes a quiet gagging sound. "I don't get how people can like eggnog. It even *sounds* gross."

"Agreed." I listen for their bedroom door closing. "I'm so sorry. I panicked. Now we have to come up with a big surprise."

"No sweat. I've got it taken care of." He nods toward the front door. "Suit up."

"Suit . . . up?" I blink at him. "What are we doing?"

He grins that frost-melting, naughty-list smile. "*Do you want to build a snowman?*"

Wyatt wins all the bonus points in the world for not saying the line, but *singing* it. Every bit of the crush I've fought against comes roaring back times infinity. In our case maybe love isn't an "open door," but one with a security alarm I'd accidentally set off. There have to be worse meet-cutes, right?

And even though I'm an indoor sports girl, I feel my mouth curl upward. "Give me three minutes." I pull on Rachel's snow gear in such a rush that I'm sweaty by the time I meet him at the door. He grins at me as he disarms it.

I suck in a breath of the night air as we step outside, him bounding into the front yard, where the remnants of their battle have disappeared under a fresh layer of snow. Flakes are still drifting down. I catch one on my tongue before I join him.

"It's good packing snow." His eyes are bright in the glow of the moon and porch lights.

It's been years since I attempted this, but I still remember how—make a snowball, then drop it. A rolling stone might not gather moss, but a snowball rolled across the ground gathers mass. It also soaks through my gloves.

I voice the world's most obvious news flash: "Snow is cold."

Wyatt grins at me over his shoulder. His snowball is at least twice the size of mine. "And that snowsuit is *bright*."

I pretend to pout. "You don't like rainbows?"

"No, rainbows are great." He swipes the back of his glove across his forehead. How is he possibly hot? I mean, besides the fact that his gear looks snow-proof and he's doing a lot more work than me. "But do they mean something?"

"Are you asking if I'm gay?" I shake my head. "No, but my best friend's sister is, and I borrowed her snowsuit."

"Ah. Cool." He gives his ball a last push, then rocks it slightly so it's settled before starting a second one.

"Are you?" Because "rainbows are great" could be meant in a lot of different ways.

He stops and sighs. "Not *every* guy dancer is queer. Some of my friends are—but some, me included, aren't."

I break off a piece of snow and chuck it at him. "Um,

before you accuse me of stereotyping, you just asked me the same question."

He laughs as he dodges my throw. "Valid point. I'm just used to people assuming."

I may not have experience with that particular dance stereotype, but I know the others—assumptions that I've got an eating disorder, that I'm a cold, snobby person, that all I do is dance.

Okay, that last one might be true.

Except Wyatt doesn't want to anymore. Or, at least he doesn't want to *at Beacon*. I've got a million questions—but this can't be the right time for them. On Christmas Eve. In the snow. When we're getting along.

"You just going to stand there? Or are you going to help?" He grins as he lifts the smaller of his balls on top of the first, then gestures to mine.

"Geez, and I thought Holly was impatient." I give my lump another flip.

He laughs. "You're so tempted to throw the whole thing at me, aren't you?"

I feign shock. "And risk my spot on the nice list this close to Christmas? I would never."

Once the head's in place, we step back and admire our handiwork. Does Wyatt realize our shoulders are touching? I mean, at least our coat sleeves are. And the clouds of our exhales are mingling.

"What do you think Holly thinks our 'big surprise' is?"

I snort, because I've been pondering this too. "I'm not so sure she thinks we had one. I kinda think she masterminded this so we'd have to come up with one."

Wyatt raises his eyebrows until they hit the edge of his hat. And how did I never know that snow hats could be so attractive on guys? His is a plain gray beanie with a ribbed cuff, but Patagonia should be calling him with endorsement deals, because, *fa-la-oooh-la-la*, does it work on him. "That evil little genius. I'm giving her snowperson a huge nose."

"*Her* snowperson?"

"It's supposed to be a 'big' surprise." He's already packing a handful together to make a new ball but aims a grin at me over his shoulder. "We just need five—five *more*." The correction is quick but accompanied with an equally fast sideways glance. And it's not like he wrote, "*And thank you for Noelle*," in his letter to Santa or dropped to his knees in a snowbank and begged me to forgive him for being less than welcoming, but this guy who's wearing llama pj's beneath his snow pants is making all sorts of amends for his first impression.

"I'll let you do Jack while I make my dad. And let's be honest, I can probably make Ginger in that time too."

I stick out my tongue at him, but he's not wrong.

He abandons his snow mound and straightens to face me. "Then that just leaves us."

I like the sound of those words on his lips. The look of snowflakes melting on his mouth and eyelashes. The scent of this air—crisp, cold, and new. We're on the cusp of Christmas and maybe on the cusp of something else too.

"Us is good. I mean, um, I'm okay with that plan."

I watch the words drift into the night, chased upward by his soft laughter. "Same."

And even though we'd agreed to divide and conquer, that's not what happens. We stay side by side, collaborating, joking, playfully knocking into each other with shoulders and hips. I stick with making the heads. I'm not even sure which one represents which person anymore, but the sixth snowperson turns out extra tall and I can't heft my ball high enough.

"Help!" I squeak, trying not to drop it or knock the other parts over.

"I got you." Wyatt comes up behind me, bracing my hands with his as he lifts the head into place, and I'm suddenly the very confused filling in a contradiction sandwich. An ice-cold person in front of me, and behind—all heat and flames. The sparks so strong they could ignite from the rasp of his snowsuit against mine. I give a shiver that feels violent, and his arms tighten around me. "C'mon, let's get you warmed up."

The upstairs lights have clicked off by the time we creep back in. Santa's cookies have been eaten, a response letter penned and left on the coffee table. There are all sorts of boxes and gift bags under the tree—and we're both trying *not* to look at them as we strip our outer layers off and hang them up; then set the small pieces to dry on the fireplace hearth.

I'm attempting to shake the feeling back into my fingers, stomp it into my feet, but do it *quietly*. It must look ridiculous, because Wyatt is doubled over in silent laughter.

He whispers, "Here," and clasps my frozen hands in his warm ones.

"Oh." The touch is so charged that I glance sideways at the tree, half expecting it to be illuminated from the electricity coming off our skin. I'd blame my reaction on pre-frostbite, except Wyatt sucked in a breath too. He shifts closer, his thumbs tracing blazing paths along the backs of my hands while his fingers light up fireworks on my palms.

I sway forward until we're almost touching and tilt my chin up. If I went en pointe, even demi-pointe, I'd be the perfect height to—

"It's late." His voice sounds gruff as he drops my hands.

I blink as I catch up. "Right." I give a breathy, self-conscious laugh and take the first step away. Then another, and another. I can't look at him as I head toward my room.

He follows! . . . except, of course he does. His room is next to mine. "Um, do you want the bathroom first? Why don't you take it. My teeth are still too chattery to brush."

He nods, but we're both still standing in our doorways, both holding on to knobs but not turning them. "It's after midnight," he says.

"Don't worry, I won't turn into a pumpkin." If he knew *Frozen* references, I assume he'll recognize *Cinderella*. But he doesn't need excuses, if I misread the moment out there, if I made him feel awkward or overstepped, then I'll apologize, recalibrate, and move on. He doesn't have to keep telling me he's tired.

"No," he says softly. "It's *after midnight*. It's Christmas."

"Oh." Earlier I'd thought there was nothing better than having Wyatt smile at me, laugh with me—but his somber attention is pretty irresistible too. And somewhere on this planet, kids are waking up to notes from Santa, stockings, and presents; they're singing "Happy Birthday" in front of nativity sets and checking to see if the reindeer left footprints in the snow or sand or whatever is outside their house. Somewhere. But it all feels so far removed from this moment.

Wyatt turns his doorknob, breaking the spell. "Merry Christmas, Noelle."

The words are so tender that after his door clicks shut, I replay them in my head. And when I go to bed, I dream of something sweeter than sugarplums. I dream of a boy with snowflakes on his eyelashes looking at me like he trusts me to keep all his secrets and copilot all his big surprises.

Babysitting Tip 13:
Expect the unexpected. Always.

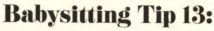

I'm an only child of only children. The closest I get to siblings is when I sleep over at Mae's house. And while the Primavera offspring may be wild, she's the youngest—so it's an entirely new, entirely disorienting experience when I'm woken up obscenely early by two small bodies jumping on my bed.

"Merry Christmas, Noelle!" *bounce, bounce.* "Merry Christmas, Noelle!"

These were the same words I'd heard before going to bed—but they were very different coming from the older brother of the hyper monsters shaking me awake.

"Get up, up, up!"

"I'm getting up," I croak in a sleep-rusty voice. Not that they actually stop bouncing to let me.

Mrs. Kahale is a laugh from my bedroom doorway. "All right, present fiends, you've done your wake-up duty. Now give these two a minute and they'll meet us out there."

These. *Two?*

My hair is in my face and my vision's still smudgy. I rub

my eyes as my assailants slide off the bed. They're whooping and running for the hallway. *"It's Christmassss!"*

My gaze tracks from their exit to the other door they've left wide open—I can see straight through the bathroom to where Wyatt's sitting on the edge of his bed, looking as dazed as I feel. "Morning," he says.

I rub my eyes again. "Good thing they're cute."

He gives a rough laugh. "C'mon, sleepyhead. Last one to the kitchen has to drink eggnog."

Wyatt's already sitting up; I'm still tangled in sheets. I practically fall out of bed in my attempt to beat him to the bathroom. I do not succeed and his chuckles echo through the door.

Well, the joke's on him. I peed when I woke up at three a.m., so I don't need to go.

I'm sitting smugly with my juice when he comes out. I push the cup of eggnog I poured for him across the counter and lift my eyebrows along with my glass. "Cheers?"

He laughs as he clinks his drink against mine.

"Are you two ready *yet?*" Holly whines. "We've been waiting *forever.* Mom said I couldn't wake you up before six."

"Have you looked outside?" asks Wyatt as he takes a slurp from his cup and tries not to grimace. "I hear there might be a big surprise out there."

Everyone else is dashing to the door and he's screwing up his face to psych up for another sip. I reach across the table and gently push his hand down. "You don't have to drink that."

"A bet's a bet," he says.

"I've seen enough Kahale boy-vomit to last a lifetime. You *really* don't have to."

"Is this *us?*" Holly calls from the doorway.

"I think so," chuckles her dad. "Pretty cool, huh?"

"That one's me! See it? Momma, that's me!" Jack is jumping as he points to the smallest snowman. It's wearing his ski hat.

"I love these. You two"—Mrs. Kahale presses a hand to her heart—"you're the best."

"Noelle's the one dancing," Holly says. "See? Her arms are like this—" She demonstrates a much better third position than we'd managed with branches. "And *I* have skis. And Mom's got—"

Her parents are uh-huhing and Jack's still bouncing.

"What are you doing, Wyatt? You're just sort of standing by Noelle." Holly rattles on, not waiting for an answer, but it takes me a minute to realize she's still talking about the snow people. Because that's an accurate description of what human-Wyatt is doing too. Standing and smiling. And taking a sip of my juice when I offer him my glass—which is weird, right? It's totally weird. I shouldn't have held it out—but then again, he didn't have to accept it. And while I don't know what *we're* doing, more than just snow people took shape last night. I'm not quite sure if Wyatt's and my final form will be friendship or fireworks—but we're on our way to something.

"Okay, stockings, *now!*" Jack's done admiring our snow handiwork. He storms into the kitchen and drags me from my chair. "They're over here."

Christmas with the Kahales feels a bit like being caught inside a holiday movie. I wasn't expecting presents. Fine, that's a lie. I assumed the Kahales would buy me one. I planned ahead and bought them some too.

But it's not one. It's a mound. A very Christmas-movie mound where I get my own designated wrapping paper and we're all in coordinated pajamas. There are carols playing, the fireplace is going, and through the window past the tree, we can watch the snow fall. The cocoa seems endless and Mrs. Kahale asks, "Do you want whipped cream on that?" No one's being yelled at for eating cookies for breakfast.

My stocking isn't loaded with LEGOs and chocolate snowmen like the littles or Wyatt's collection of ski store filler. It's got all the dollar-store items I remember from past years—a toothbrush, my favorite gel pens, a bag of dried apricots, a bath bomb in the toe. I blink at Mrs. Kahale—and ask, "How?" meaning, *How did you get it so perfect?*

She checks Jack and Holly aren't looking before mouthing "Your dad."

I hug it a little closer, glad there's some part of him here today. Glad he thought of me and pulled this together before I left. I'm missing him. I'm missing Mom too as Mrs.

Kahale twists Holly's hair into a bun and pretends to take a bite of the chocolate Jack shoves in her face before he plops in her lap.

Grief isn't a thing that leaves. Not ever. Not fully. But it gets sneakier—it creeps up on you and clamps a hand over your mouth so you suddenly can't breathe.

It steals my smile and whispers in my ear, "You will never have that again." Because just like grief, death is forever too.

Thank God for Holly and Jack, who won't let me go too far down that road. They're busy yelling at me. Apparently I "open presents too slow"—and the Kahales do that thing where they all take turns and watch whoever is peeling off wrapping paper. I guess Dad and I technically do this too, but it feels less formal when there's only two people and a few presents.

The day isn't perfect—Holly gets teary because Santa brought the book she'd just finished reading instead of the next one in the series; Mr. Kahale hits the wrong button and records his face instead of his wife's when she opens the diamond studs he bought her. There are LEGOs to step on, *batteries not included*, and Playmobil pieces to hunt down after a bag is opened too enthusiastically and minuscule forks and ice cream scoops explode into the air.

And for Wyatt, there's a much smaller mound—but also a series of envelopes where his parents spoil the surprises waiting at his mom's house. Each time he opens one, he's forced to fake excitement for whatever fancy, dance-related present is written on the slip of paper inside. Each time he opens one, I feel like I'm betraying them all.

If I'd kept my word to his parents and told them what I'd learned about him and Beacon, I could've saved him from these moments. Instead I've kept my promise to him and stayed quiet, so the best I can offer is subtle sympathy.

"This sounds great. Thanks, Dad and Ginger." He holds up the index card he'd just read aloud. I've got no clue if he's just leaving Beacon, or quitting dance entirely, and if so what he's going to do with all the high-end tights and shoes wrapped and waiting at his mom's home.

"Noelle's turn. Go!" Jack practically throws my next present. He's on a mission to get back to himself as quickly as possible.

I can tell it's a pointe shoebox by the size, but what I wasn't expecting was for there to be messages scrawled on the insoles. Good Luck! and You can do it! and We believe in you. Love, Ginger, Nick, Holly, and JAKC.

I look up with wet eyes.

"They're for your audition," says Mrs. Kahale. "We're so proud of you. Wyatt, promise you'll go cheer Noelle on."

I'm so focused on saying "Thank you" without crying that I miss his hesitation. It's not until Mrs. Kahale pauses and his dad says his name again that I register he hasn't answered.

I know why. But they don't. And now the day *really* isn't perfect because they look so disappointed in him and he's been trying so hard to impress them—popping up to fetch refills and collect wrapping paper, faking enthusiasm for each salt-in-the-wound gift.

"Oh, phew," I say. "Wyatt gets it. I wouldn't want him there—it's a dance thing. Nerves and bad luck and all that. But maybe you could call me ahead of time and say—*the French word*—*"* Yeah, I'm not swearing in front of a four-year-old on Christmas, even in a different language, and even if it means "good luck" in this context.

"Yeah," he says, "I can do that."

"Okay." His dad looks mollified and Mrs. Kahale adds, "We'll have you sign the shoes later."

Wyatt nods, but no one but me is still looking—everyone else is watching "My turn! My turn" Jack as he tears open the paper on a remote control steamroller.

Wyatt mouths "Thanks" and I barely stop myself from responding "Tell them!"

It's only a few minutes later that Mr. Kahale approaches me while I'm in the kitchen snagging a cookie—one that goes from scrumptious to sand in my mouth when he asks, "Did Wyatt say anything to you? He seems more settled today, right? Happier?"

I hold out the cookie tin with a stiff shrug. "Who could be unhappy on Christmas?"

He says, "Right. You're right. It was probably jet lag, or whatever it's called when travel makes you cranky without changing time zones. Or *Nutcracker* fatigue, or his mom." He absently eats two cookies. "You know, if you go to Beacon, maybe you two can carpool and that'll be an excuse to get my boy home more often for weekends or breaks."

"Um, maybe?" I gulp, then sigh in relief as Jack shouts it's my turn again.

After the presents have been opened and the tide of wrapping paper's been collected, there's a lull before dinner. Holly's tucked in a book, and Mrs. Kahale and Jack are working on LEGOs. Mr. Kahale and Wyatt are cooking. I slip away to call Dad. I'd already talked to him briefly before lunch while the Kahale kids called Mr. Kahale's mom, their "tūtū," in Oʻahu. Dad had had the Disney Christmas Day Parade playing in the background, so even though he was probably working, at least there was some nod to celebration. I'd teared up as I thanked him for the stocking and he'd feigned innocence. "What are you talking about? Santa fills stockings. Noelle Partridge, are you telling me you're a nonbeliever?"

This time my call goes to voice mail. I leave a message and change into dance clothes, but I'm too full of cookies and contentment to do more than a few lazy pliés before I sink onto the bed and text Mae.

Just a typical Primavera Christmas, she writes back. Remy ate some wrapping paper, Rachel announced she's applying to colleges in Europe, and Mom superglued a cut on Booker's hand.

I send a row of **?**'s

She responds, **Wrapping paper tube. Glass ornament. Baseball. He's fine.**

I chuckle. **How grounded are he and Hudson?**

Very. How's it there? Do you think Mr. Kahale would let me interview him about O'ahu for my website?

I give my Achilles a soft rub. **Fine, and probably.** I know my answers aren't satisfying, but Jack's calling me for dinner. **Got to go. Vidchat later?**

Yup. I'll tell A & C.

The meal is noisy, delicious, and ends in pie. I'm trying not to think of Dad eating alone. Would he at least do catered takeout, or was he on his deadline diet of frozen dinners? And if I leave him for Beacon, will he eat like that full-time?

The thought sticks to a bite of pie and I have a hard time swallowing it down.

Wyatt offers to do the dishes while his parents get his siblings to bed. Jack's already half drowsing at the table.

"I'll help," I say as they carry Jack and cajole Holly down the hall.

Mr. Kahale says, "Thanks," but also levels Wyatt with a stern look. "And don't forget to call your mom."

He nods grimly, but after they're out of earshot, he turns to me. "I've got a great idea for later. It's outside, but I promise it's indoor-people approved."

"Oh?" I raise my eyebrows and start stacking plates. "I'm intrigued. Tell me more."

"I don't wanna!" Both our heads swing toward the sound of Jack's voice echoing down the hallway.

Wyatt grins. "Sounds like he got his second wind."

Jack's sentiments match mine, because Dad's name just popped up on my cell phone, and I don't want to answer, at least not until I finish this conversation. But who knows when he'll be free again. "Hey, Dad. Merry Christmas."

"Hey, kiddo. I've just had a Christmas miracle, a completely bug-free test of . . ."

I point to my room and Wyatt nods. "I'll come find you after I call my mom."

The call isn't great. Dad only wants to talk about his work. I'm distracted, because—*"Mom! Geez, just—"*

The bathroom doors are closed—at least my side is, but I can still hear snatches of Wyatt's conversation when he raises his voice—which seems to be happening a lot. I wince as he repeats, "No, *no*. That's not what I said."

"Should I let you go?" Dad asks. And I realize I've been so focused on the sudden silence beyond the bathroom that I'd missed it in our conversation.

"Right. Um, probably?" I say. "The girls are supposed to vidchat soon."

"Ah. Tell them I say hi, and thank Autumn again. She's been beyond helpful."

He doesn't hear my "What?"—it's buried beneath his "Love you, kiddo. Talk soon."

But I carry all my questions to the next conversation,

as I watch my friends' faces fill up my phone screen with smiles, waiting for everyone to list off all their presents and the funny things their parents/siblings/pets had done all day. The workout I didn't do earlier will be way less enjoyable with a full stomach, but I've got curiosity to burn and the girls are so used to it that they don't even blink when I prop my phone on the dresser and begin barre exercises holding on to the bed's footboard.

"You call that a développé?" teases Coco in a faux-stern voice that must mimic her coach's. "Get that knee straight, and tell us all the news! How are you surviving the snow and ice boy's attitude?"

"He's fine—not icy, but—" I swallow and drop my leg out of its sloppy arabesque. "Autumn, are you helping my dad with something?"

The call goes quieter than should be possible for a four-way conversation. If they were in the same room, they'd be exchanging glances. In their own separate spaces, they all just sort of look away. "He—he told you about that?"

"He said to thank you." I sink into a grand plié so my face disappears off screen and take that time to collect myself before rising slowly. "How do you think it makes me feel to find out you're keeping secrets with my dad?" As I port de bras back, I catch a glimpse of the door adjoining my room to Wyatt's over my shoulder. Fine, maybe asking that question is a little absurd given my own spy-entanglements, but still. "Why wouldn't you tell me?"

"I'm sorry." Autumn is cleaning her glasses. They're not dirty, it's what she does when she's upset. "I didn't think of it that way. He needed my help testing an app—"

"Why couldn't *I* help him?" Because if he needed a teen girl to test an app, he'd had one sleeping on the other side of his office wall. Maybe if he'd bothered to include me, I'd *still* be sleeping on the other side of that wall instead of in this cabin.

"I'm not sure how much to say—it's supposed to be a surprise."

"A surprise?" My cheeks and heels lift. "My dad has a surprise for *me?* But he's barely even talked to me for months. It's been like living with a ghost."

Coco sucks in a breath, but Mae nods thoughtfully. "I knew something was up when he skipped caroling and lights. Now this trip makes so much more sense. What's going on? You okay?"

I shrug.

"I didn't know all that." Autumn chews her lip. "But he's been working super hard on this app—and if it works and does as well as it could . . . I really think you'll like the surprise he's planning. Though, if you want me to tell you, I will."

I shake my head. "I've waited this long, might as well let him do the big reveal." I bounce in relevé and consider possibilities: tickets to a real ballet, a pair of custom pointe shoes, him finally installing the barre in my bedroom! "Is it soon?"

She laughs. "Sorta. I think so. At least the reveal is."

"Great," says Coco with a pout. "Now I'm dying of impatience too. I hope it's a puppy."

"Or a trip," adds Mae. "Maybe he's taking you to a show at the Met!"

Autumn mimes zipping her lips.

I peel off my sweatshirt and spin so my other hand's on the footboard and begin the sequence on my other leg. "So, fill me in. How was Seven Fishes? Did Autumn gloat about her gingerbread win? How's Booker's hand?"

"Fishy, yes, and fine," says Mae, but Coco's eyes are wide beneath her creased forehead.

"Booker? What happened? Is he—"

"I'm knocking," Wyatt calls from the bathroom. "Do you hear me knocking?"

I laugh and say, "Come in," then mute the call, which is probably the smartest thing I've done all week, because I can only imagine what the trio on my screen said when they caught a glimpse of Wyatt.

I definitely don't want to know what my jaw-dropped expression looked like on camera. Because the llama onesie—*gone*. And he didn't replace it. I mean, he's not *naked*, but that actually takes me a moment, because my eyes get snagged on the exposed skin of his shoulders and chest and don't immediately drift lower and realize—*Oh*, he's got swim trunks on!

He tosses me a towel, loops a second one around his

shoulders. The motion making it so very apparent how seriously he trains. "Hot tub time, indoor sports girl."

It's taking all my self-control not to drool, or sigh, or blurt out, *I'm not objectifying you, I'm just swooning.* Instead I point to the screen in front of me, where my best friends are bug-eyed, their lips moving in questions I can't hear, but that will be loud and demanding when I unmute them.

"Ah." He nods. "Come out when you're done? I've got it heated up."

Instead of exiting my bedroom the way he entered, or via the door to the hallway, he passes around me, giving the camera a flirty wave and dazzling grin, and bumps my sweaty shoulder with his bare one—then opens the door to the porch. Through it I can hear the burble of water. I lean to catch another glimpse of his bare back before the door shuts.

It takes me a few tries to hit Unmute. "Uh, sorry about that."

"I'm going to need a play-by-play of what just happened," says Coco.

"I thought you hated him—or he hated you—or . . ." Autumn is holding both hands up. Her pointer fingers are raised—I'm pretty sure they represent me and Wyatt and that her sequence of bending and waggling was supposed to be a pantomime of her words, but she gives up—dropping her hands and raising her shoulders in a shrug.

Mae's mouth is still hanging open. She's shaking her head. "I thought— At first, I thought he was *naked*!"

"Me too." I give up on dancing and surrender to the giggles, leaning back on the footboard for support.

"You've been holding out on us," says Coco.

And so I tell them: shuttlebuses, snowmen, llama pj's—everything but his secrets. Those aren't mine to share.

"Wow," says Coco, and they all nod. "So is this a 'friends' hot tub thing, or him totally regretting not kissing you last night?"

"I have no idea." But I do have a preference, you know, in case this is something we get to vote on.

Autumn scrunches up her nose. "I just have one question."

I brace myself. "Okay?"

"Why are you still in here talking to us instead of in the hot tub with him finding out?"

"Um, that's a good question," I say, slipping off my fuzzy socks.

"Go!" orders Mae. "And text us later!"

I laugh as I pick up the towel, but I pause before I chase answers out the door. Wyatt's smile, the flirt, the swagger—they'd all been too bright. Dialed up from the casual jokiness in the kitchen, but in a way that didn't feel authentic. What changed since dishes? I glance at the bathroom door as I remember the explanation that seeped through it: his not-so-holly-jolly phone call. *Oh, Wyatt.* My chest aches and I know he's pretending and hiding things from his parents, but I hope he knows he doesn't have to do that with me too.

Wyatt has his head tipped against the side of the hot tub, his eyes closed. He turns as I gasp when my bare feet hit snowy deck. "You forgot something."

"My shoes?" I flinch with every step—ballet calluses are no match for fresh powder and the ice underneath it.

"A swim suit." He flicks the surface of the water toward me. "Hot tub."

"I didn't pack one." I sit on the side and tug my cropped leggings above my knees, sighing happily as I plunge my frozen feet in the water. "That feels amazing."

"I know," he says. "Hot tubs are on my top ten list of favorite things."

I came out here to get answers; this feels like a place to start. "What else is on there?"

"Um, well—" Did he just splash himself in the face? Because it sounds like he's choking. "I, uh—"

"Oh my garland." I sputter out a laugh as I piece together his sudden panic. "I'm *not* expecting you to include *me* on your list."

I haven't seen Wyatt sheepish before—and while it's not on my top ten list, it might be in the top hundred. He ducks his head and says, "Shut up." Splashing water at my shins when I continue laughing. "Keep it up and you'll land a spot on another list."

"Cool people you're jealous of?" I suggest, kicking water back at him . . . Which is risky. He's already wet, I'm hoping to stay dry.

He tickles my foot under the water. "Something like that."

"I've known you, like, three days. I'm willing to wait at least a week before demanding the top spot."

He chuckles. "With an attitude like that you'll fit right in at Beacon." The name of his school sobers him. He stops tickling, his thumb absently brushing where foot meets calf in the world's softest Achilles massage.

I want to arch my back like Coco's cat, Cabana, and purr. But I don't—and for that, Santa should bump me up a spot or two on the nice list. "You really don't want to go back to Beacon?"

He shakes his head. "It's not the right place for me anymore." I'm debating if I should pry, when he asks, "Why do you want to go there?"

"Because it's the best," I say. "I'll learn a lot and hopefully get a place with a good company. And—" All of that is true, but it's not the full truth. There are closer schools. Nonresidential places I could train and level up. "—also, because my home isn't . . . My dad—he's so busy. Like, all the time. All I ever do is interrupt and bother him. It'll just be easier if I'm not there."

Easier for *him*, not me. Autumn's words about Dad's surprise bubble up—but I'm scared to pin hope to them.

"I get it." He nods twice, then shakes his head, his hand dropping from my foot. "Actually, I don't. My mom's a brilliant oral surgeon. She's the most ambitious, goal-driven person I know. Which is great, except my goals become her goals too. So her version of 'love' means micromanaging everything I do—haircuts, clothes, workouts. Even how I stand and the turnout in my walk gets criticized in the name of 'helping.'"

I'm scared to move or breathe in case he stops talking. But he stares down at the water, his voice barely audible over the jets. "And every time I suggest taking a break from dance, she laughs it off and tells me to 'focus' and 'keep my eye on the prize.' I've been doing this for half my life—I started as a day student at Beacon when I was in first grade. Moved into the dorms in sixth grade . . . when do I get a vacation from dance?"

He scrubs a wet hand through his hair, making it stand up in a riot of whirls and spikes. "Even over winter break, she arranged for me to take classes with three different teachers without even asking. And when I protested"—he exhales—"apparently 'I'm not taking my future seriously. I have *one* chance to make something of myself and only a few years until I'll be auditioning for companies.'"

Wyatt's eyes drift from the horizon, where everything beyond the porch's light disappears into shadow. They sear into mine and I slip a little on the side of the tub before clutching the brim with both hands. "I don't want to have *one* chance—and I don't want this to be my future."

I'm simultaneously jealous and sympathetic. I dream of having a parent that interested and invested—but I can also see why it's his nightmare. "I'm sorry."

He slides over a seat and turns sideways so we're sitting parallel, pulling his legs up. His bare knee against my foot, his hand on the edge beside mine. "No. Me too. I shouldn't be tearing into Beacon. It's a great school if that's what you want to do. I just . . . don't anymore."

I want to ask a million questions; about the classes, about the dorms, about the friends he's made and what it's like to live there. But not now, not while I can see the tension he's carrying on his bare shoulders. "Why haven't you told your dad?"

Because *I* can't—I'm caught between promises—and it's killing me not to. I'm just not sure what the problem is: They love him. They know something's up. They've asked questions and given him opportunities. Why isn't he taking them?

"It's not exactly a small favor," he says. "And I feel guilty. After the divorce, Mom changed practices and moved to Alexandria to be near Beacon."

"Did they have a big custody battle?" It's pure nosiness, but the Kahales all talk about wishing they saw him more.

"Not a fight—at least not in front of me—but it wasn't friendly." The vapor of his sigh disappears quickly, but the weight of his stress lingers in the air. "Dad wanted me—but Mom offered Beacon. So when they asked, I picked Mom—but it was really the school, you know? I had my chance—and I rejected him.

"That's why I'm here this week. Before I ask, I need Dad and Ginger to want me. I need to show them I can fit in and be helpful, prove that going through a custody hassle is worth it when they already have the whole perfect family package."

My broken heart is on my face, but he doesn't see it. His eyes chase the hot tub steam toward the stars. His bare arm is so close to my leg that they keep drifting toward each other on the currents of the water, skin brushing, then us both retreating, until we stop bothering and just touch.

He settles deeper in the water, shuffling closer—deliberate contact when he leans back, his shoulder against my knee, his head grazing my hand. And I'm glad he's shut his eyes, because I'm sure the surprise on my face is comedic. There's room to seat at least six. Whatever doubts I had from the fireplace kiss-miss last night, he's in full-snuggle now.

"They'd want you." My voice sounds thick, like honey.

"Do they, though? Full-time? I don't have a bedroom in their house. I have a guest room *here*, but not in Juncture. Dad keeps offering to squeeze a bed in his home office, but Jack always insists I sleep over on the Murphy bed in his room. If I live there, am I going to share a room with a four-year-old? Is Dad giving up his office? I don't know."

"I do. They do." What I mean is, "I *do* know" and "they *do* want you," and maybe that's not clear, but maybe other interpretations are valid too.

Wyatt opens his eyes and I realize how far forward I've leaned.

I can see his thoughts in the inches between our mouths. I can choreograph all the ways this *could* play out. Him sitting up, pressing his lips to mine. An upside-down kiss wouldn't be more disorienting than this feeling. Or he slides that hand up my calf to my hip—tugs me into the hot tub, and as I'm gasping, reacting to the shock and clinging, wet clothes, he pulls me close and makes his move. Or he pivots, executes a one-eighty—pretty much an underwater chaîné turn with his knees on the seat to bring us face-to-face.

We're perched on the cusp of all these moments—all this possibility—when there's a screech and a thump. The screech *almost* sounds like a kid crying, but it's slightly too feral. The thump is Wyatt's head clunking against the side of the hot tub when I jerk my arm away and shoot upright. "What was that?"

"*That* was almost a concussion," he says, rubbing the back of his neck with a grin. "Ouch."

"No, I mean, what made that I'm-coming-to-eat-you noise?" My eyes scan the forest, the shadows no longer atmospheric and romantic.

"Probably a fox," he says. "And not only does it *not* have any interest in eating you, it's probably not anywhere close. Sound carries up here. Now can we talk about my brutal head injury?"

I'm not sure I believe him—about the fox; his head's just fine—but at least I'm closer to the door, so he's more likely to become a predator's Christmas dinner if he was wrong. "Poor baby," I tease. "Do you want a Band-Aid, a wet paper towel, or—" But the third option I offer babysitting kiddos sticks in my throat. *A kiss to make it better.*

We almost—and now . . . I pull my hands into my lap, ease away.

Because if we both get what we want—him Juncture, me Beacon—then we're satellites passing in orbit. Part of me wishes he'd never opened up, never gotten vulnerable and told me about his mom, his dad—his place between them— because it's exactly the sort of thing the Kahales asked me to report, and the promise I made him is a roadblock. I can see the perfect bridge beyond it—a few words from me and I could *fix* this. And in no universe is it my place to get involved.

No matter how much I want to.

Tell them! Tell them! The words feel dangerously close to erupting, but I've said them already. I pull my feet up onto the edge. "I should get some sleep or there's no way I'm keeping up with Jack tomorrow."

He lifts an eyebrow as he sits up. "We're totally pretending you're not running away, right?" I pause with one foot almost to the deck. I can already feel the cold radiating off it. Leaving barefoot might be as painful as staying to continue this conversation. "From the things that go bump in the night," Wyatt finishes.

"Oh." My laugh is forced, his words a little too accurate, even if it's not how he means them. I flick one last splash of water before hopping down. "Enjoy being fox food."

My attempt at making a cool exit comes to a screeching halt when I can't get the door open. The handle turns, but nothing happens when I yank. And I'm yanking as hard as I can while also hopping foot to foot, trying to keep my wet feet from making more than a second's contact with the snowy deck.

I get my wish when suddenly *neither* of my feet are touching it—because during a particularly vigorous tug, I'd managed to land one-footed on an icy patch. The ten lords a leaping got nothing on me, and for one long moment my feet—and the rest of me—are airborne. Then gravity shows up like a control freak.

"You okay?" While I'm sprawled in the snow, Wyatt practically does a tour jeté over the side of the hot tub. It's seriously cinematic, the rising steam, and the way he braces his arms against the side, one straight leg, then the other, emerging gracefully from an arc of water. He grabs our towels, wrapping one around his waist, extending a hand down to help me up. "Now we've got matching head injuries. But seriously, are you okay?"

I nod. Yes, the wind was knocked out of me by the fall, but that's not why I'm breathless as he helps me to my feet.

"Sometimes the doors up here freeze shut." But maybe even doorjamb ice melts at the sight of his bare chest, because he gets it open in seconds.

"Thanks." But he's still standing in the doorway and I pause there too.

Wyatt lifts a hand slowly—giving me plenty of time to

track it or object, even before he says, "May I?" and I nod, though I'm not sure what I'm giving permission for.

He brushes a clump of slush from my cheek, pushes back the hair that was clinging there. And then he leans in, closer, even closer, to trace his mouth across the same path.

I've been kissed twice before. Once at the eighth-grade formal and once at a pool party in Mae's backyard. Those were real kisses—on-the-mouth kisses—and neither of them had a fraction of the potency or poetry of Wyatt brushing his lips across my cheek, ending by my ear, where he murmurs, "Merry Christmas, Noelle," before stepping back, and back. Returning to the hot tub as I retreat to my room and shut the door.

There are texts on my phone—Good night, kiddo from Dad. Group ones from my friends: Update? We're dying here! And Miss Janet: Happy holidays! Did you get my voice mail? Let's chat soon.

I don't respond to any. I still don't listen to that voice mail. Instead I cling to this precious moment, cup my hand around a cheek that's still tingling from Wyatt's kiss.

Merry Christmas, Noelle. He'd been the first to say it to me at midnight; he'd be the last as well. And in all the moments in between, at least part of my attention has been diverted his way. It's not the Christmas I would've planned for myself—the Christmas I *had* planned for myself way back before Thanksgiving—but maybe life is what happens in the space between plans. Maybe this year, this is where I'm sup-posed to be.

Babysitting Tip 14:
Always, always save time for a bathroom break.
Make them try—never accept "I don't have to go."

Wyatt's pacing—I hear him passing back and forth in front of the bathroom door while I'm brushing my teeth. Since there are plenty of other bathrooms he can use, I'm pretty sure it's not because he has to pee. I knock on the door to his room.

"Come in."

His lights are dim. He's still in pajamas, passing by a bed in complete disarray. Either his night was restless, or his siblings bounced him awake again.

"Are you telling them today?"

Wyatt stops walking. He's got the rigid look of a dancer who's about to attempt a move that terrifies them. If we were in a studio, I'd intervene, because it's moments like these where dancers get hurt. When they demand their bodies try something their mind has psyched them out of. It doesn't end well.

He clears his throat. Twice. "Yeah. If I get an opening, yeah. Yesterday went well, right?" He gives a humorless laugh. "I feel like I'm auditioning to be part of my family. It's so messed up."

It really is, and it makes me think of Coco's last swim coach—a woman who snapped at her before races, saying, "Relax. Do you know how many people would kill to have your natural talent? You have nothing to worry about. Just go out there and win."

Like she hadn't seen Coco hone that "natural talent" through grueling daily practice. As much as I *want* to tell Wyatt he has "nothing to worry about"—it's because of Coach SoGladShesFired that I realize how dismissive and hurtful those words are. He's worried because this matters to him— because the outcome has life-changing implications. It would be the cruelest betrayal of his trust to imply anything different.

I offer a small smile. "I'm rooting for you."

He's giving off the type of energy I used to carry when I checked a cast list—back when Spirit's cast lists still held surprises. "I need another minute. See you at breakfast?"

I nod and slip out to the bustle of morning greetings from three people in ski pants and thermal tops—and one small boy stubbornly refusing to get out of his pajamas.

"Jack, we had a deal," says Mrs. Kahale.

Yeah, good luck with that.

He doesn't bother looking up from his toy truck. "No, we didn't."

"We did! I let you skip lessons the other day, and you promised not to whine for the rest of the week."

"Nope." Jack continues to push his bulldozer across the floor, through their neat rows of socks and gloves and hand warmers. I try not to laugh.

"Good morning." Everyone turns toward Wyatt. He's also got that half-ready ski outfit going—a waffle-knit charcoal gray Henley and a pair of black ski pants. Only on him it's a *look*.

Mr. Kahale thunks down his mug. "Wyatt!"

My spoon slips from my fingers. I haven't heard that tone of voice from him before. I'd be okay never hearing it again.

Wyatt's shoulders stiffen. "Hey, Dad. What's up?"

"What's the first rule of using the hot tub?"

"Oh, sh—" Wyatt glances at his sister and flinches. "*Sugar*. I forgot to turn it down."

"You forgot to turn it down," his dad agrees. "So it was heating the water above a hundred degrees all night. Which will do especially impressive things to the electric bill, since you also didn't fully *close the lid*."

Wyatt is still standing one foot in the hall, one foot in the kitchen. "I'm sorry, Dad. I won't do it again."

"There's a four-year-old in this house! Jack could easily have—" Mr. Kahale looks at Holly, who's all wide-eyed and eavesdropping. "You *have* to lock the lid. Every time."

While voices were raised, Mrs. Kahale managed to shoo Jack to his bedroom. The silence that follows feels extra loud without his *vrooms* or shrugging defiance.

The speech Wyatt was rehearsing in his bedroom is

definitely on pause, but I wish he'd come out to the kitchen sooner. I wish he'd seen his little brother pull a brat and bicker with his mom. I wish he wasn't in a headspace where these words are making him forget that *all* families fight. I wish I could *do* something.

"It's my fault," I blurt, but I haven't figured out what comes next. "Um, I—I got out first and Wyatt was going to stay in a while. But the door between the porch and my bedroom froze. I made him open it for me, and . . . and then we went to bed. If I hadn't distracted him, I'm sure he would've turned it down and locked the lid."

That's mostly truth.

"No! I'm not wearing pants! No pants!" At any other time, Holly would be in giggle fits over the words Jack's shouting from their bedroom, but we all ignore them.

"I appreciate what you're trying to do, Noelle, but the house rule is that whoever opens up the hot tub is responsible for making sure it gets closed down." Mr. Kahale stands, frowning as he approaches his son. "And Wyatt, it was an accident, I get that. We all make mistakes, but you've got to remember there's little kids here. And you can talk to me—you don't need to let Noelle take the blame for you. C'mon bud."

He doesn't hear my panicked "But, I—" It's buried by Wyatt's defeated "Yes, Dad."

And I know Mr. Kahale's speech and the affectionate shoulder squeeze he gave his son as he headed down the hall toward Jack's bellowing are supposed to be supportive. But I also know Wyatt only heard disappointment and blame.

That leaves Wyatt, Holly—who's wringing her hands by her ski bag—and me, the person who just made things *worse*.

"I'm sorry." I choke the words past the knots in my stomach. "I was trying to help."

"I know." His voice is tight as he pours himself juice and glugs it down. "Please, don't."

"Everyone's really cranky today," Holly says. "Well, all the boys are, at least."

"Thanks, sis," Wyatt mutters—far too quietly for her to hear, but, yeah, I'm jumping in before things escalate.

I pull a hair elastic off my wrist and hold it up. Holly knows this gesture and spins so her back is to me. "Can you do a regular braid? That's the most comfortable under my helmet."

"Sure." I finger comb her dark hair and divide it into three sections. "Are you excited about practice?"

"If I can ever get Mom and Dad out the door . . ." She kicks her bag and fidgets with the zipper on her Kringle Ski Club jacket. "We're going to work on gates and that's my favorite."

I say, "Cool," like I know what that is.

"I don't wanna wear clothes! Nooo!"

"Jack is so weird," sighs Holly.

I twist the elastic around the end of her braid as Mr. Kahale returns, throwing his hands up in exasperation. "That boy's in rare form today." He turns to Holly. "You all packed up, munchkin? Mom might have to meet us over there later."

"Oh." I give Holly's braid a final pat and step forward, because isn't this why I'm here? "I can take over with—"

My offer is cut off by a four-year-old shouting, "I want Noelle to do it!"

I shrug. "There's my cue. I'll send Mrs. Kahale out so you all can go."

Mr. Kahale gives me the smile that usually accompanies him way overpaying me. "Noelle, I don't know what we would do without you. Can we just keep you forever?"

Those words have got to burn Wyatt's ears. I can't look his way as I hurry down the hall to trade places with Mrs. Kahale.

It takes five jokes to coax Jack into clothes. Apparently he didn't realize I'm also pro—ski lessons—and the quivering-lip betrayal on his face makes me glad no one else is around to see the epic meltdown that's brewing.

Good thing I'm not above bribery.

"Let's make a deal," I say as we head to the living room. "If you go to class without whining, we'll get giant cocoas after."

Jack sucks the tip of his pointer finger. "With marsh-mallows?"

I do a goofy pantomime of pretending to think about this before announcing, "Obviously, silly." Then I begin a ridiculous victory dance after he nods to accept.

"Can I get in on this deal?"

I freeze. Then, as casually as possible, I lower my Hokey Pokey fingers and turn myself around to spot Wyatt, still sitting at the table, watching us. He grins. "I like cocoa. I also *really* like that dance. If I don't whine, will you teach it to me later?"

I'm pretty sure you could roast chestnuts on my flaming cheeks. "What are you still doing here?" The others' coats are gone. Why hadn't he left with them?

He shrugs. "Sounded like you could use some help with Jack."

Hmm. *Or*, sounds like someone's avoiding his dad.

The thought makes me wince—mine's avoiding *me*. I'd sent a hopeful text this morning: **Autumn says you've got a big surprise for me! Any hints?** But so far, Dad hasn't sent even an emoji in response.

Jack's looking between his brother and me—trying to figure out what's going on and how to make it about him.

"Hey Wyatt, how do you make a tissue dance?" He doesn't pause before delivering the punch line. "You put a little boogie in it!"

Wyatt laughs and holds up Jack's snowsuit. "C'mon, booger-breath, let's get you to lessons."

Part of me wants to prove I can handle this solo, but a much bigger part is grateful Wyatt stuck around. Maybe I need a copy of Holly's checklist, because I still find the gear overwhelming. I happily let Wyatt handle that. He slings Jack's skis over his shoulder with his own and stows it all on the bus. I assume we'll separate once we get to Kringle: Wyatt off to the big boy slopes, and me shepherding Jack to lessons. Which is why *I* unload and carry Jack's skis from the shuttle.

But Wyatt follows us to Thistle Lodge—and it's there, as I'm snapping on Jack's helmet and checking his gloves and gaiter, that I realize what's missing.

"Wyatt!" When I get panicked, my voice goes ridiculously high-pitched. It's embarrassing—but effective. He swivels toward where I'm staring at the ski rack, trying to manifest equipment into existence. "Can you do me a huge favor and sign Jack into lessons?"

"Yeah, sure. No problem," he says. "Is everything okay?"

I shake my head, already lost in it. Did we have them when we left the house? I hadn't unloaded them—were they still on the shuttle? Should I go check? "Can you rent ski poles?" I ask.

"Probably," Wyatt answers. "You can rent pretty much anything." He calls "*Why?*" after me, but I'm already half-way across the room with my phone out and dialing.

Mrs. Kahale's voice mail picks up. I take a deep breath, instructing myself to sound calm and capable: "Hi. It's Noelle, and everyone's fine. I just had a minor mishap where I forgot to bring Jack's poles for lessons. Wyatt says I can rent some, so I'm going to go ahead and do that on the card you gave me. I'm sorry—you can take it out of my paycheck. So, anyway, yeah. No need to call me back. Just wanted to give you a heads-up in case it pings you if I use the card. Thanks."

There. Totally professional.

I text the same thing to both Kahales, then hop in the rentals line. I've moved only one spot when I get a response back from Mr. Kahale.

I'll be at Thistle in five minutes. Preschoolers don't use poles. Go ahead and bring Jack to class and then wait there for me—both of you.

Oh. The tips of my ears burn. Whoops.

Well, someone might have told me that. Someone like the guy who said poles were rentable and let me go on this ridiculous quest to get Jack a pair. I mean, who else did he think needed them? Me? If I had some right now, I might whack him with them. At least poke him a little.

I duck out of the rental line. Wait—"*both of you*"? I reread Mr. Kahale's text; it was sent to me and an unknown number. I'd bet all the marshmallows in Kringle it belongs to the same guy I want to jab with a ski pole.

I spot Wyatt and his dad as soon as I step outside. Mr. Kahale's back is to me, but there's enough disapproval in his body language to make me want to play hooky. "I swear, Wyatt, if our babysitter quits because you won't stop pranking her or giving her grief—"

"Hi," I say sheepishly. "I'm really sorry I interrupted your skiing."

"Oh, Noelle, it's not your fault." Mr. Kahale's hands drop off his hips as he turns. "Ginger played me your message and it just broke her heart how panicked you sounded."

So much for "calm and professional."

"She's not as fast a skier, which is why I'm here and she's still making her way down."

"Oh, she doesn't—I didn't mean." I swallow. "I didn't know little kids don't use poles."

"No thanks to my son." Mr. Kahale's face darkens. "I'm sorry, Noelle. I don't know what's gotten into him."

"Do I get to explain myself?" Wyatt's knuckles are white around the helmet dangling from his hand.

Mr. Kahale crosses his arms. "What can you possibly say?"

Wyatt's eyes are on the mountain. He's probably wishing he could trade places with any of the skiers dotting the slopes. "I didn't get that Noelle was asking about renting poles for Jack until after she ran off."

I cringe. "I pretty much panicked that if Jack had *any* excuse for skipping lessons, he'd refuse to go. I didn't stop to listen. Sorry."

"Fine." Mr. Kahale blows out an exasperated breath. "Let's chalk it up to miscommunication and not let it ruin our day. Noelle, go take a well-earned break until Jack's done. Wyatt, you're skiing with me. Come on, let's go."

He's framing this like a punishment, but I doubt Wyatt sees it that way. Maybe it'll even be an opportunity for them to talk things out? But . . . based on the identical stubborn sets of their jaws, maybe not.

"Can't I have a minute to apologize first?" Wyatt asks.

Mr. Kahale nods and takes a few steps away.

"I'm sorry," Wyatt says. "I thought you were trying to do me a favor by asking me to bring him to lessons. Giving me a chance to be helpful with Jack or something. I really didn't get you thought he needed ski poles. And by the time I realized—"

"I'd pretty much fled?" Great job, Noelle. Super A+ work. "I didn't mean to get you in trouble."

"S'okay. You didn't do it on purpose. I would've called to clarify, but I don't have your number." He shuffles his new boots in the snow. "Just so we're clear, that's me asking for it."

I lift my chin, hoping he can't tell it's one wobbly breath away from trembling. "You still want it? You're not mad at me for messing things up with your dad . . . again?"

He shakes his head. "It was a mistake. I've made plenty, so I'll let you have this one."

My heart squeezes. "Well, the good news is, you now have my number. It's attached to the message where he yelled at us both."

"Dad's not mad at you either," Wyatt says, but I make a face. Because his dad might not be *mad*, but he can't exactly be *pleased*. "Promise. Go find your fireplace. I'll see you later."

He glances back over his shoulder as he and his dad head to the ski lift. I know, because I'm glancing back over *mine* as I head the opposite direction toward Juniper Lodge. It's long-distance across a crowd, but despite this, I can tell the smile he flashes me goes all the way to his eyes.

..*.*.*.*.*

Wyatt doesn't wait long to try out my number. He must send his first message from the ski lift, because it arrives before my cocoa order. Is it just me, or is there so much pressure to be witty over text?

I laugh and respond, Hang on, getting out my rating scale to evaluate your message—but I have mixed emotions. *Of course*, I want his attention, but he's likely sitting two feet away from the person he *should* be talking to. Am I really that irresistible, or am I being used as an excuse to avoid the hard stuff?

What's a witty way to say, Like me. But like me later?

"Does that not taste okay?" the barista asks, and I realize I'm frowning at my mug.

"Oh, it's great," I reassure her, smacking my lips and adding, "Mmm," like I'm talking to a toddler babysitting charge.

The barista says, "O-kay . . ." and backs away. So, obviously I can never order cocoa here again and now need to find a secluded couch and hide my embarrassment.

In the gaps between Wyatt's messages, I send the girls updates about last night. And I finally get a response from Dad: I wish Autumn hadn't said anything about the surprise. When I retort: Then maybe YOU shouldn't have said anything about Autumn, he replies, Probably not. I HOPE to have a big surprise, kiddo, but nothing's set yet.

Translation: *dud pile, ahoy.* Dad's always crushed and mopey when a project fails. There'll be a week of bathrobe-and-black-and-white-movies days, but then he'll bounce back—and I'll have my dad again. The version who suggests we buy every type of gum at the store and rate them on taste and bubble-blowing. We'll have Waffle Wednesday and Fondue Friday. He'll check my math homework—whether or not I ask him to—nag me about chores, and play boring science podcasts while he cooks. I don't need a big surprise if I can have him.

I respond: No worries. Miss you! Love you! to Dad and There's no such thing as too much cocoa to Wyatt.

Then I stop breathing while I panic I mixed up the recipients.

I didn't. I check this once as I put my coat back on, then again on the walk to the back of Thistle to pick up Jack. But he's not standing by the pole with the blue flag. Instead he's on Wyatt's shoulders. Both boys are waving at me, but I'm confused.

My smile feels flimsy as I walk over and wait through Jack's recitation of class highlights. "I had an awesome pizza wedge! And Benji has a dinosaur on his jacket zipper. And Renee got yelled at for eating snow. But I didn't eat it."

"Good job, bud, but shouldn't you still be in class?" I hold up my phone. "It's only eleven fifty-five. I thought lessons ended at noon."

"Renee had to go potty." Jack adds haughtily, "It's probably because she ate snow."

"Definitely," Wyatt tells him earnestly, but his eyes are

sparkling when he turns to me. "I'd just finished a run and saw them huddled at the pick-up spot. I thought I'd grab him—and the cocoa you promised if we didn't whine."

He winks at me and Jack cheers, but it takes me a moment to follow when they walk into Thistle. Wyatt is helping me babysit—again. I'm the one getting paid, and as his dad pointed out . . .

"This is your *vacation*. You don't have to stay with us." I add my coat and mittens to the pile they're making on an empty table. "I promise I can handle lunch and getting back to the cabin without any catastrophes."

"If it's *my* vacation, shouldn't I get to pick how I spend it?" As soon as Jack strips off his helmet, boots, and snowsuit, Wyatt boosts him back onto his shoulders and heads toward the food line.

"Well, yes," I concede, following behind. "But I'm working, and you should be—"

"Hanging out with the people I want to hang out with?" He lifts an eyebrow and squeezes his brother's knees, making Jack squeal and kick his striped socks. "Unless I'm in the way?"

"No!" I say quickly.

"Good." He nods toward a stack of cafeteria trays and I pick one up, loading it with all the items he and Jack indicate.

They're both sporting truly impressive cases of helmet hair, and Jack's only making Wyatt's more vertical as he tugs on it. By the time we check out, I have three burgers, three fries, a side of pasta salad, and there's just barely room for three cups of marshmallow-laden cocoa.

"We forgot the pickles!"

It's Jack's first demand after I've cut his burger in half, checked the temperature of his cocoa, and spun his plate so the ketchup is on the close side.

"Want me to?" Wyatt offers, but I wave him off.

"If you stay with him, I'll be right back."

And I'm glad Wyatt's there for another reason, because after pickles, it's applesauce. Then extra napkins for spilled cocoa. Every time I sit—every time Wyatt smiles at me and starts to say something, Jack's got a new request.

"Okay, I think we have everything you could possibly need," I say as I sit back down, smiling at Wyatt's look of shared exasperation.

Wyatt leans in. "So what are you guys going to do this afternoon?"

Is he looking for an invitation to join us? Or just making conversation? "Well, I was thinking we'd start with—"

"Noelle, I need—" Jack interrupts.

Wyatt smirks. "Let me guess." He scans the table. "You've got enough food for an army, so water? A spoon? Applesauce is a little tricky with a fork."

Oh, good call. I missed that. "I'll get a spoon," I say, but Jack shakes his head.

"No, that's not what I need."

It's my turn to guess, and babysitter bragging rights are on the line. Most guys wouldn't think "She's super close with my toddler brother" is an attractive quality, but since Wyatt *does*, I'm determined to nail this. "Dessert? You need to eat more burger first, bud."

Jack shakes his head. "Nope."

Wyatt taps his lip. "A napkin? No, *more* ketchup on your face. A red goatee to go with your cocoa mustache."

"It's not food," says Jack.

We're all laughing now, but I'm stumped. "A new joke? A hug?"

There's a competitive glint in Wyatt's eye as he considers his options. "You want a piggyback to the shuttle? To play with my phone?" When Jack shakes his head, Wyatt grins. "Then it's got to be a nap, a jumbo serving of green beans, and to go watch Holly's practice."

Jack laughs and squirms in his seat. "No! No way!" His expression suddenly turns serious. "*To go potty!*"

"Oh." I put down my burger again and stand. It's already cold, so what's a few more minutes?

"I really, really have to go." Jack's hopping from one socked foot to the other.

"Okay, Jack-a-roo, then let's do this." I swing his hand as we cross the room, but when we reach the door I thought was the bathroom, it's actually a storage closet. I pivot as Jack says, "Emergency!"

"Maybe it's over here?" Nope. That's the entrance to a medical station. "Do you know where it is, bud?" He shakes his head, but he's really whining now, so I scoop him up.

"Excuse me?" I stop in front of a mother walking with her daughter. "Can you tell me where the bathroom is?"

"Oh, it's downstairs. Such a pain." The woman points to a doorway on the other end of the room and I call "Thanks" over my shoulder as I hurry toward it.

Jack's continuous whine is a mosquito in my ear. "Reallyreallyreallyreallyreallyreally, really have to go!"

If there's a line at the ladies' room, I'll cover my eyes and bust into the men's, because clearly I should've let Wyatt take him. At least he would've known *where* to take him.

In the end, it doesn't actually matter if there's a line or not. I mean, of course there is. There *always* is in women's public bathrooms. But Jack stops whining before we reach the bottom of the stairs—and the realization of *why* is spreading like the wet spot soaking through my jeans.

It takes all my self-control not to drop him.

"Too late," Jack says in a tiny voice, before he tucks his head against my shoulder and starts to cry.

He's still crying when I get back to the table. My arms and back are burning with the strain of carrying him. Mr. and Mrs. Kahale stand up from the seats we'd vacated, alarm all over their faces. "Jackie, what happened?" asks his mom.

But his dad has reached to take him, and the answer is all too clear in the damp spot on the front of his pants. Also probably in the enormous blotch on my hip. I'm standing perfectly still, arms held out to my sides as Jack wails. "I had an accident."

"Oh no." His mom rubs his back. "I'm sorry, bud."

"Wyatt—Wyatt wouldn't let Noelle take me," Jack wails. "He was talking and talking and I-I couldn't hold it."

It doesn't matter that it isn't true. It matters that Wyatt's face crumples as his dad raises an eyebrow. It matters that Mr. Kahale is passing Jack's ski gear and the car keys to his wife. I'm reaching for Jack, because I'm already soggy. It matters that Wyatt is staying, that Holly has three more hours of practice, and that as we're walking away, Mr. Kahale is saying, "Stop making Noelle's job harder. C'mon, do a few runs with me—and don't leave me in the dust this time. I need my Wyatt-fix while you're here, because who knows when we'll see you again."

It's a good thing I spend hours each week balancing on the toe box of my pointe shoes, because it takes every ounce of my skill not to stumble over those words. Or pivot and turn back and refute them. But Jack is sniffling and wiping his nose on the hand twined in my hair, and Mrs. Kahale has her arms loaded with gear and is waiting by the door.

And my pants are wet.

When I glance over my shoulder this time, Wyatt's not looking back at me.

Babysitting Tip 15:

Brush up on your truck noises.
FYI, it's unacceptable to use the same "Vroom" for
both excavator and bulldozer!

By the time Mr. Kahale, Wyatt, and Holly get home, I'm tired. Tired of pushing toy trucks, telling jokes, and banging my head on the bottom of the table, because that's where Jack insists we play "construction site."

And I'm *really* tired of rehearsing what I want to say to them. But I'm also determined not to chicken out or let Wyatt take the blame, so they're barely through the door, coats still zipped, when I crawl out from under the table and say, "I want to apologize for earlier today."

"Oh. Hello down there." Mr. Kahale bends to wave to Jack, who beeps in reply. To me, he says, "No apology necessary, Noelle. It's all over and done."

"I know I'm probably making it into a bigger deal than it needs to be, but . . . please hear me out?"

He nods. Wyatt's eyebrows are arched as he peels off his gloves.

"I was showing off." It's a realization I had while stretching. "I should've admitted I thought I'd lost Jack's poles, or just *asked* where the bathroom was. I was trying to prove I was the perfect babysitter who could handle everything by herself. Wyatt was just trying to help and I was too stubborn to admit I needed it."

I catch his eye and he mouths "It's okay."

"Noelle, we're fairly certain you're the best babysitter on the planet. There's no one here you need to impress." Mr. Kahale smiles gently, then presses his hands together and points the tips of his fingers at each of us. "Try *less*. Both of you."

"*Oh no,*" says Holly from her spot on the floor where she's wriggling out of her snow pants. "Are Wyatt and Noelle in big trouble?"

Except the little stinker sounds less "Oh no" than "Tell me more!"

"No one is in trouble," says Mr. Kahale.

"Hmm." Holly sniffs and mutters something that sounds suspiciously like "Yet" as she picks up a sweaty heap of gaiters and gloves and heads toward the laundry room.

"God save me from that girl as a teenager." Mr. Kahale turns to Wyatt. "Think she could go away to Beacon? Maybe that'll be my new parenting strategy—ship them off for adolescence and take them back when they're full-grown."

Wyatt's smile flickers. Whatever else they did this afternoon, it's clear he didn't tell his dad about the less-than-temporary nature of his trip.

"Great, thanks. You too. Bye." Mrs. Kahale is finishing up a phone call as she approaches. She plucks a backhoe from the rug and places it on the table. "So, Wyatt, Noelle, I just got off the phone with the lodge. I called to ask what activities they have scheduled, because I thought you two might need a break from the kids . . . from all of us, really. We've spent a lot of time in this cabin and around each other."

If a blink could communicate *You're sick of me already?* then Wyatt's expression would've conveyed half the conversation he's been avoiding without him opening his mouth. But Mrs. Kahale is looking at her husband, giving him a thumbs-up. "So I registered you for a social tonight. Surprise! Jack's demanding we watch *The Grinch* for the hundredth time—save yourselves and go have fun with people your own age."

"You signed us up for a social?" Wyatt sounds as dubious as I feel.

Mr. Kahale laughs. "Oh, don't give me that. You used to love these. I'm pretty sure your first kiss was at a Junior Elves dance party at the lodge—" He coughs. "Not that that's what I'm advocating tonight!"

Mrs. Kahale's eyes dance with amusement as she puts a hand on her husband's arm. "Relax, honey. It's game night, not a kegger."

He does, but Wyatt's shaking his head. "I'm not in middle school anymore." I watch the moment he remembers he can't be a defiant houseguest, then ask to be a resident. "But it sounds like fun. Thanks for signing us up."

It's his abrupt agreement that makes Mrs. Kahale pause. "You don't have to go. I can cancel. No pressure."

His eyes are dim, but his smile's stage-bright. "Well, if my options are games or *Grinch*, hand me the dice."

They look to me. There are a lot of different versions of *The Grinch*, and I'm curious which I'd be missing, but given the choice between any movie and time with Wyatt, I know what I'm picking. "Fair warning: if there's Twister, I'm so winning."

Wyatt's phone rings as we get on the shuttle bus to Kringle Village. He curses under his breath as he slides into the molded plastic seat beside me, then answers, "Hey, Mom."

I glance sideways, but he's doing that thing where you make, like, a visor out of your hand—like you can block out the world or hide in the space between your thumb and pointer finger. "Yeah. Yeah, I saw it."

I pull out my phone and make myself unobtrusive on the seat beside him. I have a text to answer; Mae's sent me a picture of herself with Rosie and Iris Davis, two of my favorite babysitting kiddos. **LOVE these girls.**

That is zero percent surprising. At twelve and six,

they're already world-traveler adventure-seekers like their globe-hopping parents. I bet Mae's grilling them for vlog post ideas.

I type up a response, pretending I haven't noticed Wyatt's hip is pressed against mine or don't hear the relentless crash of his mom's voice, even if I can't make out her words.

"No. *No*, I haven't called. No, I'm not—I'm not going to. Because I don't— No, Mom, I don't *want* to. I don't want to be in a commercial *or* a music video. Yes—I don't care that Grant thinks I'm— Mom, are you listening? No. Don't call Dad. He's not— He's not going to agree with you." He drops his hand and sighs. "Fine. I'll sleep on it. I said I would. I'll talk to you tomorrow. Bye."

There was no part of that conversation that wasn't self-explanatory, and no part of his body language is an invitation to talk about it, so I keep texting Mae.

Wyatt rides the rest of the trip with his head tipped back against the seat, his eyes closed. He stays in his stupor when we reach Kringle Village, walking silently beside me to Juniper Lodge, where he pauses inside the door and asks, "How much of that phone call did you piece together?"

I purse my lips and consider my answer. "Your mother makes the stereotypical 'dance mom' look uninvested?"

Wyatt snorts. "Look at that, you got BINGO before we even got to game night." He fidgets with his zipper and looks sideways at me. "Does yours?"

"No." I suck in a breath and focus my attention on a couple checking in across the lobby—he's got his hand on her back, she's leaning her head against his shoulder. Their preteen son is standing *I'm-not-with-them* feet away.

I could make *"No,"* my full answer, but I can't stop looking at the couple. If Mom had lived longer, would I still be embarrassed by their PDAs? Would I have rolled my eyes, turned my back? "She died when I was eight."

It's a showstopper of an answer, one I don't normally share—but Wyatt doesn't react the typical way. He's not averting his eyes and mumbling *I didn't know*—like it was somehow about him—before making a quick topic change.

"I'm sorry," he says. "That must be harder at Christmas."

I press a hand to my chest. "It—it is." I bet my friends suspect the reason I got all in on elves and tinsel is because Mom died mid-December and the activities she'd pre-planned for me that year had been the only thing that got me through that first set of holidays. The next year, Dad and the girls' parents had replicated most of her plans to honor her memory and distract me from the calendar. The year I turned ten, I'd taken over, and Noelle's Christmas Extravaganza had begun.

I wonder what Mom would think about this year? What advice she'd have given me?

"She pre-bought all these snow globes," I tell him. "One for every year until I turn twenty-one. They're wrapped and numbered and it's the first present I open every year. I'm already dreading the Christmas there isn't one. Because what do I do then?" I lift my chin, staring up at the rafters as I blink back eyes that want to fill.

"What was this year's?" he asks.

I shake my head, too close to tears to tell him I haven't opened it yet.

Wyatt's hand lands lightly on my shoulder. "I'm sorry. It's cool if you ever want to talk about it—or tell me to shut up when I complain about my mom, because I've also got Ginger and she cancels out a lot."

"She's pretty great. And thanks." I take a deep breath and pull on a smile. "You know, I told *her* about my Beacon audition, and I haven't even told my dad."

"Isn't it in January? Like, in three weeks? When are you going to tell him?"

"It has to be soon, I guess. But I haven't had the chance. He's been totally MIA lately." My shrug feels like I'm pushing against the weight of the world, but his hand on my shoulder lightens some of the load, which is why I tell him more than I plan to. "It's part of the reason I want to go. Sometimes I just want to be the priority. I want to be more exciting than whatever what-if question or app or thingumabob is in his mind. Not all the time—I'm not saying he has to want to hear about everything that happens in ballet class or in my life, but just *sometimes*."

Wyatt gives my shoulder a squeeze and we stand there, me feeling seen and heard, until I nod. Then he pulls back and says, "And I want to be more interesting for who *I am* than what people say when I'm onstage."

We're quite the pair: him, a pawn in his mom's vicarious fame goals; me, an obstacle in my dad's obsessive experiments. We both just want to be seen; except our potential escapes are opposites, me trading Dad's house for Beacon, him leaving Beacon for his dad's. And while none of this is getting solved tonight, I feel better for having someone listen. I hope he does too.

"Okay, show me where we're going." I've learned my lesson about pretending to know things. "And I want to hear more about these elf socials where you had your first kiss."

"Not a chance." He laughs as he leads me across the enormous lobby. The sound is buoyant, echoing against the high ceilings, so I'm not surprised when it turns some heads.

"Wyatt! Wyatt Kahale, is that you?"

He pivots toward a slender blonde woman around his dad's age. She's standing up from one of the many cushioned alcoves, wearing a ski-chic outfit that makes me feel unbelievably frumpy in my leggings and sweatshirt. White-on-white-on-white—skinny jeans tucked into heeled snakeskin booties, a gorgeous tailored sweater that looks too soft to be anything but cashmere. It's all set off by a perfect red lip and a dizzying spill of gold around her neck that shines with the same highlights as her styled blonde hair. Beside her, a tall sandy-haired man and a blonde girl around Holly's age look up from a game of Uno.

"Hey, Wyatt!" The man stands and shakes his hand while the girl chirps out "Hi" and plays a card. "Dad, take two."

"Rae Ann, Kevin, Gabriella!" Wyatt smiles. "Wow, it's been a while. How are you?"

"Too long!" Rae Ann sets her champagne flute on the table beside a beer and cocoa, then steps around the couch to give him a hug. "How are you? Is your whole family here?"

"They're back at the cabin."

"I'm texting Ginger right now," she says. "We've got to do après-ski one night. And G here would love to see Holly. Now that Holly's so busy with the team, they never cross paths anymore."

"Ski club isn't as much fun without her," pipes up Gabriella.

"It's probably not nearly as daredevil either," Wyatt quips to everyone's laughter. "I'm sure they'd love to see you."

"We're all being incredibly rude," Rae Ann says with a smile in my direction. "Wyatt, introduce us to your girl-friend."

I'm not sure what his face looks like, but the smile is startled right off mine.

"She's not my girlfriend," Wyatt says. "This is the baby-sitter, Noelle."

If Rae Ann or Kevin pick up on the awkwardness of the moment, then bless them, because they gloss right over it. Kevin shaking my hand—"It's nice to meet you, Noelle"—and Rae Ann saying, "Of course Ginger would be smart enough to bring her own sitter. That means we can definitely get away one night. Perfect, perfect."

"It'll be *more* perfect if I get to see Holly," says Gabriella.

"I'm so glad we ran into you." Rae Ann takes a step back. "But we won't keep you."

"They'll be glad too," says Wyatt.

"Have a good night, you two." Kevin's giving Rae Ann this cheeky raised-eyebrow side-eye that isn't as subtle as he thinks. He totally assumes there's something scandalous happening here. I wish.

After goodbyes, Wyatt talks at me as he heads past the reception desk to a set of stairs. The lobby's second floor is all windows and railings—views of the mountains and Kringle Village on one side and views into the lobby below on the other. "The Cooks are friends of Dad and Ginger. Rae Ann used to be a dancer, so it's some sort of miracle she didn't ask about Beacon tonight."

I nod woodenly, but I totally don't care about Beacon right now. I care about how quickly he dismissed the idea I could be his girlfriend. Is it *because* I'm the babysitter? Was his distaste pointed at *me*, or at the fact his parents pay me? I'm trying not to take it personally, because it's not like he lied. But he didn't have to be so speedy with the truth.

There's a table set up at the top of the staircase, two women sitting behind it with clipboards. "Can I help you find something?" the one with glasses asks warily. "The balcony's closed for an event tonight."

"Sorry," I say. "I guess this isn't the right place."

"No, it is." Wyatt points past the array of name tags to a flyer bordered with dice and playing cards. "We're here for game night."

"It's—" The women behind the table exchange exasperated glances before one says, "It's a senior elves event."

The other woman adds, "Senior *citizens*."

"Oh. *Oh*." I giggle.

They sigh and look at each other. "They're going to have to change the name back."

Wyatt takes a deep breath and I can read his impatience at having made this trip for nothing. "Look, my stepmom signed us up—do I need to do anything, or can you just process her a refund?"

"What's going on over here?" A bald man with deep brown skin and wild gray eyebrows approaches. He's got his thumbs tucked in the yellow suspenders he's wearing over a plaid flannel shirt. "These two giving you some trouble?" His tone is as mischievous as his smile, so I'm not worried, but it still takes me a second to realize he's asking *us* and pointing to the ladies across the table, not the other way around.

"Apparently we're not, uh . . ."—Wyatt pauses—"*cool* enough for game night."

"His stepmom must've misunderstood," I explain. "She thought it was for teens."

The man laughs. "So it happened again."

"This has happened before?" I ask.

"At least once a month." He grins at me. "It's their own fault. We used to be 'Silver Snowflakes,' but *some* people said that made them feel old." He shoots a good-natured look at the women behind the table. "I keep telling them we can't have 'Tiny Elves' be five-to-nine-year-olds, 'Junior Elves' be up to thirteen, then 'Senior Elves' is fifty-plus? No way. You lucked out though—normally it happens on dance night and they're expecting a club and it's ballroom lessons. Much more awkward."

Wyatt laughs lightly. "I bet. So, we'll just—"

The man turns and calls, "Lois, come hear this. These two want to join game night."

A woman with a sleek bob steps away from a cabinet where she's unloading poker chips and playing cards—her hair is this gorgeous silver and contrasts strikingly with her black wrap dress and red framed glasses. "So?"

The women with the clipboards sputter, but Lois quells them with a look. "Honestly, what's the problem? We won't run out of space. We'll promise not to serve them any wine or spiked cider. We'll be horrible influences while we beat them at Scrabble and they teach us how to spy on our grandkids' social media."

I laugh. "Out of curiosity, what *is* the name for the teen group?"

"We just call those 'teen socials,'" says Lois. "We polled the attendees, and *they* didn't want anything twee."

One of the clipboard women sighs and mumbles, "RIP 'Teen Scene.'"

I snort and Suspenders grins at me before picking up a Sharpie. "Okay, what're your names?"

"Noelle and Wyatt, but—" I turn. Lois already has Wyatt getting game boxes off the top shelf.

"I'm George." He snags the clipboard and puts big checkmarks next to both of our names before finding our name tags. "Come on." He gestures with his head for me to circle around the table and join them.

I offer an apologetic shrug to the check-in ladies, but they laugh and shoo me on.

"Wyatt, I'm sorry to tell you this," George says with false solemnity. "But I'm borrowing your girl for the night. I need a partner for charades and Lois couldn't demonstrate the difference between a banana split and Banana Boat if you paid her."

George is watching Wyatt; Lois is too. But neither is watching him as intently as I am, because I'm expecting him to clarify I'm *not* his girl and then explain we're not staying. He hadn't seemed psyched about the social to begin with; this gives him an easy out.

Instead he says, "That okay with you?" and waits for my nod. "Okay, then I'm asking Lois. She's already told me she's a whiz at Pictionary."

"Whiz?" George scoffs. "More like *Cheese Wiz*. Noelle, you, however, lucked into a heck of a partner. What should we win first? Poker? Monopoly? Canasta? Or should we show these two how it's done with charades?"

"I'm not sure I'll be any better," I admit. "So maybe we should get that over with."

Oh, but Lois truly is awful. I'd feel bad for Wyatt as he guesses "Tree? Um, telephone pole. Post? Mailbox?" except he's making his guesses through laughter so thick he's wiping his eyes. And his partner still hasn't moved—doesn't move until the woman with the stopwatch calls out, "Time."

"I was obviously a canoe paddle!" exclaims Lois, and Wyatt doubles over so his forehead is pressed against my shoulder and I can feel his laughter against my skin.

We don't stick together. After charades, Lois leads him to Pictionary while George teaches me to play dominos.

But even when Wyatt and I are separate, he'll catch my eye from the snack table and do the best charade of the night miming to ask if I want anything. Or I peek at him over the top of my cards as George teases that my poker face is hopeless—and he's watching me from over his, three tables away.

"He's a good one, this guy." Lois unthreads her elbow from Wyatt's as they approach the table where I'm finally getting the gist of canasta. "You hang on to him, sweetie."

"Oh, I—" I very much don't have an answer for that, but Wyatt's stepping forward and holding out a hand to help me up.

"You gotta give her back now, George," Wyatt jokes as

my partner presses his hands together and faux-whispers, "Noelle, don't leave me with all these *old* people."

I'm laughing, disarmed, and off-balance when Wyatt tugs harder than I expect. The momentum carries me off my chair and into his chest. We're both knocked back a step and his other hand curves around my hip to steady me.

Lois hums conspiratorially. "Lovebirds—look up. You're standing under mistletoe."

"Kiss. Kiss. Kiss," taunts George, who I'm now realizing is a grown-up version of Jack, which explains why I like him so much. His chant is taken up by players at other tables, until it's coming from all sides. *Kiss. Kiss. Kiss.*

I smile sheepishly at Wyatt. We're still chest to chest in an embrace that's no longer balance-related. Is he game to knock me off-kilter again? I tip my chin up, offering all sorts of permissions with my eyes.

But his eyes, his smiles—they're the overbright ones from his pre-hot-tub vidcall cameo. They're for our onlookers. And when he leans in, the stamp of his lips against my cheek feels like it's for them too—quick and impersonal. Nothing like last night on the deck. No shivers, no tingles.

He steps back and drops his arms from around me. Using them instead to wave goodbye.

My smile feels as frozen as the air that's waiting outside the hotel. I tug my coat a little tighter and walk a little faster, ignoring what *might* have been an attempt by him to reach out and hold my hand.

Because you know what, it's not. Of course it's not. I may have been the one to pull away in the hot tub, but he's the one who backed off after Christmas Eve snowmen, and even a whole squad of elderly cheerleaders couldn't entice him to pucker up. Twice I've put myself out there—and both times he rejected me. It's not a mistake I'll make again. I was right last night; we're satellites passing, not lips colliding.

"Noelle." Wyatt catches up with me at the bus stop. The shuttle's already here, a line of people storing their gear and boarding. "Hey, hang on a second."

"What?" I demand. "They're loading."

He steps in front of me and waits until I meet his eyes, then tugs off a glove and reaches up to touch my cheek with his bare hand. "So much of my life is performed for an audience." His voice is soft, earnest, and he shakes his head a little. "I don't want our first kiss to be."

"Oh." It's more exhale than word. Because, *Oh.*

"Do you understand?" he asks. "I didn't mean to hurt your feelings back there."

I nod.

But now that I know the *why*, I'm full-focused on the *when*.

Babysitting Tip 16:
Just say "No" to ghost stories.

I've made a lot of macaroni and cheese when Dad's deep in obsessive-work mode. A lot of spaghetti. And, yeah, yeah, I know all about *A watched pot never boils*—but when you're starving after three hours of dance class, you want those carbs as soon as possible.

There's a moment in the water—it's not boiling yet, but it's this moment when I'm aware it's *about* to. It's a change in the surface tension, in the way the water moves. The boiling hasn't happened, but I get my noodles ready.

Wyatt and me? We're water molecules.

We haven't kissed yet—but it's coming. How can it *not* after his revelation by the shuttle last night? Maybe it would've happened at the cabin—*special moment in front of the fireplace, take two*—only his parents were waiting up. But through our story about the meaning of "Senior Elves" and Wyatt reenacting Lois's charades, there's a new energy crackling between us. As Mrs. Kahale wipes away tears of laughter and Mr. Kahale guffaws so loud I worry he'll wake Jack, Wyatt and I glance sideways, share private smiles.

It's going to happen. We just need opportunity.

Opportunity, however, feels as elusive as the missing piece of Jack's new puzzle. We've searched for it all day and never found it. And when we're back home before dinner, we're *all* back home. Jack's chatterboxing at his dad from the kitchen counter while Mr. Kahale cooks. Wyatt, Holly, and I are playing Go Fish and Mrs. Kahale is sitting in the loft, talking on the phone.

When she comes down, she beckons to Holly. "Gabriella wants to talk to you."

Once Holls is out of earshot, lying on the floor beneath the tree and giggling into the phone, Mrs. Kahale turns to me. "Noelle, we're thinking of going out tonight with the Cooks. You'd be okay with that, right?"

I refuse to look across the table at Wyatt, because I can feel his eyes on me. "Yeah, that's totally fine. It's part of why I'm here, isn't it? Have fun."

"Great. Thanks." Mrs. Kahale hesitates. "There's one more part and feel free to say no: What if Gabriella came and slept over with Holly? Is that too much?"

I shake my head. "It might even make things easier since Holly and Jack have been . . ." I search for a diplomatic word, but Wyatt cuts in—

"Fighting nonstop? I can help. We've got this."

"Thank you! You're angels. They'll drop off Gabriella and pick us up around seven. After you get the kids down, you don't have to wait up. Just set the security alarm when you go to bed."

She hurries to wrestle the phone away from Holly and confirm with Rae Ann. I kick Wyatt under the table. "You can't look that excited for them to leave," I whisper. "It's totally suspicious."

And then my eyes widen and my jaw drops open.

"What?" Wyatt chuckles. "What's going on in that head of yours?"

"Be right back." I scramble for my room, my phone already dialing. As soon as it connects, I blurt my realization to the girls: "I've become the *worst* babysitting cliché"—I'm huddled in the corner, right by the door to the balcony, and I cup my hand around the phone so I can whisper this part—"the sitter who waits until the parents leave so she can sneak a boy over."

"Wait. What about Wyatt?" shrieks Coco. "Did you meet someone on Ski Patrol or something?"

"I'm pretty sure she means Wyatt," says Autumn.

"That's technically not '*sneaking a boy over*,' " adds Mae. "It's *his* house."

"Okay, true." I admit. "But still, it's against the babysitters' rulebook."

Because, yes, we have one. Created by Autumn, of course, even though she rarely babysits. Momma Mac made her,

Mae, and me take a babysitting class at the community center last summer. Coco had been too busy swimming. Afterward Autumn compiled all the notes on choking hazards and poison control and splinter removal and burping babies into a PDF we could all store on our phones. We'd included our own rules too—and *No inviting over friends without permission* and *Definitely no inviting crushes over* were on there.

"Back up," Autumn suggests. "Start at the beginning."

"Hang on," says Mae. "I'm switching us to video."

The connection spins for a second. I take that pause to breathe, to try and calm down, but the sight of their faces popping up on my screen is better than any exhale.

"Okay, go," says Coco.

"I really miss you all," I say.

"Then don't go away again," says Autumn matter-of-factly. Coco rolls her eyes, Mae says, "Miss you too."

I catch them up: ski poles to Scrabble to "I don't want an audience" to tonight, when we finally won't have one and the only thing standing in our way will be the sacred rule of not mixing babysitting with crushes.

It's already enough, so I don't include how the Kahales asked me to report on Wyatt, how I've done the opposite—finding out and keeping his secrets. How this morning, Mrs. Kahale said, "Wyatt finally seems to be letting his guard down. Has he hinted at all about what's bugging him? I wonder if there's friend trouble at Beacon. Or if he's fighting with his mom. Nick mentioned some ridiculous plan of hers—him dancing in a music video? Maybe I should ask Wyatt again." And because I'm the worst, I'd been noncommittal and pretended Jack was calling me.

"Let's think about this logically," says Autumn, and I know she's going to tick off ideas on her fingers before she even raises her hand. "Are you planning to lock the kids in their room so you can pounce on Wyatt?"

"What? No." I sputter and laugh.

"Are you going straight from bedtime to 'lay-one-on-me'—do not pass go, find Jack's stuffed monkey, or tell Holly to put the book down?"

"No." It makes me smile that Autumn—who's also filled in for me at the Kahales—knows Holly will need that prompting. Holly *always* needs that prompting.

"And you like him? You want to kiss him?" asks Coco.

"Yes," I whisper, banging my forehead on the wall in my attempt to shuffle closer to the corner. At least I remembered to lock my bedroom doors—all three of them. There will be no Wyatt-terruptions on *this* call, thank you very much. "I like him a lot."

"Because he's a good dancer?" asks Mae.

"Not even a little because of that." It's funny how the thing that was *most* appealing about Wyatt when he was a photo on a mantel doesn't factor in now that he's a person in my life. "Because he's kind and silly, and he loves his family. He sings Disney songs about snowmen and plays charades with old people. He gives piggybacks and hates eggnog and is a gingerbread house virtuoso. He wears llama pajamas and ski helmet hair unself-consciously and does voices with bath toys and bedtime stories. He listens."

The call is silent when I finish. I lower my eyes from the rafters to my screen. Coco is beaming. Autumn lowers her hands. "I ran out of fingers."

Mae has on her head-tilt thinking face. "If you listened to what you just said, I don't think you need us to tell you what to do. You both love that family—you're not going to suddenly forget the kids. And nowhere in your list of things you like about Wyatt is 'he's so hot, I can't wait to devour his face.'"

Coco snorts. "Though, based on what I've seen, that'd be a totally valid reaction."

Mae has to wait until we stop laughing to finish her thought. "Just because you don't need us to tell *you* what to do, doesn't mean you don't have to tell *us* everything. I want an update tomorrow."

"Deal," I say, and begin unpacking strategic items from my babysitting bag as they take turns telling me about Coco's latest swim meet, the gala Autumn's helping to plan, and Mae's post about cities with the best New Year's Eve celebrations.

"You'll be home for ours, right?" Coco asks. We always have a sleepover at her house. I always dread it. New Year's means Christmas is over.

It doesn't feel right to be my typical Ebenezer about it. "A day early, even. We come back on the thirtieth." Which is only three more days. I set a bottle of nail polish on top of a picture book about trucks playing tag. Three days?

"I can't wait!" says Coco, and Autumn adds, "Seriously."

Mae says, "Not soon enough."

My smile feels frozen. Trapped behind it is my own agreement, wrapped up in a contradictory second truth, *Only three more days with Wyatt? Not long enough. Not nearly.*

If *one* eight-year-old girl is a handful, then two is a headache. I mean that in the most loving way possible, because, oh my eardrums, they are *loud*. As soon as the door shuts behind the Cook and Kahale adults, Holly and Gabriella jump on the couch, whooping and shouting.

I shoo them down. "What would your parents say if they caught you doing that?"

The girls are chagrined for about a second before their celebration goes mobile. They're running in dizzying circles around the room, leaping throw pillows. I scoop up Jack before he gets bulldozed and Wyatt positions himself in front of the tree—but there's no reason to intervene. Any energy they get out now is less they'll have at bedtime.

Across the room, Wyatt's got his phone in his hand—he winks at me as my own buzzes. I probably should've warned you: In ski club they used to call them "Hurricane Holly" and "Gale-force Gabriella."

I struggle to keep a straight face as I respond: **These sweet, calm angels? I refuse to believe it.**

Wyatt's booming laugh makes both girls freeze and look over—for at least a second—before they resume their storm.

Eventually Holly and Gabriella collapse on the couch and start planning their sleepover cliché dream: *manicures* and *movies* and *midnight snacks.*

Cocoa is next. While the girls are drinking, I ask Wyatt to give a certain pestering preschooler a bath and I break out the sheet masks and nail polish from my babysitting bag.

"Ew! I tried to sip my cocoa with my mask on and it tasted so gross!" G wails. She turns to Holly. "Try it."

Of course Holly does. How else could she add her own dramatic "Ew! I think I'm going to throw up"?

"Or I could get you both straws," I suggest, stealing all their fun.

While they're letting their polka dot pedicures dry and taking all sorts of silly selfies, I slip away to check on the guys. Jack's wrapped in a towel, and Wyatt is wearing approximately half the bathwater. "Looks like you two had fun."

Wyatt shakes his head like a puppy, spraying me with drops from his hair. "So much fun. I bet you didn't know Jack is a blue whale, who can explode water out his blowhole."

"I didn't know that." I turn to Jack. "You'll have to tell me about it."

"The explosions were like—psshhew!" He tries to gesture, but his hands are trapped burrito-style.

"Can you get the little man in pj's?" Wyatt tickles Jack through the towel. "I'm going to go find some dry clothes."

Holly has a baking sheet out when we reconvene in the kitchen. "We're making our midnight snack."

I shake my head at Wyatt when he opens his mouth to correct her. If Holly's "midnight snack" occurs at nine, I'm totally cool with that. Because there's no way *I'm* making it to midnight. I do, however, object to them arranging Bagel Bites and slice-n-bake dough on the same sheet. I save her from culinary disaster by shooing them to wash their masks off.

Then after a rowdy game of UNO, a dozen iLive videos of terrifying ski tricks (I cover Jack's eyes so he doesn't get ideas, but really it's Holly I should blindfold), a nauseating quantity of cookies, pizza bagels, and a side of salt and vinegar chips—I load three toothbrushes with Sparkle Berry and set a timer for them to get their full two minutes.

Next, it's stories and songs—Holly cutting her eyes at G and protesting that she's "too old for all that"—but then shutting up and listening as soon as I start the first page. Wyatt's yawning, and I swear he's eyeing the fourth bunk bed. Amateur.

Jack's halfway to snoring before I close the book.

The girls aren't, so I say, "It's okay if you talk, but keep it to a whisper."

Then Wyatt and I are sinking onto the couch. He's got his head tipped back, the heels of his palms pressed against his eyes, but when he lowers his hands, he's grinning. "I don't know what Jack's talking about half the time, and Holly has enough sass for an entire sitcom—but they're really the best, aren't they?"

"They really are," I agree.

"I want that every night," he says, quieter now, his smile dimming.

"You want *that* every night?"

"Maybe a little less sleepover and bath time water sports, but . . . Yeah."

I chew my bottom lip. "Are they the reason you're leaving Beacon?"

Wyatt's silent for so long that I think he's not going to answer, but finally he sighs. "They're part of it, but not the whole reason. I'm trying to be fair. If it's your dream . . ." His eyes drift over me and pause. "Achilles?"

"What?" I follow his gaze and realize I'm massaging the back of my calf. "Oh. Always, but it's not too bad right now. Just habit."

"I've got a ball in my room if you want to roll it out." He frowns, then adds, "My roommate last year had his snap. That 'pop' sound still haunts me."

I shudder. Snapped tendons are the nightmare. If they don't end your career, they at least pause it for a yearlong detour into surgery and rehab. I absently give my leg another rub. "It's really fine. Just nervous habit. But I want to know about Beacon. Please. I've read all the brochures, watched all the 'day in a life of a student' videos. But you lived there. Why don't you want to anymore?"

The fireplace isn't on, but Wyatt's staring at the empty space. "Those videos—they're not wrong. We get up, eat, go to dance class, eat, go to dance class, go to school—but my classes are a joke. It's online-charter-school, bare-minimum stuff. Then we eat again, go to dance class, do some home-work, go to bed."

"Right." So what am I missing? Because that sounds like heaven. "Are the other dancers mean?" I follow enough of them on iLive to have identified a few divas I'll be avoiding.

Wyatt scrunches his forehead. "Some are over-the-top competitive, but not any more than anywhere else." He pulls out his phone and scrolls through pictures from the past cou-ple of days until he reaches ones that are pre–ski trip. Groups in dorms and stage wings, hamming it up in costumes and in class. A striking girl in a perfect arabesque holding a pizza box, then Wyatt and a guy laughing and elbowing each other in a fight over the last slice.

"Who's he?" I point to the Black boy with short hair and a smile that's both perfectly straight and perfectly charming. He appears in the most pictures, and really, the ones where it's him *and* Wyatt are simply not fair.

"That's my roommate, Danny." Wyatt can't talk about him without grinning, so I guess that disproves my suspi-cions about him being friendless. He points out some of the other people: "That's Angelica—she was a marzipan with me. And that's Mica. They're dating Alvie—" He scrolls to another shot of Mica and a Chinese girl who looks familiar. "Alvie won YAGP nationals last year."

I blink. *That's Alva Chen!* The Youth America Grand Prix is the *biggest* ballet competition in the United States. I've seen her performances. Anyone who's into ballet has. Wyatt *trains* with her. He *eats pizza* with her and knows about her love life. It's possible I give an undignified squeak.

He politely ignores it. "And there's Justin—" It's a picture of a white guy in stage makeup. "*Nutcracker* was his last show with Beacon. He's going to apprentice with the Houston Ballet."

"They all look really cool."

He turns off his phone. "They are. If you go to Beacon, I'll introduce you to everyone." Wyatt laughs. "You can inherit the responsibility of reminding Danny to add soap to the washing machine when he does his laundry."

"I still don't understand." If anything, I understood *less*.

"I told you Justin's leaving to join Houston Ballet." I nod and he spreads his hands, palm up, like he's offering answers written inside them. "The rest of them are *jealous*. They're counting down until their own auditions and apprenticeships. I'm . . . not."

His hands drop to his lap. "When everyone else was all, 'You're so lucky' and 'I'd kill to be you,' I was thinking, 'Better you than me.' Because I don't want that anymore. I don't want to go pro, or for my whole life to be ballet. I want so much more than Beacon." He looks at my face and laughs, which I'm pretty sure means my attempt at a sympathetic expression has flopped. "You don't get it, do you?"

"I mean, I hear what you're saying, and I'm sorry you're unhappy—"

"But?" he prompts.

"But . . . Trade you?" I say with a strained laugh. I pull my left foot up on the couch, tucking my chin on my knee as I turn to face him. "My spot in town for yours at school."

"If only." He gives me a half-smile. "I'm telling them tomorrow—Dad and Ginger."

I sit up. "You are? That's great!"

"I'm going to ask them to meet me for lunch. Holls will be at practice. You'll have Jack. We can go to one of the restaurants." His eyes are on the empty fireplace as he sketches out this idea, but he turns back to me. "Tonight went well, right? That'll help."

"Tonight went great," I reassure him, bouncing on the cushion like Jack to make him smile. "I'm so glad you're telling them. This time tomorrow you could know if you're moving to Juncture." I hesitate, but add, "And then what? What are you looking forward to in post-Beacon life?"

Maybe I'll understand better if we talk about what he *wants*, instead of what he doesn't. Because all of those things: the lessons, the auditions, the life and friends built around dance and a future in a company—they all sound pretty great.

He chuckles. "I'm probably supposed to have an answer for that, right? My mom's going to want one, but—" He looks up at the beams, out the windows, at the TV. "I don't know. I want to have time to get better at video games so Holly doesn't beat me."

I snort. "To be fair, she's weirdly good for how rarely your parents let her play."

"Right? For a while I thought I was just *that bad*—and I'm bad, but she's *good*." He shakes his head. "I want to ski more without worrying my teachers will be mad. And to learn to surf next time we go see my grandparents. And rock climbing."

"Rock climbing?"

Wyatt shrugs, but his broad shoulders don't seem as burdened, like just talking of possibilities makes him lighter. "I've never tried it. Maybe soccer? I haven't played a team sport since I was six. I think I'd like it."

It makes me smile that these are all sports. Well, less so Xbox, though Holly has a strange obsession with a golf game I suspect is her dad's. "Anything else?"

"I don't know. It feels like a lot of pressure to suddenly 'choose a hobby' or whatever. Maybe an instrument or a language or something." He shrugs again and picks at the fringe of a throw blanket. "I'll probably be bad at half the things I try—and honestly, that's appealing. I want to do things and be okay with being the worst, no one correcting me every step of the way or expecting perfection."

Dad would love this conversation. He'd tell Wyatt what he always tells me: *In this family we don't fear failure, we fear not trying.* And if I present my Beacon audition that way, he'll have to support it. So what's still holding me back?

Wyatt's grin falters. "What about you? I just made Beacon *more* appealing, huh?"

I hold my thumb and pointer finger about an inch apart, because I need something *more* too. More than an apartment where I'm ignored and a dance studio where I have no one at my level to push or challenge me.

"What about me?" he asks. "Am *I* still appealing since I'm rejecting all these things you want?"

My throat feels too thick, my thoughts too heavy to answer with words. They'd come out raw, or cheesy, or I'd crack halfway through. How could I *not* want him, want him *more* after everything he's shared? I spread my fingers slightly wider—going from "a tiny bit," to "a little bit," before lifting my other hand and spreading them wide like I'm a fisherman bragging about her catch.

Wyatt laughs and reaches for my raised hands. "So it's charades again? I like this one."

Instead of clasping or lacing his fingers through mine, he guides me toward him, placing my hands on both sides of his neck. I can feel his pulse racing beneath my thumbs.

His hands trace paths down my arms to my shoulders, one stopping there, one slipping beneath my hair so his fingers grace my jaw, his thumb dancing along my cheek. His right knee is grazing the inside of my left foot, and I shift up, so that instead of my knee being trapped between us, it's on the far side of his, pressed into the back of the couch. One tug by him, one move by me and I'll topple over. It feels inevitable that we'll end up there—his lips on mine, me on him. But first: This kiss we've been waiting for—

Or.

First, a scream.

And a set of footsteps running down the hallway. Wyatt and I jerk apart as a small body throws itself into the space between us, burrowing into my lap and pressing a damp face against my shirt.

My hands, still warm from Wyatt's skin, still buzzing with that *almost*, drop to Jack's back and begin to rub circles. "You okay, buddy?" I ask. "What's going on? Did you have a bad dream?"

"I don't like the hook-hand man," he whimpers, tugging the throw blanket from the back of the couch over his head. "I don't want him to find me."

"The what-hand who?" asks Wyatt, but I've got an idea of what Jack's talking about.

"I'll be right back, buddy. I'm going to have a word with your sister about telling scary stories." Wyatt and I exchange looks as I detangle Jack from my torso and pass him to the waiting arms of his brother.

With all the interruption-adrenaline in my veins, it's not hard to locate my Stern Babysitter Gameface as I confront the girls. They're totally pretending to be asleep and innocent when I walk in and are wishing they *had* been asleep and innocent by the time I walk back out after dropping the most powerful phrase in my babysitting arsenal: *"I need to really think about whether I'm going to tell your parents."*

There is zero chance we'll hear another peep from them tonight.

But the toddler-in-chief on the couch? He's a whole different wide-awake ballgame. "One book, then back to bed," I say.

Jack's no longer white-knuckled around Wyatt's neck. He's made himself a snuggle throne in his lap. He graciously lifts the end of his blanket and waves for me to join them before pointing to the book in my hand and saying, "Read."

When I close the back, he flips it over. "Again."

Wyatt gives me a sleepy smile and a shrug, and I'm not going to say I'm jealous of the way his hands are draped so cozily around Jack, but I totally am. Maybe he's feeling it too, because he shifts, anchoring Jack more firmly in the crook of his left arm, so that his right is free to stretch along the back of the couch before settling across my shoulders. His thumb finds a home in the hollow of my collarbone, his fingers dance tiny caresses along the seam where my sleeve meets my shirt. Between the blanket and his arm around me, I'm in a cocoon of drowsy heat. I want to tip my head back, rest my cheek against Wyatt's forearm, and just close my eyes for a minute.

"Read it again," Jack demands. I yawn, and then I do.

And again.

And . . .

"Noelle. Wyatt."

I scrunch my eyes tighter and bring my hands up to stretch, jabbing my elbow into something warm and solid. Something warm and solid that says, "Oooph."

My lids fly up and I'm blinking—processing my reality in snapshots. Mrs. Kahale standing across the coffee table, calling our names. Wyatt beside me, rubbing the spot on his cheek where I elbowed him.

"We fell asleep." And in case I haven't fully demonstrated my ability to state the obvious, I add, "We didn't mean to. Jack was here too. Where *is* Jack?"

Because right now Wyatt and I are sharing a blanket, and without the preschooler on his lap and the book that's slid off mine—it looks way different than it was.

"Nick's carrying him to bed," Mrs. Kahale says. "He looked so cute snuggled in with you two. I can't tell you how often we end up in this exact formation. Did he have a bad dream?"

I unearth my legs from beneath the blanket and stand. I'm glad she knows *this* was innocent—but there's still something discomfiting about being found on the couch with the boy I'd planned to kiss there earlier. "Yeah, sorta. I can't believe we fell asleep."

"To be fair," Wyatt begins, then pauses to yawn. "*Rico the Recycler* was way less riveting by the third time you read it."

Mrs. Kahale laughs. "Well, thank you."

"All's quiet in the kids' room," Mr. Kahale reports as he emerges from the hall. He grins at us. "Looks like they wore you two out."

"Yeah," I say sheepishly. "I'm now feeling horribly guilty for all the sleepovers I've put my friends' parents through."

They laugh and Mr. Kahale says, "Why don't we all get to bed? 'Cause Lord knows they'll be up early."

Wyatt's and my bedrooms connect. It would be easy to slip through the doors between—or meet in the bathroom to finish what we'd—almost—started. But we don't. We wait in the hallway as Mrs. and Mr. Kahale's footsteps retreat up the stairs and behind a door.

Wyatt arches his eyebrow and asks a single word. "Tomorrow?"

I think of us. I think of his plans for lunch with his parents. So many things will happen then.

I roll the letters around my tongue as I echo it back, changing the end punctuation. "Tomorrow."

It's not a question anymore; it's a promise.

Babysitting Tip 17:

Secrets are a trap!
Do you keep it? Do you tell their parents?
Ugh, it depends so much on context, but it almost
always ends with someone hurt.

I'm used to waking up slowly. If Dad's sleeping in or working, I don't interact with another person until after I've showered, eaten, and gotten to school.

Mornings with the Kahales are nothing like that. The Cooks came to collect G around seven, and somehow with one *less* person in the kitchen, the noise level *grows*. But among the coffee, juice, and cereal pouring (and spilling), the finding of gloves and Matchbox cars, the trading of schedules and checking of weather reports, there's enough space and distraction for Wyatt and me to whisper undetected.

"It's *tomorrow*," I say, a giddy smile playing at the corners of my mouth.

"I've got a timer counting down until ski lessons start," he replies.

"I'm not going skiing today!" Jack singsongs from the

kitchen floor, which he's turned into his latest construction zone-slash-tripping hazard.

"Yes, you are," replies Mr. Kahale without looking up from the toast he's buttering for Holly. "Ginger, this is the last slice of bread—should we get more, or make do for two days?"

"It's being delivered this afternoon." Mrs. Kahale steps over the "road" Jack made from coasters to refill her coffee.

"Juniper lobby after drop-off?" Wyatt whispers. His hand grazes mine under the table and I wonder if anyone would notice if we clasped them. The thought is so absurd that I'm holding back a giggle.

"I'm in the mood for a spa day," announces Mrs. Kahale. "Noelle, do you want to join me? Pedicures?"

"No. No way." The laughter I'd already been fighting leaks out—because I'm not sure which is more off-limits, *pedicures* or Wyatt touching his knee to mine.

But it's not until Mrs. Kahale turns to face me—until everyone does—that I realize I need to clarify. "Oh. Um, ballet dancers don't do pedicures. The polish rubs off and makes a mess inside your pointe shoes. And you know how they want to soften your feet and buff your calluses? I need those."

"Huh. Makes sense, but I never would've thought of that." Mrs. Kahale laughs. "Mani?"

I shake my head.

The spotlight moves off me as Jack drives a steamroller up the back of his sister's chair, despite—no, *because of*—Holly's repeated requests for him to stop. She responds by swatting it across the room and my "I appreciate the offer though" is lost beneath his howls.

"Jack, leave your sister alone," Mrs. Kahale says wearily. "Holly . . . Ditto."

"Wyatt, make sure you're ready to head over when we take Holls," Mr. Kahale says. "I want to have that binding of yours checked out and there'll be less of a line when repairs first open."

"Sure, Dad." But in a soft voice for my ears only, he adds, "And if they can't fix it right away, then I guess I'll just have to find something or someone to keep me company in the lodge all morning."

My cheeks flush and I lean close to whisper back—only to have a rogue dump truck catapult onto the table, knocking Holly's spoon out of her bowl.

"It's mine now," Mr. Kahale says firmly as he plucks up the toy and wipes splashed milk. "You almost hit Noelle. Say you're sorry, and then go get dressed."

It might be sort of exhilarating to be making stealthy make-out plans—but mostly it's exasperating. I swear, the Kahales couldn't be more efficient at blocking and interrupting us if they were doing it on purpose!

"Wyatt, will you come watch me today?" Holly asks. "I'm getting so fast at slalom."

Case in point.

"Sure." He's smiling at me, touching his leg to mine

under the table in some sort of Morse code of brushes and bouncing knee.

I don't need a decoder. I speak fluent Kahale boy—it means: *I'm excited and horrible at sitting still. And did I mention excited?* If he were Jack, I'd tell some jokes to make him settle. But since he's not four, and his foot tapping is making the whole table jitter, I put a quick hand on his knee.

"I think you must be missing Beacon, Wyatt," says Mr. Kahale with a chuckle. "You've got energy to burn today. Maybe *you* should do some gates. Once that binding's fixed, let's take the gondola up and hit those double blacks."

"Don't even think of going off-piste." Mrs. Kahale points a finger at her husband. "His mom would kill us. Everyone here is going home in one piece."

"You promise?" Holly demands of Wyatt. "We're only doing them the hour before lunch, so you have to come then."

"Sure," he answers distractedly, but his knee's not bouncing anymore. I don't know if it's the mention of Beacon or his mom, but he's stiffened. "Speaking of lunch—Dad, Ginger, any chance you could meet me?"

"Yeah!" Mr. Kahale's eyes dart to his wife as his eyebrows shoot up. "Of course. That'd be great. Did you have something you want to talk to us about?"

Mrs. Kahale catches Wyatt's deer-in-headlights expression and gives her husband a significant look, pressing one palm toward the floor—the parent signal for "take it down a notch."

Mr. Kahale clears his throat. "I mean, we'll talk then. Go ahead and set it up. Wherever you want to eat."

"Okay, sure," Wyatt says softly.

Before I can give his knee another bump—this time not for thrills or warning but for encouragement, Mrs. Kahale points to the microwave clock: "Those of us not taking the shuttle over need to head out."

Wyatt's standing, out of reach and whisper range. He slides his phone from his pocket and taps out a message. I doubt anyone notices the coincidental timing of my cell vibrating, but just in case I wait until their chaotic foursome is headed out the door to read his text.

See you soon.

Wyatt's not there yet when I get to Juniper. I sink onto a lobby couch and pull up videos of last year's YAGP competition. I'm watching Alvie's winning variation—still reeling that she's Wyatt's friend and could be *my* classmate if I don't mess up at auditions—when a shadow blocks the screen.

"Noelle! Thanks again for including G last night. She had a blast." Rae Ann has a white jacket draped over her arm, but based on her pants, shoes, and purse, she's not headed to the slopes.

"You're welcome," I say. "I'm glad she had fun. Holly did too."

"What are you watching?" She glances at my phone. "Dance. Of course you're a dancer too. You and Wyatt. Do you go to Beacon?"

"Not yet, but I'm auditioning." I point to the screen with crossed fingers. "I'm trying to figure out what they'll expect, and trying not to panic about how little practice I've gotten this week."

"Do you need somewhere quiet?" She pulls a hotel key out of her purse. "Here. We have a big suite—406. No one's in it and there's plenty of room. Shove the coffee table to the side and have at it."

"That'd be—amazing." I haven't heard from Wyatt. Either he's still waiting at ski repair or his dad's dragged him off to double diamonds. In which case maybe they'll talk things out *now*, and lunch can be celebratory. "Wyatt said you were a dancer too."

Rae Ann smiles and moves into first position. "Dance was my world when I was your age."

"Why'd you stop?" This question has been on loop in my mind lately. How does someone—Rae Ann, Wyatt, me—go from ballet being their life to figuring out who they are without it?

She lowers her arms and adjusts her purse on her shoulder. "In high school I made the cheerleading squad. I didn't have time for both."

"Do you ever regret it?"

She pauses to consider, then shakes her head. "No. I

don't. I made great friends on that squad, it connected me to my school and was important to me. Dance was important to me too—in a different time in my life. I enjoyed it, then moved on. No regrets or sad feelings." She laughs. "Well, one sad feeling: Gabriella hates ballet! No mother-daughter *Nutcracker* pictures for us. But maybe she'll change her mind someday. Or maybe I'll take an adult dance class and force her to come to *my* recitals."

I nod like I get it, but I don't. "What do you do now?"

"I'm an exec at a pharmaceuticals company," she says, her shoulders back, her chin high with pride. My surprise must not be subtle, because she laughs. "I didn't *just* dance and cheer—I was an honor roll junkie, in all AP classes."

I think guiltily of the schedule I'd chosen for its low-homework potential and how appealing Wyatt's description of "bare minimum" school had sounded. "I don't think I have it in me to be both a scholar and a dancer."

"Noelle, you can be anything . . . But you can also be *lots* of things. And I hope that all young girls know that. I hate the idea of people being boxed in so early, being told they have to pick a path and not deviate. Gabriella already has friends with private sports coaches—at eight! It's why I have so much respect for people like Ginger and Nick—they're letting Holly do the ski team, but they've also got her in dance and art and piano too. Kids need to be exposed to lots of ideas and options."

I nod slowly, knowing I'll be thinking of her words long after this trip.

Rae Ann glances at her phone—making me jealous that hers has buzzed when mine hasn't. "Speaking of Ginger, she's waiting for me at the spa. I'll see you later!"

"Thanks." I hold up the room card. "Four-oh-six?"

"Yes, and sure! Just leave the key in the room when you leave."

In her suite, I do exactly what she suggests—push the furniture to the sides and then dance like the doubts in my mind are chasing me. Like they'll latch on if I pause for a moment. Wyatt wants *more*. Rae Ann's *lots of things* advice is the opposite of Beacon. And maybe the reason I told *her* I'm auditioning—when I haven't told Miss Janet or my dad—is because I'm terrified of their reaction. I'm not sure if I want Dad to forbid or support it, Miss Janet to tell me I'm ready or judge me for leaving. Do I want confirmation I should *go* or a reason to *stay*?

When my phone buzzes with Finally! I'm in the lobby. Where are you? I'm panting and dizzy from too many à la seconde turns. I'm ready for something else to make my head spin. And if that something can be *Wyatt*, well, that's practically perfection.

"Hey!" I say, dropping my coat on the table in front of him. He's already standing to hug me, already coatless and I sink into the softness of his sweatshirt and the firmness of his grip.

"I spent that whole time at repairs trying not to panic about lunch and wanting to be here with you." He pulls me tighter before letting go and nodding at the poinsettia tree. "Do you know the first time I wanted to kiss you was in this lobby?"

"Because of my fancy skills at charades?"

He laughs. "No, before that. You were spinning around admiring the decorations, then throwing a fit about missing the tree lighting." My eyes go wide, but he keeps talking, smiling at the memory, oblivious to the fact that he's blown my mind by changing up the time line. "I haven't forgotten about the lighting, by the way. Let's come back here tonight and watch it."

I nod and manage, "Okay."

"Were you practicing?" Wyatt traces a finger through the dampness at my hairline. Maybe I should feel self-conscious about sweating, but I don't. I've spent too much of my life as a bunhead to see sweat as anything but a sign of hard work. Whether or not Wyatt's staying at Beacon, he'd get that. He has to have the same mentality and work ethic to have gotten in and excelled there for so long.

Dance is our common language, our common culture—a shortcut to a place where I'm not insecure about my turned-out penguin walk and can be proud of my gross pedicureless feet, because we both know the work that went into building each one of those calluses and the skills they represent.

"Yeah, a little practice." I don't tell him about the doubts that are starting to creep in—at least not the complicated ones. He's got enough on his plate with his upcoming lunch conversation. It feels safe to share the basics though—the fear every dancer knows. "I hate auditions. I hope I'm good enough."

"Noelle." He shakes his head and chuckles. "You're good enough."

"That's nice, but . . ." I shrug and do a châiné turn around him. "You can't know that."

He closes the gap between us with a glissade. "I've seen you dance."

In my mind I see a million pas de deux we'll never get to have. I'm so distracted by this thought that it takes me a minute to process what he said. "What are you talking about?"

"I was at Holly and Jack's spring recital last year." He reaches for my hand. "You danced the Queen of Dryads variation from *Don Quixote* and blew me away. At the time, I didn't know you were their babysitter. I didn't make the connection until after Ginger mentioned your Beacon audition. I've seen you dance—you're incredible."

I'm speechless, but maybe I don't need words right now. I bourrée closer and tilt my head up.

It's going to happen this time! I can feel it. It's in the way he's looking at my mouth. In the way his fingers tighten around mine. In how his other hand reaches out to touch my face. It's in the air, in the decreasing space between our lips as he moves closer. Until I'm shutting my eyes, practically vibrating from anticipation.

No. Wait.

I'm actually vibrating. Or at least my butt is. Because that's where my phone is ringing. When I startle at the sensation, Wyatt freezes, giving me space, but by the time I get it out of my pocket, I've missed the call.

I'm about to call Mrs. Kahale back when Wyatt's phone rings. He rolls his eyes and squeezes my hand as he answers. "Hey, Dad."

But his fingers quickly slide off mine as he raises them to block his other ear. His grip on the phone tightens and he steps away from me. "Dad, slow down. I can't understand you. What happened to—"

"Noelle!"

I pivot from Wyatt to where Mrs. Kahale is shuffling across the lobby at a pace that defies the foam flip-flops on her feet. She's got her boots in one hand and her phone in the other. Rae Ann is beside her, carrying their coats and purses.

"Hey, it's the lovebirds!" Lois is passing our table, ski-geared to the hilt and oblivious. "You two back for more board games—or for another crack at that mistletoe? Oh, is Romeo on the phone? Well, I'll leave you to it!" She winks, and waves, and keeps walking, but Mrs. Kahale's eyes are even wider as she approaches. There's zero chance she missed those comments or their implications, but less than zero chance it's important right now.

"What's wrong?" I ask.

She pauses to shove her wet toes in her boots. "We have to go."

"Is that Ginger?" Mr. Kahale's voice booms out of Wyatt's phone. "Where the heck are you?"

"Holly fell. She hit her head," Mrs. Kahale finishes as Wyatt says, "Holly's asking for *me*?" He curses and everything about him crumples, his face, his posture, as he whispers, "*I promised.*"

Okay. Crisis. I can do this. I have a babysitting certificate that tells me so. I shove on my coat and take Mrs. Kahale's, grabbing her purse from Rae Ann, who's hugging her and saying, "I'm sure she's fine. She's a tough, strong girl. You'll call me later. I'm praying."

Since Wyatt's frozen, I tug his phone from his hand. "Mr. Kahale, it's Noelle. I have everyone with me. Where should we go?"

"I'm with Ski Patrol. We're bringing her to the medical station. It's on the far side of Thistle Lodge."

Right. I'd seen it during the great bathroom hunt. "I know where that is. We'll be there in three minutes." I tilt my head toward the door and start walking, Wyatt puts his arm around his stepmom as they follow. "Do you need anything else?"

"Have Ginger call—" Mr. Kahale is interrupted by someone asking him a question and the line goes dead. But we're already outside, already halfway down the path, nearly in a run, despite Mrs. Kahale's unlaced boots and Wyatt's coat being in his arms, not on them.

We beat the snow patrol to the medical center. The dispatcher at the desk shares that a girl took a spill on the slalom course and hit her head on the ground. "She was slow to get up and crying but never lost consciousness—that's all I know."

I reassure them that this is a good sign—repeating Rae Ann's words about how strong and brave Holly is. But I'm not sure they hear me.

Mrs. Kahale's eyes well up when the door at the far end of the room opens and two people in red jackets carry Holly in. Her dad follows right behind, holding her empty helmet in his hands. She's strapped to a backboard and looks impossibly small beneath the red bindings, her feet nowhere near the end of the orange board, her head and neck encased in yellow foam.

None of which stops her from trying to crane them to see us. "Mom, I got to ride down on the rescue toboggan."

"Stay still, sweetie." Mrs. Kahale grips Holly's hand as soon as they set the backboard on a cot. The Ski Patrol are giving a report to the paramedics in the room and Mr. Kahale is listening in. Wyatt's sitting in a chair by the wall with his head in his hands.

I catch snatches of their conversation—*Head injury protocol. Err on the side of caution. Airways, Breathing, Circulation. Alert and attentive. Initially crying and complaining of pain, but—Recommend. Ambulance. Follow-up.*

One of the Ski Patrol members steps over to where Holly can see her. She lifts her goggles and says, "I hope you feel better soon."

"I'm feeling better already," chirps Holly. "Do you think they'll unstrap me soon? My nose itches."

Everyone laughs—everyone but Wyatt. I take the seat beside him as Mrs. Kahale does her best to zero in on Holly's itchy spot. "She's going to be okay," I tell him.

I'm not lying. By the time my phone buzzes twenty minutes later with a reminder to collect Jack, Holly is sitting up. Drinking Gatorade. She's recited the alphabet and as many states as she can remember—"We haven't learned them all yet, but I can tell you all of Jack's *Paw Patrol* characters or name a bunch of Pokémon."

The paramedics have backed off the idea of calling an ambulance but are still encouraging the Kahales to check in with Holly's pediatrician or a local doctor. Knowing the Kahales, they'll do both. As I stand to slip out the door, Holly's angling to go back to practice while her parents are being given a list of warning signs to watch for. "If she experiences *any* of these, head straight to the emergency room."

"I've got to go. Can you text me and let me know if I should bring Jack here or back to the cabin?" I ask Wyatt, pairing the question with a quick hand squeeze. Or, it was supposed to be quick, but he grasps on like I'm a lifeline and my heart twists. He should be headed to lunch with his parents, telling them he wants to move in.

"It'll be okay," I tell him.

"What are you two whispering about?" asks Holly. "You're *always* whispering."

The room quiets and I'm so aware of my hand still in Wyatt's, that this is the first time Holly's addressed either of us, even though she's been cracking up the paramedics and easing some of the worry off her parents' faces with her antics.

"I—I was saying I'm going to get Jack." As casually as I can, I disentangle my hand from her brother's and shove it in my pocket. "And asking Wyatt to find out if I should bring him here or back to the cabin."

"Thanks, Noelle. Why don't you go ahead and take the shuttle," says Mr. Kahale. "I'm not sure how long we'll be or if we're coming directly home."

"There's no need to say anything that'll worry Jack," adds Mrs. Kahale. "Wyatt, if you want to go with—"

"Why doesn't he stay," interrupts his dad. His eyes are narrowed on the space between us, questions written on the creases of his forehead. "We might need his help."

Wyatt nods, Holly says something snarky, and I leave—because my role here is babysitter. The only assistance I can offer right now is removing Jack from the list of things they need to worry about.

But based on Mr. Kahale's probing look and Lois's mistletoe comment that Mrs. Kahale overheard, I'm worried Wyatt and I might be on that list too.

At the very least, there's a feeling of concern? Curiosity? I can't identify their emotions when they return to the cabin, but I'm so *aware* that they're watching Wyatt and me as they get Holly situated. Their eyes follow us over balcony railings and peek back around corners. Obviously, he and I need to talk—but how? When? I don't know what went down after I left. I can't tell what he's thinking or feeling behind the placid stage-expression he's wearing. It makes the two of us as awkward as we were the first day we met, only instead of ignoring each other while decorating a gingerbread house, we're now avoiding each other in this one—him leaving the kitchen when I go get a can of seltzer. Me faking total engrossment in Jack's story when Wyatt comes into the living room to get his sweatshirt from the couch behind us.

The Kahales' scrutiny kicks up another notch once Holly's settled in their room for a nap—they decided she'll sleep there tonight too so they can keep an eye on her before a follow-up doctor's appointment in the morning. Mr. Kahale's voice is firm when he says, "Wyatt will bunk in with Jack tonight so he's not scared."

His younger son—who's sitting in my lap reading a book—claps at the announcement, almost whacking me in the nose, but Wyatt just nods.

"You hungry, Jackaroo?" Mrs. Kahale hands him a bowl of apple slices, then puts on a movie for him. Once it's playing, she says, "Noelle, will you join Nick, Wyatt, and me in the kitchen? We need to talk."

I reluctantly ease Jack off my knee—it's probably not fair to use him as a shield—and follow her and Mr. Kahale to the table. Wyatt's still standing. Taking painfully long to fill a glass of water.

"What do you want to talk about?" I keep my voice low, even though Jack's fully enmeshed in the movie about scheming babies. "Is it Holly?"

"No." Mrs. Kahale rubs her forehead. "The consensus is she was more scared than hurt. That's why she was crying after her fall."

"Being overtired from her sleepover probably didn't help," says Mr. Kahale, "but she was also upset Wyatt wasn't there. Ski Patrol told me she kept insisting he must be with the other people watching and that they find him."

Wyatt dumps the glass he'd just filled down the sink and slumps against the counter. "I forgot I'd promised I'd come see her do gates."

"You forgot," Mr. Kahale repeats, before he turns to point at me, "because you were with Noelle."

Mrs. Kahale cuts in, "Holly's fall is not your fault, Wyatt. Your dad's not saying that."

"No, of course not," Mr. Kahale says. "It's not anyone's fault. Skiers fall. And she seems fine. You heard the paramedics; tomorrow we'll take her in and she'll likely get the all-clear to go back to practice."

Wyatt nods in acknowledgment of their words, but it's clear he doesn't believe them.

"Noelle." Mrs. Kahale turns toward me. "When Wyatt first arrived, we asked you to tell us if you found out something was going on with him—" Wyatt's eyes fly to me, wide and betrayed, but when I try and catch his gaze, he looks away. "And all week we've asked you for updates. Even yesterday when I brought up that he was smiling more and seemed happier, you claimed to have no idea why. I think maybe you *do* know."

I stammer, "I—um, I—"

She gives me a gentle, probing look. "I think maybe *you're* the why."

My cheeks burn. At least he knows I haven't told them about Beacon? Though I'm not sure this conclusion is any better.

"I feel like a fool," Mr. Kahale says. "When Rae Ann and Kevin told us they suspected something between you two, I told them they'd been watching too many rom-coms. 'I *know* my son,' I said. 'He'd tell me. He wouldn't sneak around behind my back.'"

"And I would've thought the same of you, Noelle." I feel Mrs. Kahale's sigh like a gut punch. "Has this been going on since the beginning? Since back when we were worried Wyatt wasn't being welcoming or was getting in your way?"

"No! Not at all. He's—I'm—" I look to Wyatt for backup, but he's just . . . defeated. Staring down at his feet and seeing his future in their turnout. Or pissed? All I know is he isn't talking and won't look at me. "This has nothing to do with my babysitting. Not Jack's accident or the hot tub lid, or—"

Mrs. Kahale's eyes go wide and she touches the hands I'm knotting on the tabletop. "No, of course not! No one is saying that." She nudges her husband. "Right?"

But Mr. Kahale's not listening. He's shaking his head at his son. "Wyatt, I don't know what's going on with you lately, bud. I thought you were here to spend time with your family—but you've barely skied with me. You've barely *talked* to me all week. Your mom says you've been being defiant, and I don't know, I don't see that, but *something* is up. It feels like you're keeping so many secrets." He scrubs his hands down his face and looks so much like his elder son as they wear matching slumps to their shoulders. "I miss the days when you'd talk to me. I was so excited for our lunch today."

Wyatt is barely audible when he says, "Me too."

And there's nothing angry about his dad's words, but they're hardly an invitation. How can Wyatt open up *now*, when they're not starting in a place of neutrality? When everyone's already at DEFCON levels of emotional drain.

Mr. Kahale chuckles into a sigh. "I like to think I'm a pretty in-touch dad, but I've got to admit, I did *not* see you two happening."

I struggle to find words to clarify. *Nothing's happened* feels false, but *We haven't even kissed,* isn't right either. It implies we *want* to and confirms their suspicions. My hand strays to my bracelet. No matter what it says, I'm just their babysitter—a replaceable employee. The stakes are so much higher for him. I stand to lose a job—Wyatt stands to lose his parents' trust and the place he wants in their home.

I open and close my mouth a few times before managing, "It's not like that."

"I want something to be crystal clear." Mrs. Kahale pauses until our attention is secure. "My problem is *not* with the fact that you two are or aren't dating or whatever they call it these days. I love you both. No part of what we're objecting to is the idea of you together." She takes a deep breath. "It's the secrecy that bothers us. I wish you'd just been open and honest with us; this was not the best way to find out."

"Agreed," says Mr. Kahale. "That, and time. I wish you'd managed yours a little better, Wyatt, because when you're back at Beacon, this isn't how I want your siblings remembering their big brother, as a person who doesn't show up for them." The unintentional cruelty in Mr. Kahale's words makes me flinch. "Holly already suspects something—I mean, let's be real, her default mood is suspicious—but she's hurt and jealous that you blew her off today."

"I get it," says Wyatt thickly. "I totally get it. And I'm sorry." He throws his hands up and lets them slap down on his thighs before leaving the room.

Any of us could go after him—and maybe I should, but I don't want to make things worse. So I offer, "I'm sorry too," and join Jack on the couch. I let them debate it, let them decide to "Give Wyatt space," and I keep my opinion to myself—*any more space and you'll lose him forever.*

It takes until halfway through dinner for Holly to forget she's mad at Wyatt and stop giving him attitude. Then her focus switches to coaxing everyone ten and up out of our sullen moods. When she realizes her efforts are failing and sighs, Mrs. Kahale goes red alert. "Are you okay? Is your head hurting? Nick, where's the paper with the warning signs?"

"I'm fine, Mom." Holly sulks. "Everyone's just so grumpy."

"Noelle didn't even laugh at *Boss Baby*," Jack accuses, and we force chuckles.

"It's called 'sleepover fallout,'" Mr. Kahale says with a thin smile. "Everyone will get to bed early tonight and things will look better tomorrow. Right, Wyatt? Noelle?"

"Right," we chorus obediently, but we do it without looking at each other, and Holly's expression remains unconvinced.

Which seems fair. I'm unconvinced too.

I want my mom. I want her hugs and her advice . . . but I don't even know what she'd say. I was Holly's age when she died; I hadn't thought to ask ahead for her pointers on heartache. There are so many things I never got the chance to ask about. So many things I'll have to figure out on my own. My memories of Mom are getting fuzzy around the corners, and I can't tell what's true and what I'm filling in—borrowing from photographs and Dad's stories to try to keep them vivid. Sometimes it feels like pain is the last true thing I have to hold on to. Pain and snow globes.

Also, a finely tuned sense of self-preservation, so I don't just look away when Mrs. Kahale leans over to kiss Holly's forehead, I excuse myself from the table.

I call Dad and get his voice mail. "Just wanted to say hi. You don't have to call me back." But my voice is wobbly, and I hope he will.

As Jack's getting ready for bed and Wyatt's packing things to bring with him when he bunks down the hall, it occurs to me that the changed sleeping assignments were likely more about our adjoining rooms than they were about Jack's potential fears. The lack of trust feels like a stab in the gut; we haven't done anything to warrant it.

But while our rooms still connect, I'm making use of that—knocking, but not pausing—as I ease into his.

He looks up from unplugging his phone charger. "What do you want? Here to spy on me again?"

"I didn't," I protest. "They asked me to, but I didn't say a word."

"No. You just pressured *me* to tell them. I thought you were trying to support me—but you were just trying to help them. God forbid you're not the perfect babysitter."

"That's not true!" I object . . . but isn't it? At least partially? I had hated being in the middle, in the impossible situation of failing them all. "Besides, you do need to tell them about school and moving in. You've *got to*, Wyatt. You're running out of time, and can't you see that it's making everything worse?"

He scoffs, and I almost can't recognize the face of the boy who'd been an inch from kissing me in the sneer he's currently wearing. "Do you even listen to yourself? You're such a hypocrite. You're all over me to talk, but you still haven't clued your dad in about Beacon. When are *you* going to say something? Once you're packed and need a ride? Or will you just leave and see if he notices? Wake up! Your big plan to run away to Beacon isn't going to fix things."

I take a step back, banging my elbow against the doorframe, but the pain is dull by comparison. Wyatt's not wrong, but he didn't have to be so accurate in targeting my biggest fear: that just like Dad hadn't cared about me going away for Christmas, he might be indifferent when I tell him I'm leaving for good.

I force my chin up as I lie to him. "You don't know what you're talking about."

"Don't I?" he challenges, his voice raw. "I may not have been 'spying,' but I've been paying attention. Even if your dad's on some sort of selfish parenting hiatus, I've heard you with your friends and seen you with my dad and Ginger, Jack and Holly—you have a family. Beacon's nothing like that. It's lonely. And you'll get in, Noelle, but I don't want you to."

Everything he's saying makes me wince and hug myself a little tighter. It's too much to process at once, but his last words resonate cruelly in the air between us. My voice is tiny when I ask, "Why are you so mad at me?"

"I'm not mad at you." But he says it through gritted teeth.

"I'm mad at *me* for not realizing that while I've been trying so hard this week to be the type of person they'd want around, you all have been teaming up against me like I'm a problem to solve. Meanwhile, you've got your own problems—so maybe focus on those."

I straighten my spine. "I *wish* my problems were as easy as yours. There's zero chance your dad isn't thrilled to have you move in. It's not my fault that they're ready to listen, but you're not ready to ask for what you want."

He shakes his head. "Maybe that was true at the beginning of the week, maybe they would've wanted me then—but that was before *you*. Did you not see his face out there? They don't trust me at all. Not anymore. They can't wait to send me back to school." I follow his gaze to a scuffed Beacon sticker on the suitcase in the corner. "And, hey, at least I'd been planning to tell them. I'd made lunch reservations. What have you done?"

My lack of answer fills the silence between us before he sighs and continues. "Looking at you is the worst kind of reminder, because I thought you were on *my* side, but I was just a distraction so you don't have to face your own life. I need you to leave me alone."

I have lots of experience with that request. Maybe he can make a sign like Dad's office door: DON'T APPROACH UNLESS YOU'RE BLEEDING OR THE CABIN'S ON FIRE. Luckily heartbreak is a bloodless injury. Pretty soon we'll be gone from Vermont and he can have hundreds of miles of distance. Except, what about Beacon? If I go, if he doesn't talk to his dad and he's still there, will I be a reminder of Juncture and what could've been? Will he ignore me and make me feel as invisible at Beacon as I do at home? I raise both of my hands as I step into the bathroom. "Look at that—progress. You asked for something, and I'm going to give it to you: this is me leaving you alone."

He throws a "Noelle, I'm sorry" at my retreating back, but I shut the door on his apology—on anything that could make this night worse.

Babysitting Tip 18:
Just because someone is little doesn't mean
their problems feel small to them.
Listen.

"I'm not going skiing today," Jack announces between
bites of Cheerios.

It feels like déjà vu of every other morning, only it's
not. Everything's different. I was up most of the night, waiting for my dad to not call me back, wondering how much of
what Wyatt said about me was true. *Hypocrite. You have a
family. Face your own life. Say something* . . .

I found honesty as the sun started to rise: *all of it.*

Wyatt had said Beacon was me running away, and he
wasn't wrong, but he'd missed something that was so obvious
in hindsight. This week, this trip, was running away too. And
it hadn't fixed anything. Hadn't changed Dad. Hadn't made
him miss me more or brought us closer.

So why would Beacon? I thought I needed to talk to
Dad about going there . . . but I'm not sure I want to anymore. Beacon's not the only path to a professional career;
it's just the one that allowed me to escape my problems. I

keep saying I miss our team, but a team only functions if the players work together. Dad might be sitting out this round, but I've been hiding in the locker room, making plans to quit.

My stomach twists and clenches with way-too-late empathy for Wyatt. I get his reluctance now in a way I didn't before. It's going to be uncomfortable and awkward and potentially awful, but, I still need to initiate this conversation. Wyatt was right. He'd at least made a lunch reservation; all I'd done was hint and wait for Dad to approach me. And he didn't.

So I will. Even if that means spending Jack's whole lesson hitting redial until Dad answers.

I want to tell Wyatt about it—apologize. But even though I can't stop looking at him, he *won't* look at me. I half wonder if he's blatantly ignoring me to win brownie points with his dad.

"I'm really not going," says Jack.

No one stops eating, no one looks shocked. Probably because he's said the same thing every morning. Or possibly they're preoccupied with Holly's doctor's appointment. If I had to make a judgment based on the enormous breakfast she'd inhaled or the flip over the back of the couch she'd done afterward, I'd guess Holly's feeling just fine. At least I hope so. Some kids aren't meant to be sidelined or sedentary. The possibility of Holly being told she can't get back out there breaks my heart a little.

"I mean it," Jack says. "I really do."

And even though we've successfully coaxed, cajoled, or bribed him into his boots every other day, this time Mrs. Kahale pinches the bridge of her nose and says, "You know what, pal? I cannot fight another battle right now. If you don't want to ski, don't. You and Noelle can stay here."

Which means I don't get a break. Which means this phone call with my dad is going to have an audience. I don't care; I'm not delaying. I'll be home tomorrow and I don't want my problems to be waiting when I arrive. I don't want to give myself a chance to chicken out.

"No skiing!" Jack hops down from his seat and begins his victory lap with a somersault.

When Holly stands, her mom fixes her with a gaze. "Don't even think about it. In fact, go get your shoes."

Holly pouts. "Just so you know, I'm bringing my ski stuff. That way when they say I'm cleared, we can go right to practice."

Mrs. Kahale holds up her crossed fingers.

"You ready, Wyatt?" Mr. Kahale asks. "You're skiing with me today. All day. We'll get them to drop us at the mountain."

"Oh." Wyatt glances my way so quickly I almost think I imagined it. His face is blank as he nods. "Yeah, let's go."

I stand in the kitchen and hope that *both* exiting Kahale kids get the answers they want in the conversations they're about to have.

As soon as the door shuts behind them, Jack tugs on my hand. "Let's make a fort!"

I get it. I want to hide away right now too. We strip the cushions from the couch and use them to prop blankets we drape over the dining room table, but I can't keep playing pretend. If Wyatt goes back to Beacon or his mom's house because he's too cowardly to say anything to his father, that's his choice. I'm making a different one.

I shimmy out of the fort, leaving Jack "reading" books to his stuffed monkey. Beacon's a great school, but maybe it's another hiding place. I can wrap it in excuses about skills I'd learn there, but it's also a fancy, expensive way to avoid facing my problems. And if I go now, I won't be ready, I won't get everything I could out of the experience—because everything unsaid and unfixed at home will be weighing on each pirouette.

Speaking of avoiding things, Miss Janet's voice mail still waits on my phone. So before I call Dad, I play it. I figure it can be a facing-my-problems warm-up (or a delay tactic). But, after listening to her message, I realize that maybe my choices aren't as black and white as I thought. It's not just stagnate or Beacon, stay or grow. She offers me an opportunity I'd never considered, one that makes me pause—and smile.

Which doesn't mean my fingers are any less trembly as I hit the button to call Dad. It just gives me yet another thing to think about.

"Hey kiddo." Dad answers sounding groggy and distracted—so, pretty much his usual. "I thought you weren't free until nine? I was going to call you back then."

Oh. I didn't expect him to have noticed or remembered that. "Jack's not going to lessons today."

"Ah. Got it. Sorry I missed your call. I've been pulling all-nighters to finish and crashed early. I didn't even hear it ring. You okay? You sounded sad."

I didn't expect him to notice that either, and it throws me. "I'm ready to come home."

"You and me both, kiddo." Dad had been doing *something* in the background. Dishes, maybe? Tinkering with a prototype or circuitry? Whatever it was, the clinking and clanking stops. "It's too quiet around here."

"Yeah, like you even noticed. You've been busy working 'all-nighters.'" I'm not pulling any punches or wasting any time, because who knows how long I'll have his attention for—or how long until Jack demands mine.

"I was," he admits, defensively. "But it's done now. The app is finished. It actually—it launched yesterday. It's doing really well so far. *Really* well. I can send you the link—"

It launched? You finished? I swallow down my questions and excitement for him, because I can't get sidetracked. "Meanwhile you had time for Autumn."

"She tested it for me!" he says. "Noelle, *you* suggested it. You said, 'Maybe you need to take organization lessons from Autumn.' And I did. This app combines to-do lists, goal-setting, and schedules. You set it with whatever you want to achieve, and it reverse engineers the steps you need to get there. Mini-goals and benchmarks, accountability dates. It's called *GoalBusters*—like ghosts, but . . . goals."

"I could've helped." I mean, fine, I did say that and this is so Autumn, but I have goals too. I could've shared them with him if he'd asked or picked up on any of my blatant hints. Hello, can it get more obvious than brochures on the toilet or under your pillow?

"I needed it to launch before January first. Resolutions and all that. You've been so busy with dance and babysitting and you *hate* all things New Year's. I didn't think you'd want to work on it. But conveniently you had this trip."

"*Conveniently?*" I shake my fists at an empty room, no one here to commiserate or catch my exasperation.

"Yeah." He says it like this is obvious. Like I haven't felt banished. "I mean, I would've preferred if you'd given me some notice and not sprung it on me at your show, but it all worked out."

Oh, he did *not* just chuckle. "When, Dad? Because you've been so available lately. When was I supposed to ask? On the days I went without seeing you? When you could barely make it to my *Nutcracker* performance?"

"I was there." He's upset, but so am I.

"I know!" I'm trying—and failing—not to raise my voice. "And it shocked the heck out of me."

"Noelle."

"No. You don't get to *Noelle* me. I've barely seen you all fall—"

"You're busy too." He sounds hurt and a selfish part of me thinks, *Good!* "And you're the one who told me to butt out of your schedule. That you're in high school and don't need me."

"I'm fourteen! Of course I said that. Of course I need you." This feels like something Mom would've understood, but Dad scoffs defensively and I push on. "We haven't done anything on my Extravaganza list. You didn't even take out Mom's snow globes. We don't have a tree!"

"We do! I got one. I don't understand what's bothering you, we agreed to do Christmas later." He sounds accusatory when he adds, "This ski trip was *your* idea."

"You were supposed to care!" I shout, then glance at Jack's fort and lower my voice. "You were supposed to say 'no.' "

My heart hammers in the silence that follows. It's out there. I said it, and now I can't take it back. And it feels . . . terrifying and satisfying, so I say it again, "You were supposed to say '*no.*' "

"How was I supposed to guess that?" Dad asks. "You always say how much you love the Kahales. I thought you wanted to go."

"I don't always *know* what I want." Not about Beacon, or dance, or from him. Except attention. That's clear. I want to feel seen and valued by him, but I'm fighting against old habits and my impulse to end the call because it's hard and it hurts. "I don't know what I'm doing half the time, except I'm always messing things up."

"Hey." Dad's voice has gone gentle, and for the first time in this conversation, it feels like he's hearing me. "You know the Team Partridge rule—in our house we don't fear failure, we fear not trying. You may end up with bruises and blisters, and I've got a heck of a dud pile, but you stuck with it and nailed your tour jeté and I've got an app that's in the top ten right now. Whatever you're messing up, you'll figure it out."

"Top ten?" I say, momentarily derailed. "That's awesome, Dad."

"Thanks. And, kiddo? I don't know what I'm doing either. I've never been a dad to a high schooler before—frankly, it terrifies me. I wish your mom were here to help, because I have no idea how to figure out if I'm being a helicopter parent or giving you too much freedom. You said to butt out, and that you wanted to go on this ski trip—I thought I was doing the right thing by respecting your voice and autonomy. I've been hoping this app would help me keep track of you from afar.

"But then I got an earful from Autumn. She said you're unhappy and, 'Don't ever listen to your kid when she tells you to back off.' I thought she was exaggerating, or you were mad I wouldn't tell you about your Christmas present surprise, but then I woke up to your voice mail." He pauses to take a deep breath, but my head is spinning too fast for me to jump in. Autumn did a dad-tervention? That explains the Just checking on you text she'd sent this morning.

"But I *want* to listen to you when you tell me what you want," he continues. "That's how teams work. So, how do we do this?"

"I—I guess we start with me being honest with you?" The words are a squeak. "I never wanted you to abandon me. I was just mad."

"Abandon you?" Dad sucks in a breath. "Is that how you felt?"

I squeeze my hand tight around a die-cast dump truck and force the words out. "I know we're not the family we were before, but now we're barely even a family. I already lost Mom, I feel like I'm losing you too." Which is maybe why I wanted to leave—so I didn't get left behind. I choke on the thought, which feels too true to swallow back down, then force out the rest between sniffles. "We're supposed to be a team. You said we were a team, but now . . . we're not. We're just, *not*."

"I-I don't even know what to say." Dad sounds stunned and there's a long, sighing silence. So long that I check we weren't disconnected. "I'll start with 'I'm sorry,' because I had no idea you felt like that. I'm really sorry, Noelle. You are the most important thing to me, and it guts me you didn't feel that."

It's possible he's sniffling too, which makes my eyes well more, so that I'm hunting for where Mrs. Kahale keeps tissues. "When you get home, let's talk about this. A lot. Because this is something we're fixing, kiddo."

"Oh." I'm feeling small and also wrong, because Wyatt was right to call me a hypocrite. I'd been all over him about how easy his conversation would be—how much his parents would care and listen. But none of this is easy, even *if* they care and listen. And even as I say "Okay," I know it's not a quick fix.

"Do you have time now, Noelle? We can talk—we don't have to wait."

"Actually, I don't." Jack's probably only ten seconds away from needing a snack or a playmate. I'm only seven away from bawling.

"Tomorrow, then," he says. "And I really am sorry, kiddo. It's killing me that you felt this way and I didn't know."

"I guess it isn't all on you," I concede. "I could've said something sooner."

"I'm glad you did now. Love you, Noelle," says Dad. "More than anything."

I get off the phone feeling relieved but still a little sad. I don't want to think of Dad as flawed but trying. It's easier when I cast him as hapless or villainous. It's harder to handle gray areas. And if he's going to try—really, truly try—then I need to too.

"You were talking to your dad?" Jack knocks over two couch cushions and emerges, wearing a face too serious for a four-year-old. "It made you sad?"

I snuggle him to my side, grateful for the warm weight of his hug. "Sometimes we have to say hard things—not to hurt people's feelings but because ours hurt. I told my dad it made me sad not to see him on Christmas."

He frowns. "Like—like, telling Momma I don't like my snowsuit?"

I almost laugh, but instinct tells me not to. This isn't a kid who has problems rejecting five shirts or trying on three pairs of pajamas. I crouch down to his level. "What don't you like about it?"

"I can't get up when I fall in the snow," he says. "And I can't do the zipper. It's tricky. I have accidents."

"That's tough." I keep my face sympathetic, hide away all the flashbulbs going off in my mind. "Why do you think your mom would care if you didn't like it?"

"Because it was Holly's." He sucks on a finger. "It's for big kid skiing."

I nod slowly. "I think your mom would be happy if you told her this. And if you want me to be there, I will." Because today feels like the day for revelations and hard conversations. And lessons learned from four-year-olds about listening and asking questions. And maybe I can't blame Dad—at least not entirely—because I haven't been half as vocal or honest about my needs as this preschooler's been about his. And even with him shouting—we hadn't heard.

"Hey, loves!" Mrs. Kahale pops in the door but doesn't take off her coat. "The good news is Holly's cleared to return to practice. The bad news is, she lost her mouthguard on the hill yesterday, so I need to find her backup."

"That's awesome," I say. "But where is she?"

"In the car doing a vidchat with Gabriella." She gives me a wry smile. "The way that girl searches for something is by tearing a room apart. I figured I'd keep her busy instead."

"There's no Jack here," calls a voice from inside our fort, and I bite back a laugh.

"That's too bad," says his mom. "I was hoping there was a Jack. I was hoping he'd give me a big hug and help me look for Holly's old mouthguard."

"Surprise!" He bounds out and says, "I'll check my truck bin."

"Actually—" I give him a meaningful look and point to where his snowsuit is hanging. "Jack has something he wants to tell you. We both do, but I'll let him go first."

"Oh?" She unzips her coat and turns to him. "What's up, bud?"

"I need snow pants," he announces, then dives back under the table.

Mrs. Kahale turns to me, so I guess I'm his designated clarifier. "He hates ski lessons because of his snowsuit." I explain about the difficulties with falling and potty breaks and zippers as she checks the kids' bathroom and the shelves around Holly's bunk.

"Wow. Well, that's— You've solved the mystery. Go, you." She shakes her head as she shuts the storage drawers beneath Holly's bed. "And that's an easy fix—we can get him new ones today. He can try them out tomorrow before we leave."

She's rooting around in the hall closet now, among spare toothbrushes and blister Band-Aids. The sight of those make me wince, because it's a reminder of the rude awakening that awaits me when I put my pointe shoes back on. Future Noelle is going to hate current me when she's soaking in an Epsom salts bath, too sore to climb out or use her toes to turn on the hot faucet after the water goes cold. I should not have slacked so much this week. There's *a lot* of things this week I should've done differently.

"Well, if all else fails, we can mold another one." Mrs. Kahale holds up a new mouthguard still in its packaging. "Did you say you needed to talk to me about something too?"

I do. But if it's hard to confront Dad—who *has* to love me—it's harder to confront this woman who I adore and respect. "I have a question—" I take a breath. "If Holly or Jack wanted to go to Beacon when they were older, would you let them?"

"No." There's zero hesitation, and those two letters are her whole answer. "Come with me to the kitchen. I need to put the kettle on."

I trail after her, frowning. "But Wyatt—"

"Stepparenting is *hard*. I love Wyatt and can express my opinion or be here for advice, but I don't get veto power over his mom. I have to respect Leilani's decisions." She opens the mouthguard package and pulls out the directions. "But Jack and Holly, absolutely not. It might make me selfish, but kids are only kids for a short time. I'm not willing to give up any of those years."

"You let Holly do this scary ski thing?" I press. "And she wasn't hurt, but she could've been."

Mrs. Kahale fills the tea kettle under the faucet. "I want my kids, all three of them, to live their dreams. I wish I could wrap them in bubbles and keep them safe from injuries and hurt feelings and broken hearts"—the look she shoots my way feels pointed—"but I can't. So the best I can do is protect them and be there—even if it means driving to Vermont every weekend for ski team. And it kills me that Beacon keeps me from being there for Wyatt the way I'd like to."

Outside, the car beeps. I point to the door. "Should I go—"

"She has legs. If she wants something, she can come in." Mrs. Kahale levels me with a knowing look. "Now ask your *real* question, Noelle."

I feel as unbalanced as my first time en pointe when I blurt out: "Do you think I shouldn't go to Beacon?"

"I think that's not my decision to make. Every person, every family is different. You will be so missed if you leave, but the bigger question is: Will you be happy if you stay?"

Holly beeps again, and her mom shakes her head and turns the stove on. In our fort, Jack is building towers with his wooden blocks, then crashing them down. That feels a lot like my Beacon plans—I thought they were so sturdy, but one little poke and they're crumbling.

And I'm grateful to have Mrs. Kahale for these sorts of conversations, but it's not the same. I'm not telling her everything—not Wyatt's insights, my doubts, Dad's words, Rae Ann's comments, or the voice mail from Miss Janet. I can't pretend yesterday didn't change things between us.

Or, I could—past-me would've—but I don't want to be that person anymore. The one who cares more about people-pleasing than her conscience. Who runs rather than speaks. If I'd used my voice to object when they first asked me to report on Wyatt, then my chest might not feel so hollow. Wyatt might not feel so hopeless.

So I take another deep breath. A poorly timed one, because she'd just pulled out the trash can to drop in the mouthguard's packaging. But if my face looks disgusted, maybe that's fitting. "You know, it wasn't fair of you and Mr. Kahale to ask me to spy on Wyatt. And, yes, he *does* have something going on—and, *no*, I'm not going to tell you what. Because it's *not my place.*"

Mrs. Kahale is kneading the unmolded rubber. "You're right," she says, flinching when Jack crashes down another tower.

"And yesterday you said you didn't mind if Wyatt and I

were . . . 'whatever'; you were just mad we were keeping it secret." I fold my arms across my heart that's both racing and bruised. "But here's the thing: we weren't trying to hurt your feelings. That wasn't why we didn't tell you."

She nods for me to continue.

"I didn't say anything about Wyatt—because I didn't know *what* to say. How could I tell you what we were, when *I* didn't know yet? We haven't even—" My exhale is shaky.

Mrs. Kahale brushes back a piece of my hair and rubs my shoulder. "Oh, sweetie. I was not entirely fair to you yesterday. And I need to have this conversation with Wyatt too. Emotions were running high, we were so worried about Holly—and that's not an excuse. I was not fair to you. You and Wyatt don't *owe me* that trust or owe me information about your personal lives. You're entitled to secrets and privacy. And if we insinuated differently, or made you feel like we doubted your ability as our babysitter, then we were wrong and I am so sorry. We all adore you and are beyond lucky to have you in our lives. I truly apologize."

"I adore you all too." I sniffle, and when Mrs. Kahale sniffles back, it's game over.

Holly barges in thirty seconds later. "Why are you hugging? And what's taking so long? Wait. Are you *crying?* Mom, I'm *fine.* The doctor said so."

Mrs. Kahale and I both laugh and wipe at our cheeks—she lifts a hand and waves for Holly to join us. And even though Holly grumbles, she's an enthusiastic participant in the group hug—for at least two whole seconds before she says, "*Now can we go to practice?*"

"Wait!" calls Jack. "Me! Me too!" And so the four of us—plus Jack's recycling truck—hug it out before Holly bites into warm rubber. The new mouthguard hardens in a glass of ice water while Jack and I layer up. Then we head over to Kringle Village, where one non-concussed eight-year-old is going to slay the gates that took her down yesterday, and the remaining three of us are on a potty-friendly snow pants mission.

And if both these kiddos can confront their obstacles, I'm going to get over myself and handle the last of mine. As soon as Wyatt Kahale is off the mountain, he and I are going to talk.

Babysitting Tip 19:

It doesn't sound as bad if you call it an "incentive" instead of a "bribe."

"**L**adies and gentlemen, get the boy a runway," I tease as Jack struts out of the dressing room in a pair of fluorescent yellow snow pants that look like they were dip-dyed at a highlighter factory. They manage to out-bright even Rachel's rainbow getup.

So, of course he loves them.

"And the zipper?" I mean for him to give me a thumbs-up or thumbs-down, instead he drops the zipper—and the pants. So it's a very good thing he's got sweats on underneath, because we're standing in the middle of a ski supply store.

His mom had been right behind him when he emerged to show me the winning pants—but she's ducked behind a clothing rack and has her phone pressed to her ear. When she hangs up, her smile looks distracted.

"Is everything okay?" I ask. "Is it Holly?"

"She's fine." Mrs. Kahale gives me a probing look. "That was Nick. He says Wyatt wants to talk to both of us. I want to ask you what that's about—but I won't."

"Good." I mean it on so many different levels.

She laughs at my smirk. "Can you finish up here? Just charge the pants to the card I gave you, then take Jack to get a sugar cookie or fudge."

Jack tilts his head. "How about *both?*"

"How about, 'dinner's in a half hour, so be glad you're getting any treat,' " she counters, kissing the top of his head. "Meet us at Fireside at five fifteen. It's the restaurant just past Juniper."

"Sure." I'm already crossing my fingers. Not for myself—with a fudge bribe pending, Jack will be angelic—but for Wyatt and the conversation he's about to have. Once he puts this out there, it can't be taken back. For better or for worse, it's going to change his family.

✳ ✳ ✳ ✳ ✳ ✳ ✳ ✳

Holly is flush-cheeked and victorious when we convene at the door to Fireside. Her dad's inside putting his name down for a table, and she makes us wait for him before she'll tell us why.

He's barely out the door when she pulls something from her pocket and waves it around. "I got my fastest time on the course!" The "something" is U-shaped molded plastic, which Holly gives a dramatic smooch. "This is a lucky mouthguard—I'm never not wearing it!"

Mrs. Kahale laughs and wrinkles her nose. "Then let's try

to be a little better about keeping it in a case. But, congrats, sweetie! I knew you'd show that hill who's boss."

"We'll have a cocoa toast to celebrate Holly's great time and Jack's new pants," Mr. Kahale says. "But, unfortunately there's a wait. So we won't be having that toast for another forty-five minutes or so."

Jack and Holly are groaning. Their parents are hushing. Me? I'm spending all my energy not looking at Wyatt. His hair is a fabulous array of helmet flat and finger-combed spikes. And his eyes—they're the world's most sensitive security alarm, because every time I glance his way, he catches me. Which, how is that even possible?

Unless he was already looking at me?

That feels like wishful thinking.

"So, we have some choices to make," Mr. Kahale says. "We can wait here. In the cold, just standing around, or . . . we can go skating."

His question is drowned out by cheers. Jack grasps my hand and starts towing me down the path, but his mom steps in front of us. "Jackie, slow down. I don't know if Noelle's coming with us."

"Oh, I skate," I say. "I know it's an 'outdoor sport' here, but I learned indoors. Or because of ballet?" Which is the reason I gave for not skiing. It's the reason I've given for a lot of things—and right now it feels more restrictive than protective.

"Not because of ballet. Because of me. Can we talk?"

It's the first time Wyatt's spoken since our groups merged, and I don't miss the look he exchanged with his dad, the deep breath he took before speaking, or Mrs. Kahale's nod of encouragement.

That last one was aimed at me, so I pass Jack to his mom and now I'm the one swallowing before I answer. "I could be persuaded to skip skating."

"I'm not above bribing you with cocoa." Wyatt takes a step closer. "And I think I was once promised a dance lesson—it went something like this—" He does an absurd Hokey Pokey variation that I recognize from a lifetime ago, back before Jack's first lesson. When I was the one offering cocoa coercion. I laugh as I let our eyes catch. Catch and hold, even though we have an audience. Even though mine might start brimming.

"You two are so *weird!*" huffs Holly. She stomps toward the rink. Her parents laugh and scoop up Jack as they follow, seemingly oblivious to the fact they're leaving us behind. But there's no chance it was anything but deliberate. Perhaps even planned ahead of time.

"I think you mentioned cocoa?" My voice isn't cooperating; it refuses to sound glib.

"Right, of course." Wyatt steps closer, his hand hovering in the air like it might touch my shoulder . . . Instead it drops by his side. "Have you tried it from the kiosk past Santa's house? It's the best in Kringle."

"I didn't know there was a Santa's house."

"It's on the other side of the tree." He takes a deep breath and holds out his hand. "The big guy's still there for one more night if you want to get a picture with him. And I promised you the tree lighting. Is it going to feel anticlimactic if both those things happen after Christmas?"

"Right now, I don't know how I'll feel," I say honestly, "about anything."

He nods and looks away, but his hand's still out, so I take it and add, "I'll only do the picture with Santa if you'll be in it with me." Maybe we're getting too old for photos with Santa on McGinty Farm, but this feels different. I want a record of this night with this guy. If Santa has to be in it too, I guess that's fine.

Wyatt must be worried I'll change my mind, because his grip is firm and his feet are fast, guiding us through the crowd and past the skating pond where his family waves, to the tree, and around it. We join the end of the Santa line—and there *is* a line, even on December twenty-ninth. There's also a waitress taking cocoa orders on a mobile tablet.

Once ours are placed, Wyatt turns to face me, giving our clasped hands a squeeze—one that tingles even through our gloves. Or maybe it's the earnest look in his eyes that's causing them. "We have until she gets back with our drinks to decide what we're going to cheers about—I'm hoping it might be that you'll accept my apology."

"I should've told them I wouldn't spy on you," I say. "And I should've told you they'd asked. It must've really hurt to hear about conversations that took place behind your back."

"Yeah." He swallows. "But that doesn't excuse what I said. It wasn't fair to blame you for my mistakes this week. You being close with Jack and Holly and Dad and Ginger isn't the reason I'm *not*. That's on me. I'm sorry for attacking when you were encouraging me to talk to them."

I squeeze his hand. "So did you?"

"Yeah. Though it was less being brave and more not having a choice. Dad confronted me as soon as our feet were off the ground on the chairlift." He shakes his head. "Longest fifteen minutes of my life. But it could've been worse—it could've been in a gondola with an audience."

"Excuse me." The waitress is back with red cardboard cups. "One double chocolate, extra whip, and one peppermint twist."

We thank her and I let go of Wyatt's hand to take both cups. He meets my eyes with a confused smirk. "You double-fisting? I'll share."

I shake my head. "You're not getting this until you fast-forward to the conclusion. What'd they say? Are you moving to Juncture?"

He nods and his smile stretches wide, until it's brighter than fairy lights or tinsel. It's the first time I've seen him without any shadows in his eyes. This is Wyatt, unlocked. Alive in a way I've only witnessed when watching tapes of his dance performances—which feels ironic, since the reason he looks that way is because he won't be dancing anymore. At least not at Beacon . . . I wonder how'd he'd feel about being the only guy past puberty at Spirit.

I hand over his cup and tap mine against it. "Welcome to PA. Welcome *home*. And when you get to the high school cafeteria, know the only edible foods are pizza, fries, or bagels."

"They can't screw up carbs. Got it." He clinks our cups again. "It's not a done deal. I don't know how Mom will take it. Technically she has primary custody, but I'm never there anymore. I spend as many of my breaks and holidays as I can with Dad, and I've done Beacon's summer intensive the past four years. I'll probably see *more* of her if I move in with Dad." His words are coming out in the breathless tumble I associate with Jack and Holly. The Kahale enthusiasm is just as endearing on him. "And Dad agrees I don't have to go back to Beacon. And the bedroom thing—he didn't even blink. He's going to finish part of the basement for his office. Apparently they've been talking about doing it anyway."

"They have," I confirm. "Home theater, gym, and it would totally make sense to have his office down where it'll be quieter."

"And Ginger—she said—" His smile doesn't fade, but his voice is thicker and he pinches the bridge of his nose before he can continue. "She said this is what she's always wanted. That they made that bedroom an office so she wouldn't have to walk by it and remember I wasn't—"

His voice cracks and I drop his hand again—this time so I can give him a hug. And sure our cocoas are squished between us and my nose is cold and someone nearby keeps sneezing, but it's still pretty perfect. I have no intention of letting go.

The family behind us clears their throats. "The line's moving."

We laugh and close the gap and I'm giddy with the same disorienting relief that comes from nailing a long sequence of fouetté turns . . . which, if we trade places and I end up at the school he's leaving, may be how I'm spending many future hours. But will I still feel as giddy if, when I stop spinning, my whole life and landscape are dance? If there's no Saturday mornings at Coco's swim meets, or afternoons watching Mae's travel documentaries? No cake tastings or bounce-houses with Autumn's family when they're trying new companies for their party-planning business. No Friday nights with the Kahales, the Diazes, the Davises, or any of my babysitting clients. No chance to fix things with Dad or Wednesday waffle dinners where whipped cream is practically its own entree and we talk about the weirdest news headlines we've read that week.

"I called my dad," I say. "I'm not sure about Beacon anymore." We're still five families away from the front of the line and maybe that's enough time to get this out.

"Is it because of what I said?" Wyatt winces. "I was being

a jerk. It's a great school and you'd do great there . . . just make sure you're going for the right reasons."

"You weren't wrong." My sip of cocoa is as careful as my word choice. I don't want to burn my tongue or have anything hurtful slip off it. "And my reasons are messy. I need to untangle them and figure out what I want. Miss Janet—my ballet teacher—she's been trying to get in touch with me. I finally listened to her message. I thought it'd be about Beacon, because she's been telling me I need a 'new challenge' and in my mind that could *only* mean Beacon."

"But it wasn't?" Wyatt guides me around a spot on the sidewalk where a spilled drink has frozen into a slick puddle.

"She wants me to teach a class. Jack's, actually." I shake my head, still trying to sort out my reaction to this. "If I was meant to go to Beacon, I wouldn't be more excited about the idea of eating waffles with my dad and teaching four-year-olds, would I?"

"I can't answer that for you," he says.

"Yeah, I know." I pretend to pout. "I called my friends and filled them in—and they wouldn't give me any answers either. Of course, I made that call from inside a blanket fort and Jack insisted on giving everyone in the vidchat shark heads, so it wasn't exactly the setup for a serious discussion." I shrug again and lean into Wyatt. "I'm sure they'll have more thoughts tomorrow when we meet up for carol karaoke. Autumn offered to transcribe my pros-cons list."

But I realize I don't need her to. And while they'd held my hand when I signed up for the audition, once I was alone tonight, I was going to cancel it. My choice.

"They sound like good friends," he says. "But back up a minute, what's 'carol karaoke'?"

I laugh. "It's exactly what it sounds like. We normally do it on Christmas Eve, but they waited until I'm back."

"I can't wait to meet them."

It's so weird to think he *will*. That he'll be in school and classes with them. I wonder if that thought is as strange to him as it was when he offered to introduce me to his dance friends and Alvie stopped being this YAGP winner I'd seen in videos and started to be a person.

"You're up," says an elf. There's a salt line halfway up her red, curled-toe shoes, and her green-and-white-striped leggings are faded. It's a costume that's ready to be retired, a reminder that Christmas is over.

Wyatt squeezes my hand and we climb to where a white-bearded man is sitting on a gold-painted throne. "Ho, ho, ho," he puffs out. "Have you been good this year?"

"Mostly," I answer. But instead of sitting on his knee, I eye the space beside the chair and look at Wyatt. "Arabesque penché?"

He grins. And in the photo there's Santa looking jolly on his throne while Wyatt's on one knee beside him—supporting me with two hands on my waist as I'm bent toward him, my weight balanced on my right foot as I extend and lift my left into a vertical split. The space between our mouths is no more than an inch—kissing-close, but we're too busy smiling.

"That's a new one," says the elf who hands us the printed picture. "Merry Christmas."

We're laughing so hard we're leaning into each other as we exit Santa's village. There's barely anyone else waiting around for a tree lighting on December twenty-ninth; I guess that's a perk of post-Christmas Christmas celebrations. We claim a spot right against the fence and Wyatt texts me a picture of the digital download code printed at the bottom of our photo before carefully tucking the original in his inside pocket.

But there's something sobering about the sound of him zipping his coat back up. Something that makes my laughter fizzle, even before he asks, "So where does all this leave us?"

"With you hopefully coming to Juncture and me . . ." I shrug helplessly. "I don't think I'll audition now, but I can't promise I never will. And I don't know what you want."

He reaches for the hand I'm pointing between us and presses it against his chest. "You. I want to be with you. Wherever you are. Wherever I am. If you go to Beacon, you're not going to have a ton of free time, but I know that going in. I've lived it. I can be patient. And if I'm stuck at my mom's—at least I'll be closer to Beacon. And if I'm at Dad's—if you're home or on break—"

I flex my fingers on his chest. There's my glove, a coat, and several shirts between our skin. I can't sense his heartbeat, but I can feel the heaves of his breaths—like this conversation is as demanding as a series of barrel turns or cabrioles. "Have you already thought through *all* the scenarios?" I ask.

"Hey, one of us went to bed the same time as a four-year-old last night." He takes a step closer. "I've had a lot of time to think."

"Too much time to think." I reach my other hand up, glad he's not wearing a hat so I can tease the flyaway chaos of his hair. "What if we trust that we can tackle any obstacles—geographical or other—when we reach them? We are *dancers* after all—isn't defying odds and gravity and pain thresholds and physiology pretty much what we do?"

He's still chuckling when I settle my palm on the back of his neck, pulling him down and pushing up on my toes—pressing our lips together—*finally.*

There's a moment before the Juncture tree lighting, when everyone's holding their breath and the music's been paused—and then they hit the switch. You think you know what it'll look like, and you think you're prepared for the beauty. You're wrong. It's not until the lights are blazing that you realize how dark it had been the moment before. How different things look now in the bright glow.

That's how it feels when Wyatt kisses me—like I've been illuminated with a thousand sparks of light. A thousand sensations. And everything before—I'd been so in the dark. I had no idea kissing could feel like this. It's the buzz of audience applause, the dizzy spin of a manège, the relief of a hot bath on exhausted muscles, the fizz of sparkling cider after a show, the confidence of putting on a perfect-fitting costume for the first time and feeling beautiful even before you look in the mirror. It's the line of his jaw beneath my palm, the press of his hand against my back.

It's the realization, when we open our eyes to breathe and marvel at each other, that we're doing so by the light of so many tiny bulbs. That we've missed *yet another* tree lighting. And laughing about it—because maybe we were the spectacle this time. Maybe the tree gets to bear witness to us.

Babysitting Tip 20:

Remember, whether a sitting job goes amazing or awful, it ends.
Make your time count, because this is the best job in the world.

"I can't believe I never got you on skis," Wyatt says early the next morning as he's zipping his backpack. It's on his bed bedside a duffel bag (mostly empty) and a suitcase (mostly full). "It's not too late, you know. You and Jack could do a lesson together before you head home. I'll be en route to Dulles, but I bet Ginger would send me pictures."

I point to my chest. "Indoor sports girl." *Tired* indoor sports girl, who stayed up way too late texting her friends about a certain ballet boy who's as talented with kisses as he is on a stage.

Wyatt takes my hand and uses it to pull me toward him. "*My* indoor sports girl." He pauses and scrunches his forehead. "That sounds a little caveman, doesn't it?"

I crinkle my nose and laugh. "A lot caveman. We'll pretend you never said it."

"Good plan." He punctuates the statement with a kiss. A quick one since everyone is scurrying in and out of his room with belongings he has to sort into the duffel going with him on the plane to DC or the suitcase going in the car to Pennsylvania. The hope is that he'll be reunited with his suitcase—and all of us—soon!

Despite Wyatt's teasing, I don't feel any pressure to get on skis. I've been brave enough this week. I've taken other risks—flown and fallen in other areas.

I'm proud of Holly's fierce fearlessness as she flies down the mountain, and her ability to get back out there after a crash. But maybe fearlessness isn't always so obvious. Courage isn't just speed and skill—it's calling home and being honest. It's sharing your truth in front of an unlit tree, letting down your guard on a ski lift. It's telling someone that you need new pants and more potty breaks. It's realizing that secrets only have power when you're keeping them. And that I had people willing to listen when I was ready to share.

Courage is kissing this boy goodbye in front of his family and a waiting Uber. Despite his sister pretending to gag, his brother giggling, and his parents being way too amused. Despite the fact that we don't know what our future holds in terms of geography or when we'll get to do this again.

Wyatt rumples Holly's hair and tells her to watch for attacking gates; he reminds Jack to take Dramamine on the car ride home. He hugs his parents. And me? He asks for my help carrying his stuff to the car. Since he's got his backpack on and his bag is practically empty, I'm pretty sure everyone knows this is an excuse for him to kiss me again. Or, at least his parents know, because as they're shutting the front door behind us, I catch them shooing the kids away from waving at the windows.

Our goodbye kiss is brief, but fierce, his hand on my chin, mine in his hair. And the sum total of our relationship is shorter than twelve days of Christmas: we've shared nine kisses, spent eight days together, held hands seven times, built six snow people, played five games at game night, drank four cocoas, missed three tree lightings, survived two hot tub "head injuries," and decorated one gingerbread house. It doesn't feel like enough, but only because I want so many more verses and choruses.

"Soon," he says as he climbs in the car. And I echo the word back—not entirely sure if the unsaid part is "talk" or "see you" or "let's do that again" or "we'll have answers"—or even all of the above. But as his car pulls out of the driveway, I lower my arm and say it again—this time as a wish.

Soon.

On the drive back to Juncture, there are zero songs about juice boxes—mostly because Jack is passed out cold. It's possible this is because he exhausted himself during his last morning lesson—one he didn't complain about attending—thank you, magic snow pants. It's also possible that the Dramamine Mrs. Kahale picked up for the drive back was *not* nondrowsy.

Dad is waiting outside when we pull into the parking lot of our apartment building. He's not alone. Coco, Autumn, and Mae have signs that read *Welcome Back Noelle*—or *Welcome Noelle Back*, once Coco impatiently pushes her way out of alignment to hug me sooner.

"You might want to move a little faster getting your stuff out of the car." Autumn consults her watch. "We have two minutes left on the timer before the cinnamon buns burn."

But even with delays to hug Holly and Mrs. Kahale, and the hauling of all my stuff upstairs, the cinnamon rolls are perfectly toasted when Mae pulls them out of the oven and sets them on a trivet beside a plate of bacon, a bowl of eggs, and a ginormous fruit salad.

She says, "It's Boxing Day Brunch . . . for dinner, on not–Boxing Day. We wanted to wait for you."

The hand I've got pressed to my heart is squeezed tight, like I can hold all my big feelings inside. "You are the best!"

Coco is over by the TV, plugging in the karaoke machine from Autumn's house. "Some things just aren't the same without you."

"*Christmas* isn't the same without you, kiddo," says Dad. And normally I'd be all sorts of embarrassed and annoyed if he tried to hug me in front of my friends. But I let him today, let him spin me in the most awkward pirouette to face the corner. Where there was an empty tree stand when I left is now a short, chubby spruce. It's *my* favorite kind of tree, not his. "I decorated it—but I left the star for you. And I haven't plugged it in yet. Do you want to do the honors? I should warn you, I forgot to test the lights before putting them up, so this may be anticlimactic."

It's not.

I finally get my tree lighting. It's only a five-foot spruce, but it lacks none of the magic or majesty of the trees ten times its height in Juncture's town center or Kringle Village. In fact, I might even like it better.

And under the tree are two presents. One is a box wrapped in paper that's six years old, with my name and the year written in handwriting I still miss on lunchbox notes. Dad picks up the other one. "Here's the 'big surprise' that *someone* tried to spoil." He winks at Autumn and kisses the top of my head as he hands me an envelope. "Merry Christmas, kiddo."

My heart clenches as I take in the red logo. "Beacon?" I hadn't told Dad about my plan—because it wasn't my plan anymore. My audition is canceled, but had they already mailed something to the house?

Dad chuckles. "Your hints weren't exactly subtle, Noelle. I think the brochure *inside* the coffee canister was my favorite. But it's expensive." His smile slips. "I didn't want to say anything if we couldn't afford it. Saving up for what's in that envelope was actually my inspiration for the app. And it's because GoalBusters is knocking it out of the park that we can. Now, c'mon. Open it!"

I slide a shaking finger under the backflap. Will he be crushed if I tell him I'm not ready? That I love the gift but want to defer a year or so? I look at the girls with wide, panicked eyes; Autumn gives her head a subtle shake and flashes me a thumbs-up.

I pull out a few folded pieces of paper. *Congratulations, Noelle Partridge, on your acceptance into Beacon Academy of Dance's Summer Intensive Ballet Program. Your acceptance is a reflection of the dedication and skill demonstrated in your application video as well as the glowing references from your ballet instructor, Janet Smith of Spirit Ballet . . .*

"The summer intensive?" I have to read it twice to be sure, then laugh. "I'm going to Beacon's Summer Intensive?!"

"Yeah." Dad's face is confused. "Isn't that what you wanted? Tell me I didn't accidentally send two Beacon brochures through the wash for some other reason. Miss Janet already had the application materials prepared, so I thought you two had talked about this."

It's a six-week program. Residential. Beacon teachers. Beacon classes. A hard work, low-commitment trial run of the school.

"Dad, it's perfect!" This time I'm the one to initiate a hug.

Autumn grins at me over his shoulder. "Told you you'd like his surprise."

She can have a free pass for that I-told-you-so, because I'm too busy rereading the letter—convincing myself it's real—to stick out my tongue or roll my eyes.

I'm leaving my other present—Mom's snow globe—under the tree until I have less of an audience. And they all know that; they're not going to make me say it. Instead Mae announces, "The cinnamon rolls are congealing . . ."

I thank Dad again before he slips off to his office—not to escape into work but to give us space for our friend dinner.

"Another reason I'm glad you're home," says Mae between bites of bacon, "I've been babysitting my butt off. *So* many of your families have been calling me this week, asking me to fill in."

"Even I got calls," says Autumn. "Not that I took them. It's party season. I've been working so hard that I'm pretty sure my moms are violating child labor laws."

"Whatever," I say. Party-planning runs in her blood. "You love it."

She nods. "I really do. Now if I could only convince them to let me work there more . . ."

"Well, nobody called me to babysit." Coco does a seated victory dance. "Because I didn't take the babysitting course with you all. Ha!"

"I don't think I'm giving the Davis family back, by the way," says Mae. "Rosie and Iris belong to me now."

Coco snorts. "I think that Noelle might be okay with that. After all, she's now got *three* Kahale kids to occupy her nights."

Autumn taps her lip. "Will you have to raise your rates for them? Or will they now need a sitter for their babysitter? A chaperone?"

I demonstrate my maturity by not responding with words—I throw a grape at her instead. But if I think the teasing ends when we clear our plates, I'm so wrong.

Mae's smile is pure Primavera mischief when she says, "So, we may have prepared a special song to kick off carol karaoke."

And while I'm super glad it's not "Drummer Boy" or "Twelve Days of Christmas," or any of the other tracks from a certain guy's repeat playlist, I'm wholly unprepared for them to bust out with a modified version of a classic. They're grinning as they lean toward me and sing, "I'm dreaming of a *Wyatt* Christmas."

Before I join in—because I so am—I pause the music. "I'd like to go on record stating that you guys are brats—and the absolute best." Also, their song isn't true. Not anymore. Before I'd been dreaming—of the perfect guy, the perfect dance school. The truth is messier . . . and a lot more appealing.

I'll always have dreams, and not just about boys and ballet, but I'm not letting them stop me from appreciating the here and now. Because this moment, with them giggling over the microphone and Dad in his office, is better than any Extravaganza plan, and I'm going to savor it while it lasts.

A dozen songs later, Autumn's being extra efficient at packing up. "So everyone should come to Coco's by four tomorrow," she says. "I really think this is going to be our best New Year's slumber party yet." She darts a glance my way. "And I know it's your least favorite holiday, but this year you're not allowed to be cranky about it, because we haven't seen you in forever."

"I won't be. Promise." I hold up my hands to show I'm not crossing my fingers, and Coco takes it as an invitation to steal another hug.

"Ohh. We missed you! But also, your butt is vibrating."

This time I let the girls officially "meet" Wyatt over vid-chat. Mae is shy, Autumn's assertive, Coco is brazen. Wyatt is . . . calm and charming.

He's also visibly relieved when they leave and it's finally just me and him, in the glow of my tree, with the letter from Beacon and Mom's snow globe beneath it.

Dad pops out of his office to fumble noisily in the kitchen—but then hands me a mug of cocoa and a note before disappearing again. I unfold it: *Come find me when you're free, kiddo. Let's start talking. -x Dad*

"Did you open your bag yet?" Wyatt asks.

"The one I brought to Kringle?" It's still sitting in a heap by the door with all my presents from the Kahales. I unzip it. Right on top is a small gift-wrapped box. A sprig of mistletoe is tucked in the bow. "Oh. It's beautiful."

"I didn't wrap it," Wyatt disclaims. "I had them do it at the store. Believe me, next time I give you a gift, if I wrap it myself—it'll be all lumpy and crooked and you'll know I did it."

I'm caught on "next time" and that there was even a *this time.* "When did you get this? And why?"

"Christmas present." He sheepishly shrugs off the words. "I hope you like it."

Untying the knots around the mistletoe requires both hands, so I prop the phone. When the ribbons and wrapping paper are gone, it's a tan box the size of a mug. Nestled on the tissue paper inside is a snow globe.

"Oh, Wyatt." My voice is immediately thick, my eyes wet. I run to get a tissue, because I'm going to need it.

"I thought maybe you should start adding your own snow globes to the collection." He can't see me nodding, swiping at the tears dripping onto my smile, so there's some panic in his voice when he adds, "I hope that's okay. I know it's a special thing from your mom, but when I saw this one had Mount Kringle and the lit-up tree at the bottom—I thought maybe you could use some from your *now*, not just memories looking back. And then when you do hit that first Christmas when there isn't one from her—you'll still have *your* part of the tradition to carry forward."

I'm trying—and failing—to sniffle delicately as I sit back down. "It's perfect. I love it."

"It's *almost* perfect," he grumbles. "I wanted it to play 'Little Drummer Boy.'"

I snort. That first morning—the alarm, his awful playlist, our gingerbread house—it feels like a lifetime ago. I turn the globe over and twist the bronze knob. "I swear, if this plays 'The Twelve Days of Christmas' . . ." My voice trails off as the first notes of *The Nutcracker* spill out.

And now I'm laughing and sniffling again. Missing him.

"When's your dad coming?" I ask.

"Day after tomorrow." Wyatt sighs. "I'm going to talk to my mom today. Dad wanted her to have some time to process before he shows up and the three of us sit down together. If all goes well, I can pack some bags and come back with him that night. If not . . . They'll call their lawyers and it'll take a little longer."

"I'm crossing my fingers," I say.

"Me too." He gives a quick, disbelieving laugh. "You know, if things go well, I could be—be *home* for New Year's Day." And I wonder if this is the first time he's called Juncture "home" or if he's always seen it that way and just never dared to express it.

"Well, I hope you're resting up," I say. "Because there are several people here who are super excited to meet you in person—and remember how exhausting that sleepover for eight-year-olds was? Consider that training for when you meet my best friends' families."

"Put me in, Coach," he says. "I'm ready."

I'm still laughing when I hear a voice in his background. "Wyatt? Are you in there? Who are you talking to? Wyatt Makoa Kahale, answer me."

"Mom's home from Pilates," he says. "I should go get this over with."

"Good luck," I tell him. "Call me later."

If the conversation he's having right now goes well, *he*

could be here New Year's Day. I might have to rethink that whole "least favorite holiday" thing. Not because Wyatt might be coming to town, but because he's right: I shouldn't always be looking back—not with snow globes and not with holidays. Instead of mourning the fact that Christmas is over, why not look ahead to a new year, new beginnings? New challenges in new dance classes—both the wriggly four-year-olds I'll be helping to teach *and* the new partnering class I don't think I'll have any trouble talking Wyatt or Miss Janet into starting.

I don't have to go to Beacon to find new things to learn, to find my pas de deux—but I'm glad that I'll get to. And if I love the Summer Intensive . . . well, I can investigate the doors it opens then. Decide if they're ones I want to walk through.

Regardless, it will be a more informed decision—not one I feel pushed into because I've outgrown Spirit or feel unwelcome at home.

I shake the snow globe one more time before placing it at the center of our mantel. Sometimes the things we think we want aren't what we imagine at all. And sometimes—like with Wyatt—they're even better. I don't have all the answers yet. I don't know what challenges and triumphs this new year will hold, but I'm going into it with so many people on my side. And pretty soon the ornaments will be packed away, the tree turned to mulch, and even the stalest Christmas cookies dipped in cocoa and eaten—but instead of looking backward, I'm keeping my eyes on the horizon. I'll find my spot, go en pointe, take a deep breath—and dance.

Acknowledgments

I started writing this book the week our world stopped. My twins and toddler were out of school for spring break, but Disney World closed the day before we were supposed to arrive. Spring break stretched, then turned into virtual school. They'd be completing third grade and preschool at home, while I completed this book. My first thank-you is to them and to their teachers—for persistently and creatively meeting all the new obstacles this year has thrown at us.

I've skied and taken ballet before, but it would be generous to describe my skills at either as "skills." And all my bright plans to visit ski lodges and ballet classes quickly proved impossible as slopes and studios shut down. This means you're spared humiliating video of me on skis and in ballet slippers—but it also means I'd hit some serious research roadblocks.

I'm eternally grateful for the people in my life who stepped up to share their wisdom and time with me. From ski team schedules, to safety patrol protocol, to ski lodge culture, huge thank-yous to Katie Locke, Connor Burnett, Keira, Colby, and Amy Rieszer.

Haley Zelesko, from *Dance Academy* recommendations to patiently answering pages of questions about ballet to responding to my calls and texts about phrasing (and also about *Dance Academy*) to demonstrating moves and loaning me the pristine and destroyed pointe shoes that have sat on my desk through every step of drafting and editing—you are a godsend. You're also Rascal's favorite babysitter. I could—literally—not have written this book without you.

I'm also grateful to all the young dancers who share their triumphs, challenges, and day-to-day lives on their various social media platforms—your drive and dedication are inspiring.

Jessica Spotswood and Annie Gaughen, I owe you platters of Christmas cookies for your thoughtful insights on my drafts and calls of encouragement.

I'm forever raising a mug of cocoa to toast my agent-extraordinaire Kate Testerman. No matter how upside down and sideways the world turned, you have been a calm, steady place. That has meant more than I can say. Thank you.

I've never been caroling. I'm not sure it actually sounds enjoyable? But if I went with any of the following people, we'd be laughing all the way. Stacey, Jenn, Kristin, Carly, Shannon, Rae Ann, Jen, Michelle, Nancy, Courtney, Emily, Tip, Jenny, Susie, Amy, and Elisabeth, thank you for your friendship.

I am so thankful for my team at Abrams: Jessica Gotz, Anne Heltzel, Brooke Shearouse, Marie Oishi, Melanie Chang, Jenny Choy, Kim Lauber, Trish McNamara O'Neill, Nicole Schaefer, Megan Evans, Hana Nakamura, Jade Rector, Brenda Angelilli, Amy Vreeland, and Penelope Cray—Andrew Smith, you get an extra shout-out for being my title hero. If I could, I'd have you all over for a Christmas movie marathon where we wear animal-print holiday onesies or ugly Christmas sweaters and eat too many cookies. In this sprinted marathon of a year, you have all been amazing and supportive, and my gratitude is endless.

And to my family, thank you for indulging me in a gingerbread house contest on Easter weekend, endless repetitions of *The Nutcracker* score, and many, many mid-May cups of cocoa.

In a time when so much was scary and uncertain, writing this story was my happy place. I hope it becomes one of yours. While Buddy the Elf (from *Elf*, the best Christmas movie of all time) says smiling's his favorite, you, reader, are one of mine! Thank you for choosing this book and giving it a chance.

May your days be bookish and bright—and may all your Christmases be . . . exactly your preferred weather configuration.